MURDER ON THE TOR

AN EXHAM-ON-SEA MYSTERY

1

GLASTONBURY TOR

Sunlight bathed the ruined tower in gold. Libby leaned on a stile at the base of Glastonbury Tor, looking up at the summit far above, Bear by her side. The huge sheepdog panted, tongue lolling, keen to begin their favourite climb. 'Wait, Bear.' Libby's fingers sank into coarse, thick fur round the dog's neck as, mesmerised, she watched the first pearly wisps of mist rise, shift and coalesce. Soon, a heavy grey blanket cloaked the hill, blotting out the tower on the summit and the sun's rays.

She loved to walk on the Tor in the early morning. Her first visit had been years ago, when she'd spent a holiday in Exham on Sea with Trevor, her late husband, and the children. The whole family had loved the windy climb to the top to see Somerset spread below.

Those had been happy days, before Trevor became so difficult and controlling.

Bear barked, shattering the silence. He slid from under Libby's hand and bounded up the slope, mouth wide, paws muffled on the grass. Libby ran, breath rasping, legs trembling with effort. 'Come back,' she called, but the dog disappeared into the mist without a backward glance. Libby ran a few more steps and stopped to breathe, suddenly reluctant to follow.

What was that? A single howl drifted out from the cloud. Libby took a step into the damp mass and the mist closed in, chilling her lungs. Strands of wet hair clung to her cheeks, but she brushed them aside and climbed higher, isolated and blind, sliding on the grass. Her feet stumbled on to a solid path and she followed the easier track, expecting every moment to break through the mist. Time and distance shifted, until she had no idea how long she'd been walking.

Just as she began to think she'd be stuck in the white wilderness all day, she burst through a swirl of damp cotton wool cloud into a blaze of light. She blinked, blinded by the sudden glare, and the tense knot in her stomach unwound. Glorious sunshine bathed the top of the Tor, warm on her face. In the brilliant morning light, St Michael's Tower stood out, sharp against a blue sky. In a burst of relief, energised, legs no longer tired, Libby followed a series of steps cut into the hill, climbing fast. 'Bear? Where are you?' Her voice carried, thin and high in the morning air, but the dog was out of sight.

Libby sank onto a wooden bench, watching the mist below. A sound at her back brought her to her feet, nerves jangling. A small girl, hair a tangled mass of black curls, stared, motionless, eyes wide, clutching a furry brown toy monkey. Libby smiled. 'Hello. You made me jump.' The child snuggled a cheek into the monkey's fur. Libby tried again. 'Is Mummy here?' The girl shook her head. 'Daddy?' The round eyes slid away from Libby's face. 'You're not alone, are you?' The child stuck a thumb in her mouth and sucked.

Libby remembered Bear. 'Did you see my dog? A big, cuddly one. He's up here, somewhere.' The girl smiled, showing tiny white teeth, and pointed up the hill to the tower. Libby screwed up her eyes against the sun but saw no sign of Bear. A finger of ice crept up her back. She shivered and turned to speak to the child but the words froze on her tongue. The girl had disappeared.

'This is ridiculous.' Libby spoke out loud. She was letting the Tor get on her nerves. The child must have wandered down through the mist to a waiting parent. She wouldn't come to much harm on the Tor.

Libby marched on up the hill, as fast as her wobbly legs allowed, determined to shake off her unease. She'd been reading too many stories of Glastonbury and King Arthur's ghost.

She turned the final corner of the zig-zag path in record time, with no further stops. Such a feat would normally fill her with pride, but today, Libby was too worried about Bear. She covered the remaining few yards at a run and stepped into the cool, dark, deserted interior of St Michael's Tower.

Crossing the flagstones in three quick strides, she was back in daylight. Bear lay on the grass, ears flat, tail twitching. 'There you are.' The dog's tail flickered as he staggered to his feet. 'What's wrong?' His head hung low, the fur of his neck standing out in a prickly ruff.

Libby knelt by Bear's side and slipped her arms round his chest. 'Are you hurt?' She ran gentle fingers over the animal's body, searching for lumps and bumps, finding none. She lifted the coarse top layer of hair and inspected the soft inner coat for blood, but there was no injury to be seen. She scrambled to her feet and, hands on hips, gazed over the mist that hid the nearby fields and woods to a range of distant hills, shimmering blue in the sunshine.

A stiff breeze sent her to seek shelter on the other side of the Tower, where she sank on to the grass, back propped against the ancient stones, and drew both knees up to her chest. Her gaze swept in an arc, searching for signs of company. No one appeared but at least she had Bear as a companion. Libby pulled the huge animal close, glad of his earthy, doggy smell. 'What happened, Bear? What frightened you?' She rubbed the dog's head. 'This place gives me the creeps.'

Her right leg hurt. She shifted position, rubbing her calf, and searched in the grass, curious, expecting to find an abandoned shard of glass or the ring from a beer can. Instead, her fingers closed on one smooth, round pebble, then another. She searched until she'd uncovered a handful of muddy beads joined by a length of rusty wire.

Libby rubbed the stones and the mud fell away to reveal a necklace of even, smooth beads that glowed golden-red, as radiant as the sunshine. *Amber.* Libby dropped them into her pocket and called to the dog. 'Come on, Bear. Time to go.'

* * *

Listless, the dog plodded down the hill, staying close to Libby's side, tail tucked under his body. The mist still blocked their path and Libby hesitated, reluctant to step back into the clammy white blanket. Bear whined. 'You don't like it either, do you? I wish we could find another way down.' Unless they intended to stay on the Tor until every last trace of murk had dispersed, she'd have to face it. 'Take a deep breath, Bear, and follow me.'

She pulled her jacket tight. 'Right, here we go.' This time, she took only half a dozen steps before bursting out into the June sunshine, laughing, relieved beyond common sense. She reached over to pat the dog. 'That wasn't so scary, was it?'

Bear whined, shivering despite the warmth of the sun. He coughed. 'You can't have caught a cold, not in just half an hour.' The dog coughed once more and slowed his pace, struggling to keep up with Libby. Every few paces, he stopped to sniff the ground. 'Did you see something that frightened you?' Libby asked. 'I can't take you back in this state. What will Max say? I only borrowed you because I wanted to stretch my legs and everyone else was busy.'

When she'd called to collect the dog for their walk, early that morning, Libby found Max Ramshore engaged in an animated phone conversation. He opened the door, grinned, winked and gave a thumbs-up sign. By the time Libby finished snapping Bear's lead to his collar, Max was scribbling notes on a pad of paper. He'd taken early retirement from his banking career and now undertook various consultancies. Libby had only a vague idea what this meant. Max had a habit of avoiding her questions, admitting only to tracking shady financial deals. He was too engrossed in the call to stop and talk, so Libby waved and led Bear to her small, battered but much loved purple Citroen.

The noise of a car, brakes squealing as it screeched to a halt, brought Libby back to the present. Doors slammed. Raised voices floated up the hill and, in a flurry of movement and shouting, two figures burst from the woods. The uniformed police officer in the lead ignored Libby and staggered on up the Hill. A policeman in plain clothes followed and Libby groaned. Blond, blue eyed, the man was easily recognisable as Max's son.

Detective Sergeant Joe Ramshore stopped in front of Libby; weary exasperation written on his face. 'I don't believe it, Mrs Forest. Always in on the action, aren't you?' He waved to his companion, urging him to keep running. Libby recognised Constable Evans, older, stouter and less fit than Joe, round face brick-red with effort, panting and gasping as he stumbled higher.

Joe groaned. 'I might have known you'd be involved, Mrs Forest. Did you phone it in?' His raised eyebrows and folded arms made Libby feel like a criminal. It must be a trick he learned at police college. Her fingers closed on the beads, safe in her pocket. Did he intend to accuse her of theft?

More police appeared; too many, surely, to search for a single string of amber beads. Close to the summit, a fitter, younger officer overtook Evans. A dreadful thought struck Libby, turning her hands clammy. 'Has something happened to the little girl?'

'Girl? What girl? We had a call about a dead man on the Tor. Was it you on the phone? Did you see him?'

Libby pulled out her phone, waving it at the detective. 'I haven't made any calls today.'

Joe narrowed his eyes, reluctant to believe anything without proof. 'Well, someone did. You need to go, Mrs Forest. We're about to cordon off the Tor.'

'There was a child on the hill, but she disappeared.' The mist seemed to thicken again. Or was it Libby's eyes, as they strained to focus against the sun? She took a step towards the Tower.

Joe swung round. 'Keep away, now. This is a police matter.'

2

SWEET TEA

Libby dragged a listless Bear back to the car, fear lying heavy in her chest. A death on the hill. *Not the child, please. Not that little girl.* Libby's lips shaped the words, repeating them under her breath as though they were a mantra.

Joe said it was a man. A dead man. Libby clung to the thought, but her heart still thudded and bile rose in her throat. If something dreadful happened to the curly haired girl, it would be Libby's fault; her responsibility. She should have grabbed one of the small hands, chaperoned the child into town and refused to rest until she found the parents.

Channels on the car radio buzzed and blared as Libby drove back to Exham. The local station was playing a jaunty tune that ended abruptly, cut off. A presenter's broad Bristolian vowels made the announcement, his words drawn out, savouring the drama. 'A body has been discovered on Glastonbury Tor. Police have yet to make a statement. The body's believed to be that of an elderly man, but we have no confirmation as yet. Our reporter is at the scene and we'll bring you breaking news as it happens...' Libby's hands gripped the steering wheel until they hurt. A rush of relief brought hot tears to her eyes, scorching the eyelids. An old man had died but at least the little girl was safe.

Bear whined, dragging Libby back to the present. She forced a shaky hand from the wheel and fumbled the key out of the ignition. Her thoughts raced. How did the body come to be on the Tor? 'Did you see anything strange, Bear? Something I missed?' She glanced over one shoulder. The dog whined again, and Libby touched his nose. It felt hot and dry. 'Poor old fellow, you don't seem at all well.'

She snatched a glance at her phone. Ten thirty? That couldn't be right. Had the battery given out or something? She switched off the phone and waited, counting to five before hitting the restart button, but there was no mistake. Most of the morning had slipped away despite their expedition starting so early. Libby calculated. A six thirty arrival and the climb to the summit; a brief conversation with the child; a rest at the top while she found the necklace. How could that have lasted four hours?

She must have wandered in the mist, following a circular path, disorientated, for longer than she realised. No wonder her legs ached. She shivered, one hand resting on Bear's head. She'd never seen the dog so exhausted. Bred to walk for hours in the mountains of Romania, he was usually a ball of boundless energy. 'I can't take you back to Max in this state.' There was a veterinary practice on the road leading to the beach. Before Libby took Bear home, she'd get him checked over. She'd never forgive herself if anything happened to the animal.

* * *

Bear hung back at the door of the surgery, reluctant, eyes mournful. 'I can't carry you. You're far too heavy. It's no good looking so miserable.' It took Libby a combination of pushing, pulling and pleading to coax him through the door.

'Poor thing,' murmured the receptionist, a cheerful, middle-aged woman. 'Isn't that the dog old Mr Thomson used to own? I'm sure Tanya will fit him in straight away. It's a quiet day, today.' She muttered into a telephone. After a moment the vet appeared, pulling on a pair of blue disposable gloves and beckoning Libby and Bear into a consulting room.

Tanya Ross, the vet, had a wiry, lean body that hinted at a jogging habit, despite the woman's apparent age. *Older than me. In much better shape, too.* Libby pulled in her stomach. Only five foot, four inches, tall, she knew every ounce of spare flesh on her body showed. The vet must be well over retirement age, judging by the ruddy, outdoor complexion and collection of crows' feet round her eyes, but she skipped across the floor, quick and light, eyes robin-bright, to examine the dog with firm but gentle fingers. Bear lifted his head and licked her hand.

Libby's spirits rose. 'He's feeling better, already. Must be your magic touch.' By the time the vet finished weighing, measuring and inspecting the dog, Bear looked far more cheerful; almost back to normal. 'What do you think was the matter?'

Tanya Ross fondled Bear's ears. 'His temperature's low but he seems to be recovering fast. What happened? Has he had a shock, or been chilled?'

Libby swallowed. 'It sounds stupid, but when the mist came down on the Tor, we lost our way. We were on the hill far longer than I thought, in the damp and cold. I can't understand how it happened. We must have been there for an hour or more, wandering round the sides of the Tor. It gave me the creeps, to be honest, and we'd only just got out of the mist when the police arrived. They told me about an accident on the hill; about the man who died.'

Tanya Ross put her head on one side. 'I heard it on the news. If you were on the hill when that poor man died, it must have given you a nasty shock. I think you need a nice hot cup of tea. Have a seat in the waiting room, and I'll make one. I could do with a brew.'

She disappeared through another door while Libby and Bear returned to the waiting room, which smelled of dog and disinfectant. Libby passed the time looking at cute photos of kittens and puppies, reading a poster that warned of the danger of ticks, and admiring a row of framed certificates. She examined all four, one for each of the vets in the practice. She'd guessed Tanya Ross's age accurately. The oldest of the team, she'd graduated from Bristol University way back in 1971 The newest vet, younger than Libby's son, Robert, had been in practice for no more than two years.

There was nothing else to read and Libby settled on a hard, wooden chair. At once, the receptionist stopped pretending to work at a computer and took off her glasses, bursting with news. Her eyes sparkled. 'Have you heard about the dead man?'

'I just came from Glastonbury Tor,' Libby admitted.

She soon wished she'd held her tongue for the woman licked her lips and, face alight with excitement, whispered, 'Did you see the body?'

'No. It was misty on the hill.' Libby kept her answer brief, hoping to shut down the conversation, but she was disappointed. The receptionist, thrilled, drew a long breath through pursed lips. 'Ooh, you be careful, m'dear. You don't want to be going up the Tor, not in the mist. Anyone will tell you that.'

Libby raised an eyebrow, suddenly intrigued. 'Why not?'

The receptionist leaned over the counter. 'You're new around here – I forgot. You see, some say there are tunnels under the Tor and King Arthur walks there every midsummer, guarded by the little people. Folk around here don't go up on the hill, then. They reckon if one of the fairies appears, it heralds a death.' Before Libby, stunned, could reply, the vet reappeared. The receptionist snatched up her spectacles, replaced them on her nose and resumed typing.

'Here.' Tanya Ross offered Libby a battered mug. 'Strong, with milk and two sugars.' Libby took a polite sip, trying not to wrinkle her nose. She hated sugar in tea. The vet leaned an elbow on the counter. 'I bet Mrs White's been telling you tales about strange happenings on the Tor.' The receptionist typed harder; eyes fixed on the screen. 'Oh, yes,' the vet went on. 'Everyone round here will tell you that local people keep away when the mist comes down.' She raised her voice. 'Don't they, Mrs White?'

The receptionist pretended not to hear. Tanya rolled her eyes. 'Take no notice of her, Mrs Forest. The stories are meant to excite the tourists, though I bet there weren't many other walkers up there today.'

'No. Oddly enough, there weren't. Bear and I were alone at first. Then we met a little girl. And the dead man—'

'You saw him?'

Libby drained the mug, trying not to shudder. 'No. He wasn't on the hill when we arrived, and I can't understand how he managed to reach the top unseen.'

'Ah. He must have climbed up the other path.'

Libby started. 'There's another one?'

'Oh yes. There's the easy way, through the woods...'

'That's the route I took.'

'And there's another entrance further down the road. The second path is shorter, but steeper.'

Libby's laugh was shaky. 'So, I'm not crazy. He came from the other direction. I didn't see him because I was lost in the mist.'

'Any idea how he died?'

'The police didn't say.'

'A heart attack, that's most likely. It's a steepish climb if you're not used to exercise.'

An elderly lady burst through the surgery door, struggling to control two perfectly matched Scottie dogs, as neat as a pair of white porcelain figurines. Tanya Ross handed Libby a small box. 'Put a couple of these tablets in Bear's food. They'll keep him calm for the next few hours and he'll be right as rain soon.'

She presented a hefty bill. Libby blinked, recovered, paid and left, the dog trotting at her side, tail in the air as though nothing had ever been wrong.

'You're a fraud,' Libby hissed, 'and an expensive one, at that.'

3

MAX

'Imagine, Max, while Bear and I were on the Tor, someone died.' Max's open French doors led to a vast, well maintained garden. Bear, his usual rude health restored, chased imaginary rabbits under bushes. He nudged aside a voluptuous peony's blowsy pink and white flowers and scrabbled at the earth beneath, sending up a shower of soil. Triumphant, he galloped back to drop a filthy, bedraggled tennis ball at Libby's feet. 'The mist, and Bear vanishing, and seeing that strange little girl.' Libby shivered. 'No wonder Bear had a funny turn.'

Max scoffed. 'He tired himself and got cold. Nothing strange about it. It sounds as though you wandered around, confused, for a lot longer than you realised.'

'I think I panicked a bit,' Libby admitted. 'I lost my bearings. I thought I was on a path.'

'You were. It's the ancient way up the hill. The remains of seven terraces still spiral round the Tor, like a maze. They're visible from a helicopter, but hard to see when you're walking. Legend suggests the monks from the Abbey took that path, when they processed up the hill to the Tower. It takes a while to reach the top, because it's an indirect route, but it's easier than climbing straight up. The steps you used at the top are recent additions, intended to make it easier for visitors. You walked the ancient route.'

Libby grunted. 'I didn't enjoy it, and nor did Bear.'

Max looked serious. 'Don't forget, Bear's an old fellow and he won't be with us for ever. In dog years, he must be getting on for ninety. I'll miss the old chap as much as you when he goes, but I'm not surprised he feels under the weather from time to time.'

'At least he recovered quickly. I didn't want to bring him back in that state.' Libby wiped mud from the ball. 'Tanya Ross's receptionist would like me to believe some kind of curse jinxed poor Bear. Something to do with Glastonbury's special relationship with the spirit world.'

'Don't let local people hear you scoff, because we're fond of our Glastonbury legends around here. We all know King Arthur's buried under the Tor.'

Libby threw Bear's ball at Max. Damp and grubby, it left a smudge of mud on his shoulder. 'Oops. Sorry.' She scrubbed at Max's jacket with a tissue, making matters worse. 'The Once and Future King is also rumoured to be buried in about five other places in England, according to the stories.'

She gave up on the mud stain. 'Joking apart, it was strange and scary on the hill today. In that thick mist, I lost all sense of time and place. I could have walked in circles for hours. It made me shiver, and I'm not given to imagining things.'

Max tossed the ball to Bear, who loped down the garden in pursuit. 'There's no one more down to earth than you.'

'Thank you.' She guessed that was meant to be some sort of compliment, though it made Libby sound dull. 'Anyway, after we came out of the mist, Joe arrived. The police spread out all over the hill, looking for the body. It gave me a shock, so soon after meeting that funny little girl.'

Max closed the doors and rested a pair of size twelve feet on the coffee table. 'I bet that child ran straight down to the nearest play park. Kids scuttle up and down the Tor all the time. The parents are always near – just don't have the puff to keep up.'

His easy explanation infuriated Libby. He wasn't taking her seriously. 'Max, someone died up there. I can't just ignore it.'

'You could leave it to the police.'

Libby made a face. 'They're most likely to write it off as an accident.'

Max sighed. 'It's none of our business.'

Libby took a breath, and Max raised his hands, as if warding off a blow. 'Don't shout at me. The police are perfectly capable of investigating a sudden death, especially if the man died from a heart attack. But the history of the Tor's interesting. I've got a book, somewhere...' He covered the floor in two strides and ran his hand over a long shelf.

Dozens of volumes, crammed in at all angles, jostled for every inch of space. 'No, must have left it in the study. Come with me.' Curious, Libby followed Max out of the room. He grinned over one shoulder. 'Don't often take people into my study. Ignore the mess if you can.'

On three sides of the tiny room, shelves ran from floor to ceiling. A haphazard mix of ancient, saggy, mismatched chairs hinted at long, comfortable reading sessions. An oak desk occupied most of the floor space. Intrigued, Libby tilted her head to one side, trying to read the spines on a heap of books that teetered on a nearby stool. *International*

Corporate Finance. Max straightened the pile. 'Work, I'm afraid.'

'Sorry. Didn't mean to pry. It's one of my bad habits. My children tell me I'm nosy.'

'Nonsense. Curiosity's a great quality. What with that and your brain power, it's no wonder you can't resist problem solving. Especially when you think other people aren't taking the issue seriously.' Max shot her a grin as he brushed crumbs and dog hairs from a chair. 'Would you like the guided tour?'

'No, the Glastonbury book first, if you don't mind.'

'Well, come and look round another time. This is a favourite place of mine.' Max waved an arm round the room. 'See, there's your cookbook.' Libby fingered *More Baking at the Beach,* a second collection of her favourite cake recipes. She had to admit, Christian, her publisher, had made a good job of the book in the end. She'd forgive him for the ceaseless phone calls and emails asking her to explain her recipes. Max was kind to buy a copy; she couldn't imagine him ever making use of it.

Max's finger traced the volumes on the shelves, stopping at a green, leather covered tome. 'Here. *Myths and Legends of the West Country*. You can borrow it, if you want.'

'Thanks.' She took the book, smooth and cool under her fingers. 'I love this room. It's cosy.' Every object looked right, from the rows of books, to the massive dog basket in one corner.

'Me too. I rattle around in the rest of this place. Can't imagine why I bought such a big house.' He waved at the ceiling. 'An old rectory like this should be full of life, with dozens of kids running up the stairs, kicking the walls and fighting. A grumpy old retired banker has no right to live here alone.'

Satisfied the chair was sufficiently clean, Max plumped up

the cushions and waved Libby to sit. 'Read *Myths and Legends* and you'll understand how lucky you've been to escape the grip of the Tor. Why, you could have been whisked away to Fairyland.' Max grinned. His old fisherman's sweater was unravelling round the neck, giving him the appearance of a North Sea trawler captain. Libby caught a whiff of woody aftershave.

'Incidentally,' Max fiddled with documents on the desk, not meeting Libby's eye. 'I'm going to a photography exhibition tomorrow. I wondered if you'd be interested.' He dropped the papers in a drawer and paced round the room.

A smile tugged at the corners of Libby's mouth. 'What photos?' She giggled as a blush crept over Max's face. 'Yours? Don't tell me you're an ace photographer?'

He stopped walking and settled into a battered old chair; long legs stretched across the floor. 'Nothing so grand, I'm afraid, but you can't live in the West Country and not be tempted to take a snap or two. I've submitted a few pictures to the show. Most of the exhibitors are keen amateurs, but a local man, John Williams, is a professional, selling pictures to magazines like Country Life. He's showing some of his earliest work. A retrospective, I believe, is the proper term.'

Libby was more interested in the sudden glimpse into one of Max's passions. 'Can I see your photos?'

'Not now. I'd be embarrassed. Come to the show, tomorrow. The hall's in Glastonbury, funnily enough, and the exhibition's the brainchild of Chesterton Wendlebury and the company he works for, Pritchards. It's called Somerset Secrets. The idea is to show off the county for the summer visitors.'

Libby groaned. She'd met Wendlebury, a wealthy businessman with a finger stuck firmly in most local pies, many times. He sat on the boards of several big, ruthless and avaricious companies. She'd suspected Pritchards, Wendlebury's biggest business, of planning to take over the Exham bakery, putting Libby, her lodger, Mandy, and Frank Brown, the baker, out of business.

Libby disliked Mr Wendlebury more every time they met.

* * *

The doorbell interrupted. 'I thought I'd find you here.' Max waved his son, Detective Sergeant Joe, into the hall. The policeman stepped inside, awkward, as though he hadn't been near his father's home for a while. 'Haven't got much time,' he said. 'Can't stop long. Wanted to let you know about the body on Glastonbury Tor.'

Joe was a younger edition of his father. He'd inherited the enigmatic, crooked smile and a pair of ice-blue eyes, the legacy of a Norwegian ancestry. At least the two of them were talking these days. By all accounts, they'd spent most of Joe's adult life at daggers drawn, since Max's divorce from Joe's mother.

'I heard the brief details on the radio,' Libby said. 'But they didn't say much. Just that it was an elderly man. What happened? Who was he?'

'The name's John Williams. He had a wallet in his pocket with his address. He lives – lived alone.'

Max paused in the act of opening a bag of coffee. 'John Williams? The photographer?'

'Is he?'

'Half the exhibition tomorrow is his work.' Max was thoughtful. 'I wonder if it'll go ahead?'

Libby interrupted. 'How did he die, Joe?'

Joe thrust his hands in his pockets. 'Suicide.'

Libby snorted.

'I know what you're thinking, Mrs Forest. You'd prefer it to be murder, but he had a note in his pocket.'

'You think he killed himself? The day before his exhibition?' Libby didn't even try to hide her disbelief.

The police officer wagged a finger, infuriating Libby. 'Mrs Forest, everything points to suicide.'

'You've said that before.' Libby had twice proved murder when the police had dismissed a death, calling it an accident.

'It's an open and shut case.'

Libby folded her arms. 'It's too easy to write off every death as accident or suicide.'

Max intervened, grinning, clearly enjoying the argument. 'You can't blame the police. Funding, lack of time, shortage of manpower...'

'What about justice? Doesn't every sudden death deserve investigation?'

Joe groaned. 'In a perfect world,' he said, 'of course they do. The world isn't perfect, though. We can't waste hundreds of police hours trying to prove a man was murdered when he left a perfectly clear note.'

He shrugged. 'And before you ask, it's in his own handwriting. We checked it with shopping lists and so on. And he tied a plastic bag round his head. Easy to do it yourself if you're determined enough – not that I'm offering tips. No one else need be involved. So, unless someone provides evidence to the contrary, suicide it is. My constable's doing the paperwork, right now.'

Max laid a restraining hand on Libby's arm. 'And you came to tell us because...?'

Joe coloured. 'Ah. Thought you'd be interested.'

Max said, ‘You mean, you’ve got a few doubts of your own and you wouldn’t mind if we poked around?’

Joe’s face was impassive. ‘I couldn’t possibly ask it of a pair of civilians.’

‘Of course, you can’t. And you haven’t, have you?’ Max winked.

‘Will the exhibition go ahead tomorrow?’ Libby asked.

Max grunted. ‘If I know Chesterton Wendlebury, he won’t let a little thing like a tragedy get in the way of a money making venture. He’ll be hoping John Williams’ death makes the show more profitable.’

Joe rubbed his chin. ‘Maybe I’ll send someone along to keep an eye on things. We can spare a community support officer for an hour or two.’

Libby asked, ‘Did you find the girl I saw?’

‘We spoke to a couple of local people.’ Joe gave a short laugh. ‘Amazing how news can spread. There were crowds in Glastonbury by the time the body was removed. At least it saved us some legwork.’

‘The child…’ she prompted.

‘Well, we heard the usual tales about fairies whose appearance heralds untimely death, of course, but aside from those, there are no reports of any missing children. I don’t think you need worry.’

His radio buzzed. He flicked a switch and listened. ‘I’ve got to get back to the station. Keep your ears to the ground, will you?’

4

MANDY

As she tidied the kitchen after breakfast the next day, Libby related her adventures on the Tor to her lodger and fellow baker's assistant, Mandy. Exham's resident teenage Goth flicked her head. A lock of black hair fell back over one side of her face. Libby closed one eye, trying to decide which side of Mandy's head looked oddest; the left, shaved close to the skull, or the right with its single long, limp strand reaching to the girl's chin. Libby longed to push in a hair clip.

Mandy jigged from one foot to the other. 'Are you going to investigate the dead man? Can I help?'

'There's little to go on at the moment. We're off to the photographic exhibition today, to see some of his work.'

'We? Max is going, too?' Mandy examined her fingernails, selected one and nibbled the corner. 'So, you're going on a date with him.'

'It's not a date, it's an investigation. You can come, too, if you like.'

'Not likely. I'm off to one of Steve's rehearsals after work.'

'Band or orchestra?'

'Band. His mate lent him a new mouthpiece for the saxophone.' Steve, Mandy's boyfriend, was a talented musician headed for the Royal College of Music in September. Meanwhile, he divided his skills. Sometimes, neatly suited, he played classical clarinet in an orchestra with other soon-to-be professional musicians. On other days, in black t-shirt and nose rings, he contributed the saxophone part to a local band called Effluvium.

'Why does he need a new mouthpiece?'

'It's metal. Makes more noise.' Libby winced and Mandy giggled. 'Yeah. It's loud. His mum won't let him play it in the house. Anyway, Mrs F, don't change the subject. You've got a date.'

'It's not a date.'

Mandy giggled. 'Saying it don't make it true. Bet you a tenner he comes in the Jag. You can't go on a proper date in that old Land Rover.' It was true, Max's favourite vehicle did smell a little of dog and ancient leather.

'Ten pounds? It's a deal.'

'Don't forget your meeting with Jumbles, that posh shop in Bath, this afternoon.'

'I'll be there,' Libby promised. 'I'll have plenty of time. I'll nip back here, pick up the samples and get to the meeting with time to spare.'

Last night, Libby's experiment with new chocolate flavours had extended well into the early hours of the morning. Samples of new orange and geranium creams sat in neat boxes in the shiny, professional standard kitchen, along with Exham's favourites, lemon meringue and mint. Libby had prepared everything for today's meeting. She wasn't leaving matters to chance. If Jumbles put in a big order, *Mrs Forest's Chocolates* would be on the way to making a decent profit.

Mandy, selecting a new finger to bite, raised heavy black eyebrows. 'Whatever.'

Libby chewed her lower lip. Mandy was turning into a real asset in the fast growing chocolate business, despite her weird appearance. Could Libby afford to take her on full time? Frank's bakery, the main outlet, was doing well. The business had gone from strength to strength lately. Frank, the owner, was so delighted he'd offered Libby a partnership. That would mean changes.

Libby wouldn't have time to manage all the development, manufacture and packaging herself much longer, never mind the marketing and advertising, especially if outlets like Jumbles put in regular orders. She'd been thinking of setting up a proper apprenticeship. She'd talk to Frank, sure he'd agree.

Would Mandy commit to it? 'We need a proper business meeting soon. I'd like to run a few ideas past you.'

'So long as you provide cake for the meeting, Mrs F. Oh, there's the door. I'll get it.'

'No...' Too late.

Mandy raced down the hall and threw open the door. 'Mr Ramshore. You look wicked.' She edged round the new arrival to take a peek at his car. 'You've brought your new Jag. How very – er – appropriate.'

Max looked puzzled. 'Swallowed a dictionary, have you, Mandy?'

The girl held out a hand, palm up, to Libby, who sighed and scrabbled in the handbag hooked on to the banister. 'Little bet, that's all,' Libby muttered, and pressed a folded ten pound note into Mandy's outstretched hand.

* * *

'These are terrific. I'd no idea there were so many fantastic beauty spots near Exham.' Libby and Max sauntered down the rows of photographs. 'I love that sunset on Exham beach. The one with the lighthouse in the distance.'

He didn't answer. 'Max, are you listening?' She'd never seen him so embarrassed. 'It's one of yours, isn't it? I'm going to buy it.'

'I'll give you a copy if you really want it.'

'No, you bought my book, so I'll buy your photograph. Oh, here's Chesterton.' Chesterton Wendlebury, burly with a yellow waistcoat, a thatch of grey hair and an impressive Roman nose, appeared beside Max. Libby's friend, Marina, splendid in a floor length orange and green dress, a red and yellow pashmina, and a string of purple beads, followed hard on his heels accompanied by a small, balding, elderly man in a formal suit. If ever there was an odd couple, it was Marina and Henry, her mild mannered husband.

Libby more often met Marina accompanied by the powerful, larger-than-life Chesterton Wendlebury than by Henry. She suspected they were more than friends.

'Henry.' Marina possessed an ear shattering, retired deputy head teacher voice. 'You simply have to buy this one. It's utterly perfect for your study.'

'Sorry, Marina,' Libby intervened. 'It's taken. I'm afraid I got here first.'

Marina looked down her substantial nose. 'I don't see any little red dot.'

'I haven't had a chance to finalise the deal.' Libby stood her ground.

'Well, you're too late, because I'm determined to have it. Chester, here's my card. Put a red dot on the picture, right now. Libby won't mind, will you, dear?'

Marina, as ever, expected her own way but Libby wouldn't give up without a fight. She wanted Max's photograph. 'In fact, I do mind, Marina. I saw it first.' They stood toe to toe, hands on hips, like children in a school playground.

Libby pasted a wide smile on her face. 'I was wondering if you still wanted me to take Shipley out for a walk tomorrow?' Marina would rather die than take her own dog for a walk. 'You know, I'm so busy these days, it's getting hard to find the time...'

Marina took the hint. 'Of course, you must have the picture, darling.' She waved an arm that jangled with bracelets, making a quick recovery. 'I wouldn't dream of standing in your way if it means so much to you.' She peered at the printed label below the photograph. 'M.R. That wouldn't be you, Max, by any chance?' She laughed, reminding Libby of the donkey whose loud braying call sounded across the fields in the early summer mornings. 'Maybe Henry and I will choose another of your efforts, Max. I'm sure we can find a nice one somewhere. Won't we, Henry?'

'Yes, dear. Perhaps we will.' Marina departed like a frigate in full sail as Chesterton Wendlebury stuck the all-important red dot to the photograph.

Max took Libby's arm. 'I think a cup of tea might be a good idea before you start a fight.'

He steered Libby to the single unoccupied table in the refreshment corner. The hall had filled almost to capacity, now the news of John Williams' death was out. Who could resist an exhibition of photographs by a man who'd died only the day before? The place hummed with excitement. Near the entrance, high visibility jackets marked the presence of a pair of police community support officers. It was their frustrating task to field a constant stream of theories, for everyone had an opinion on the affair, no matter how little they knew the dead photographer.

Chesterton Wendlebury stalked the rows of easels, hands behind his back, every smug inch the man in charge of a successful event. The till clanged and dinged. At this rate, all the exhibits would be sold in less than an hour.

Libby took a sip of weak, lukewarm coffee, made a wry face and replaced the sturdy green cup in its saucer. *I think I'll wait.*

'That's Catriona.' The muttered exclamation caught Libby's attention. At the end of a row of prints on stands, a short woman, so squat as to be almost square, had pressed a hand to her mouth, stifling her exclamation. The woman sent a quick, furtive glance around the room, as though checking for observers, before grabbing the photo and sliding it inside her coat.

She hurried down the row, removing one photo after another from its display easel.

She was stealing.

Libby shouted. 'Hey! What are you doing? Are those your photos?'

The woman, caught off balance, stumbled. Her foot nudged one leg of the nearest picture stand. It wobbled. She turned away, walking fast, head held high. Eyes fixed on the door, looking neither to right nor left, she cannoned into Libby's table sending coffee splashing across the surface.

Libby, transfixed, ignored the coffee as the picture stand rocked, teetered, righted itself for a split second and at last, in slow motion, toppled over.

It crashed onto the next stand.

The second easel fell against a third and momentum built down the row.

One after another, each easel thundering into the next, they fell like a set of dominoes. The last stand in the row collapsed on the floor in a muddle of wooden legs and photographic prints.

The woman who'd taken the photographs dodged a knot of stunned spectators as she made a dash for the door. She would have got clear away but for Chesterton Wendlebury, who stepped out, his bulk filling the exit doors, to stop the woman in her tracks. 'Not so fast, madam.'

5

JEMIMA

The culprit's eyes, enormous behind the lenses of a pair of glasses rimmed with tortoiseshell, filled with tears. 'Oh dear,' she murmured. 'Dear me. I didn't mean to...'

She sniffed, fumbled in her bag, pulled out a handkerchief and blew her nose. 'It was an accident. I – I tripped over an easel, and then – then they all started to fall, and I – well, I suppose I panicked.' She shot a sly glance at Wendlebury, as if assessing the effect of her words.

Wendlebury was too busy enjoying his favourite role as a genial, kindly gentleman to notice as the woman slipped photos from inside her coat into a large brown handbag strapped across her chest. He patted her shoulder. 'Never mind, madam. No damage done. Accidents happen. Get yourself a nice cup of tea and forget the whole thing.'

Libby mopped spilled coffee. 'Max. Did you see? That woman grabbed some of the prints.'

'Really? I was looking at Wendlebury. Got to admire the man. He's quite an operator.' He handed Libby another paper towel. 'The woman's not just clumsy, then.'

Libby nudged him. 'Don't let her leave.'

Max winked, covered the ground in a few long strides and caught up with the culprit, just as Wendlebury turned away. Max grabbed the woman's elbow. 'Not so fast. You've got a bit of explaining to do.'

Marina, Exham's most prolific gossip, had migrated to the cafe area, well away from the clear-up operation. Libby murmured in her ear, 'Do you know that woman?'

Marina's tinkly laugh rose above the hubbub in the hall. 'Of course, I do, darling, she lives in Wells. Jemima Bakewell. Recognise her from years ago, when I was teaching.'

'At the same school?'

'No. Come to think of it, I don't believe we ever had a proper conversation. She taught Classics. Dresses the part, don't you think? A spinster, of course.' Marina drifted away, losing interest and heading for Chesterton Wendlebury.

Max steered the woman towards Libby.

It was true she didn't appear to care much for fashion. Short iron grey hair, a small but conspicuous moustache, sensible brogues and a thick brown jacket stretched almost to bursting across her chest, did nothing for the woman's appearance. Her nails were broken and discoloured. *A gardener, perhaps.*

She shook Max's hand from her elbow with an irritated shrug but made no attempt to move away. Nevertheless, he positioned himself between the teacher and the door. 'Stealing photos? A teacher? Pillar of the establishment? I suggest you explain before we mention it to the community support workers. Luckily for you, they're busy helping to clean up your mess.'

The woman inspected every inch of Max, from the top of his head to the soles of his shoes, snorted her disapproval and turned away to focus on Libby. The fluffy elderly woman act had disappeared, the experienced teacher far too shrewd a judge of character to try it with either Max or Libby. 'I've seen you before, young lady. Now, where was it? I never forget a face.' She pursed her lips. 'I know, you were selling chocolates at the County Show.'

Chocolates. Oh, no. Libby gasped. She'd forgotten about the meeting in Bath. She was going to be horribly late.

As panic set in, Libby's phone trilled. She scrambled to find it at the bottom of her bag, extricated it and detached an old, fluffy mint from the screen. A message waited.

You haven't forgotten the appointment with Jumbles, have you? Mandy.

Libby swore under her breath. Even if she left right now, she'd still be late, and she'd miss the chance to find out more about Miss Bakewell and the photographs.

She hit the buttons on her phone. 'Mandy, this is your big moment. I'm stuck here and I need you to take my place. Use a taxi. It'll cost a fortune but I'll pay you back. Just get yourself and the chocolates to Bath as fast as you can.'

She heard Mandy take a deep breath on the other end of the phone. 'Okay, Mrs F. No worries. Will do.'

* * *

Max pointed at Miss Bakewell's bag. 'Shall we take a look at the photographs you stole?'

The woman fiddled with the strap, twisting the end round her hand. 'Photographs? What do you mean?'

Libby held out a hand. 'I saw you take pictures from the

easels and hide them in your coat and transfer them to your bag. You can't deny it, so you might as well explain why you wanted them. Come on, hand them over.'

For a moment, the teacher looked ready to refuse. Neither Libby nor Max had any authority to force the issue and Libby was already looking for the police workers, when Miss Bakewell sighed, delved into the bag and handed over a small stack of prints.

'I don't believe it,' Libby muttered.

Max leaned over her shoulder. 'Glastonbury Tor. Nothing odd in that. You can see plenty of photos of the Tor in the exhibition. There are more prints of the hill than anything else.'

'That's not what I mean. Look.' Libby pointed to the child in the picture, the small face dwarfed by a cloud of curly black hair, whipped to a thatch by the wind. 'That's the little girl I met on the hill.'

Miss Bakewell muttered, under her breath, 'So, it's not her, after all.'

'That's the child I met.'

The woman laughed in a high pitched voice, sounding on the verge of hysteria. 'It's all a silly mistake. Just a photograph. Not what I thought, at all.'

She made a grab for the print but Libby whisked it away. 'The photograph was taken recently. Look at the date. Oh—'

Max said, 'Now what's the matter?'

'I found that necklace on top of the Tor. I'm sure of it. The photo's dated June the twelfth last year, and the little girl's wearing the beads round her neck.'

Max rounded on the teacher. 'You'd better tell us why you took the photos. Otherwise, we'll be tempted to give them to the police; they're private property, you know. I expect you'd rather not be charged with theft.'

The woman folded her arms, scowling, but said nothing.

Max flipped through the pile. 'Most of these date back a long time. To the late sixties, I'd guess.'

'You're right.' Libby pointed. 'Look at the clothes on that couple.' The two people in the photograph, smiling at the camera, were unmistakable hippies, all long hair and necklaces.

Libby gasped. 'There's the necklace again. Look, Max, it's in the old photos as well.'

6

THE NECKLACE

Max pulled three chairs round a table and introduced Libby. Jemima Bakewell shot him a look fierce enough to curdle milk and spoke to Libby. 'Very well. I can see you're a sensible woman, Mrs Forest, so I'll explain. I found the necklace many years ago. I should have handed it in, but I didn't. I became rather fond of it.'

Libby frowned. Was she confessing to jewellery theft? It seemed unlikely.

The woman clenched her hands until the knuckles turned white. 'I assure you, young woman, it's true. I went for a walk one day, found the necklace on the Tor, liked it, popped it in my pocket and forgot about it.' She rubbed her nose. 'No one reported it missing. I would have returned it at once, if so. I'd no idea the beads had historical importance until, several weeks later, I emptied my pockets, ready to send the coat to be cleaned, and looked at the necklace more carefully.'

She swallowed and Libby frowned, confused. *She's lying, but why?* 'What do you mean by historical significance?' she asked.

'I'm a teacher of Classics. I've devoted many years to the study of ancient texts. In fact, my treatise on a comparison between the Iron Age in Britain and the later Roman civilisation was exceptionally well received.' Libby nodded, trying to look impressed. Max sighed and tapped an impatient finger on his knee, but Libby glared, sending a signal to let the woman talk.

Miss Bakewell gained in confidence as she explained her work. 'In my paper, I point out the importance of certain items of jewellery to early settlers. The necklace is a case in point. It would have formed part of the grave furniture of a high status woman, in 250BC.' The teacher broke off. 'That's right, Mrs Forest. You may well gasp. Those beads date back more than 2,000 years. Archaeologists must have discovered them when they explored the remains of the Glastonbury Lake Village settlement.' Her neck turned pink. 'I should have handed the necklace in to the authorities but I'd grown fond of the beads and no one seemed to know about them.'

The fingers of one of Miss Bakewell's hands scratched at the back of the other until Libby feared she might draw blood.

'What was so special about the beads?'

'Special?' The woman looked down, snatched her hands apart and gripped the seat of her chair. 'Oh, just their age, of course.' The attempt at nonchalance wouldn't fool a child. 'That was all. They're important because they're so old, but no one was looking for them. I thought I could keep them safe but a few weeks ago, I heard the University was planning another excavation at the site. I decided to hand them back, but...'

'But you lost them?'

Miss Bakewell cleared her throat. 'I – I took a walk up the

Tor, for old times' sake, and I wore the beads. They're threaded on a piece of wire, not gold or silver, so they don't count as Treasure Trove. The wire was old and thin and I suppose it must have broken because when I returned home, I'd lost the beads.' She spread her hands and sighed.

Libby said, 'As a matter of fact, I have them.'

Miss Bakewell's head flew up, eyelids stretched wide, jaw slack.

'Yes, I found them on the Tor.' *That wiped the sanctimonious expression off your face.* 'Of course,' Libby added, 'I'll return them to the proper owner when I find out who that is. If there's a new excavation, I can hand them in myself.' From the corner of her eye she saw the flash of a grin on Max's face.

Miss Bakewell scraped her chair back, grasped the handbag to her chest and took a step towards the door.

'Wait.' Libby took her arm. 'We haven't finished.'

'No, no. I have to go.' The woman's hand was trembling. 'Here's my address.' She shook off Libby's hand, scribbled on a scrap of paper, and threw the note down on the muddle of photographs. With a surprising turn of speed, she shuffled across the room and out of the door, leaving Libby standing.

Max reached for the address and whistled. 'She's quite a character.'

'She didn't think much of you,' Libby pointed out, 'and finding out I have those beads spooked her. Do you think anything she told us was true?'

'Parts of it. I reckon she made up most of the story for our benefit, probably because she's ashamed of taking the beads. I wonder where she really found them?' Max rubbed his hands. 'Let me have a look at them when we get back to Exham. Don't you love it when peculiar things happen? The Case of the Ancient Beads. That's something else for

Ramshore and Forest, Detectives Extraordinaire, to investigate, don't you think?'

'I think it's all very suspicious. The man who photographed people wearing the beads died just one day before he shows the photos. It gives me the creeps. D'you think she knew him?'

Max's eyes glittered. 'We need to learn a bit more about those beads. Miss Bakewell said they came from an excavation and I'm tempted to believe that part of the story. The dig must be documented.'

'I know how we can find out more about Somerset's past.'

Max closed his eyes for a beat and groaned. 'Oh no. Definitely not. I'm not going anywhere near the local history society. I've been there once, and that was more than enough. Those women terrify me.'

'It's the best place to start. They know absolutely everything about Somerset.'

He was shaking his head. 'When Marina Sellworthy gives me the once-over I feel like a grubby and unimportant fossil from Kilve beach, and the rest of your history society friends are the biggest gossips in the West Country.'

'What do you have to hide? Are you telling me you can pull the wool over the eyes of international criminals, but you're too chicken to face the history society?'

'That's about right. A man can only withstand so much.'

'OK, I'll talk to them. There's a meeting in a couple of days, and I still provide the cakes.' Libby gathered up the photos. 'That was Marina's fault, by the way. She nabbed me about a week after I arrived, almost as though she was lying in wait. She persuaded me it would provide good advertising for my business. She can be very persuasive, and once I'd agreed it got harder to back out.'

'What flavour are you offering this time?'

'Cardamom and ginger. Tempted?'

Max grimaced. 'Sounds good, but not great enough to get me in that room. You might save me a slice, but I'll leave the society to you. I'll do some internet searches, and we can compare notes. First, though, we'd better return the photos Miss Bakewell left behind.'

Max stopped talking. She'd seen that look on his face before. 'Max? What are you cooking up?'

He took the pile of photos from Libby's hands. 'There's no hurry. We'll hand these prints over to John Williams' estate in a couple of days, but first, let's have another look at them. Maybe we'll see why they mattered so much to Miss Bakewell. I don't buy the historically valuable ancient beads story. It's not as if the police were on her trail for stealing them forty years ago.'

'You're right. She kept glancing at the photos while we were talking, as though she saw something she didn't want us to notice. I don't suppose it will hurt to keep them for a while.'

'Joe told me John Williams was single and lived alone, so there's no wife or kids wanting the photos for sentimental reasons.'

The hall had emptied, visitors at last persuaded to leave, to embellish their stories at home. Max slipped the pictures inside his jacket. 'We can't study these photos properly here. Are you free tomorrow?'

'It depends how Mandy got on this afternoon. I had to send her to Jumbles with the chocolate samples. They've talked about stocking our products, but if the meeting went horribly wrong I might need to build bridges.'

'That girl could sell nuts to Brazil if she set her mind to it.

I'd like to be a fly on the wall when the Jumbles staff see her tattoos. Isn't it an old-fashioned business?'

'That's what bothers me, though their marketing girl sounded younger than I'd expected. I'd better get back home and prepare for the worst. Fingers crossed, see you tomorrow.'

* * *

Libby walked into the kitchen and her jaw dropped. 'Is that really you?' Mandy had brushed her hair until it shone. A demure hair band held the long side out of her eyes and hid most of the shaved area. She'd dabbed a subtle hint of pink blusher on her cheeks and removed most of the facial nuts and bolts, leaving only two or three earrings in each ear. Even the skull tattoo had disappeared; a fake, as Libby suspected. She recognised the pink silk shirt and pencil skirt, though. 'Are you wearing my clothes?'

Mandy swore, kicked off a pair of six inch Jimmy Choo's, the only pair of designer shoes Libby owned, and rubbed a bright red spot on her toe joint. 'Blimey, how do you wear these babies, Mrs F? They're giving me bunions.'

'Those shoes are strictly 'car to bar.' I've never tried to walk any distance in them. I just tottered across the road, sat down for dinner, and limped back to the car. Best with tights and some of those gel pads, by the way, for future reference.'

The shoes hadn't seen the light of day for years. Trevor, Libby's late husband, hadn't frequented bars. At least, she amended, he hadn't taken Libby to them. She'd recently realised she hadn't known Trevor at all, for under his respectable insurance salesman front, he'd been part of a web of fraud. His role had been laundering money through property deals.

Libby winced, remembering some of the lies he'd told.

Mandy was talking. 'Does that mean I get to wear the shoes again?'

'A little out of character for a Goth, aren't they?'

'I suppose. Anyway, I don't wear tights. Well, not those flesh coloured things.' Mandy's legwear was restricted to thick black tights. 'My toes are all, like, screwed up. Look at them.' She hoisted a bare foot on to the tabletop.

Libby shrieked. 'Don't do that. I'll lose my five star food hygiene certificate.'

'Only if an inspector happens to look in the window, and if they're snooping about at this time of night, we'll call Max's son, grumpy Detective Sergeant Joe.'

Libby shooed Mandy out of the kitchen into the living room, wiping the table with Dettol on the way. The girl stood in the hall, hopping from one bare foot to the other. 'Don't you want to know how I got on, then?'

'I'm beside myself. Judging by your face, it went well.'

'They loved me, Jumbles did. Ate all the chocs, told me I did you credit, and said you were to give me a raise.'

'Oh, yeah?'

'Maybe not the last bit. But they've put in an order. Look.'

Mandy extracted a crumpled sheet of paper from her bag. A column of figures marched down the page and Libby whistled. 'This is easily the biggest order we've had yet.'

'It's not just for now, either. They want to try these out for starters, and if they sell, they want a repeat every month.'

'Mandy!' Libby collapsed onto the sofa, infuriating her marmalade cat. Fuzzy stalked away and slunk upstairs to hide in the airing cupboard.

'Can we do it? Fulfil the order, I mean?'

Dates and preparation times swirled round Libby's head.

She sat up, taking a deep, steadying breath. 'Of course, we can. Now, I'll need your help. I've got a proposition. I've been meaning to talk to Frank about setting up an apprenticeship, and if he agrees—'

'And he always agrees with you – ever since you saved the business—'

'If he agrees, I think you'd be a great apprentice.'

'What? You mean, like, official? With qualifications and everything?'

'Absolutely.'

Mandy whooped, threw her arms in the air and jigged round the room, giggling. At last, breathless, she flopped backwards over the arm of a chair, leaving her bare feet dangling.

'When do I start? Frank's taken on a couple of new girls, so he won't mind me moving across to the chocolate side of the business.'

'In a week, and only if Frank goes along with it. That'll give us time to get the paperwork done.'

Libby darted back to the kitchen, retrieved a bottle of chilled New Zealand Chardonnay from the fridge and poured two large glasses.

'Don't gulp, sip,' She insisted as Mandy took a huge mouthful. 'We're going to be busy, supplying Jumbles as well as the bakery. Are you up for it?'

'Watch me. Oh, nearly forgot. Your iPad's been dinging. Can't you turn the noise off?'

'Haven't got around to it.' The machine was new, and Libby hadn't got to grips with it. She flipped up the cover and checked her emails, finding one from Max, headed *The Beads.* 'He's sent photos. How do I open them?'

'Just tap.' Mandy emptied her glass and broke pieces off a

bar of Cadbury's Dairy Milk, giggling at Libby's horrified double take. 'Your chocs are wonderful, Mrs F, but sometimes a girl needs, like, a proper bar of chocolate.'

As the first photograph opened, Libby studied the set of amber beads arranged on a table alongside other artefacts. She compared them to the ones she'd found on the Tor. They were identical. Alongside the necklace, Libby recognised a sharpened stone as a spear head. Max had added a note.

Found the photo online. If your beads are the same, it seems they came from an excavation near the Tor about forty years ago.

Libby smiled. Miss Bakewell had a few more questions to answer.

Max's second photo showed the Tor rising from a mist that ended just below St Michael's Tower, blocking out half the hill.

Libby said, 'The Tor looked like that when Bear and I were there.'

'Spooky,' Mandy said. 'Makes you shiver.'

7

2,000 YEARS

'Did you bring the necklace?' Max asked.

Libby and Mandy cradled mugs of coffee in Max's living room, while Bear stretched across as many feet as possible, grunting with pleasure. Libby placed her mug out of reach of the dog's tail and unzipped a small pocket in her handbag, pulling out a silk jewellery pouch that once contained a silver brooch. The amber stones felt warm against her skin. 'I've been terrified of losing them. I kept moving them around, hiding them in different places. In the end, I decided my bag's the safest place. I never go anywhere without it.'

Max agreed. 'It would take a better man than me to part a woman from her handbag.' Libby laid the beads on the coffee table.

'More than 2,000 years,' Mandy murmured. 'You wouldn't know it. They just look old and dusty, really.'

Max had spent the previous evening googling amber beads. He shared his findings. 'Amber's a strange medium. It's actually tree resin, compressed for hundreds of years. Sometimes, it traps insects or flowers, preserving them inside the amber for ever.'

Mandy giggled. 'Or until someone takes the DNA and makes dinosaurs. Like in Jurassic Park.'

Max grinned. 'I'm not sure the science of that idea holds water, but amber's been valued as a precious stone for hundreds of years. It's even thought to have healing properties.'

'I'm not surprised folk are fascinated.' Libby picked up the beads and with a sigh, slid them back into the silk pouch, zipping them in the side of her bag. 'I wish I could hang on to them but I suppose I should find the real owner and hand them back. At least they aren't part of a hoard of gold or diamonds, or Miss Bakewell would really be in trouble.'

She laid Max's *Myths and Legends* book on the table. 'I was up all night reading this. Glastonbury seems to have as many legends as ancient Greece.'

Mandy grabbed it, skimming the text. 'Well, the Tor's pretty cool, with that old ruin on top. St Michael's Tower,' she read. 'Never knew that was its name.' She pointed to a sticky note. 'What's all this about a curse?'

'It keeps cropping up.' Libby took the book and thumbed through the pages, pointing to other marked areas. 'Here, you see, and on this page. Look. Amber beads figure in the tales of King Arthur and Guinevere. Guinevere was King Arthur's young wife, but she fell in love with Lancelot, one of the twelve knights. According to the story, he travelled far and wide searching for the Holy Grail, and on the way he found a dozen 'perfect gems' which he gave to the beautiful Queen. She hid them from her husband, for fear he'd suspect her love for Lancelot, but forgot where she'd left them.'

'You'd think she'd take care of a present like that.' Mandy put in.

Remembering something, Libby scanned her notes. 'Look, she was only a teenager. Not even as old as you. I suppose girls were as forgetful then as they are now.' Mandy made a face. 'Present company excepted,' Libby added.

'Are you going to finish the story?' Max tapped a foot, impatient. Mandy rolled her eyes at Libby and mouthed, 'Men.'

'I saw that,' Max said.

Libby went on, 'One day, the beads appeared on a golden platter at dinner. Guinevere, frightened one of her household knew of her secret love and planned to inform the King, made up a story about a child finding them at the foot of a great hill. King Arthur believed her and ruled they must be kept at Glastonbury for ever. Because Guinevere lied to her husband, the story goes, bad luck would fall on anyone who touched the beads.'

Max looked from Libby to Mandy and laughed. 'I wish you could see your faces. Anyone would think you believed all this mumbo-jumbo.'

'Of course, we don't,' Libby said. 'It's just a legend. Good story, though.'

Mandy interrupted. 'So, who put the beads on the serving platter?'

'Doesn't say in the records. Someone knew about the affair with Lancelot and wanted to cause trouble. Even in Arthur's court, there were arguments and jealousies. Maybe one of her ladies wanted Lancelot for herself. Rivalry's inevitable, I think, where people live close together.'

'Like Exham on Sea?' Mandy suggested.

Max laughed, but Libby glanced at her bag, thinking

about the beads. Trouble seemed to surround them, even now.

'Libby, you've gone quiet.'

'Sorry. I was thinking about jealousy and quarrels, and bad luck.'

Mandy's eyes were round. 'What do you mean?'

Libby gave a short laugh. 'I'm not sure, really, except that John Williams took photographs of people wearing the beads and now he's dead.'

* * *

Mandy pulled on a jacket, ready to leave for a shift at the bakery. 'It's so unfair. You two can carry on drinking coffee and sleuthing, while I'm slaving in the bakery. Those new girls Frank brought in are so-o-o slow.'

'Help Frank train them up, so you can start that apprenticeship.'

Mandy mounted her bike. 'Can't wait. Don't uncover the murderer before I get back, will you?'

'Tell you what,' Libby said. 'We'll invite Max for dinner and talk more, then.'

Mandy wobbled in a circle, narrowly missing the trunk of an old ash tree as Bear tried to lick her ankles. 'By the way, what's on the menu?'

'Sticky spiced chicken. It's already in the fridge, at home. We'll just need rice. Bring Steve, if you like.'

'Young love,' Max murmured, hauling the dog indoors and kicking the door shut in one practised movement. 'I wonder how long it'll last.'

'Steve's leaving for music college in a few months. Things

may fizzle out, especially if Mandy's busy with the apprenticeship. I'd be sorry, though. They're very happy.'

'At their age, they'll be changing partners every few months. Didn't you have plenty of boyfriends when you were young?'

Libby threw a ball for Bear to hide hot cheeks. 'Not really. Trevor sort of took me over, when we met. He was very persistent.'

'And he bullied you?'

'Not at first. A little, maybe, later,' she admitted. In fact, towards the end of their marriage, her husband had convinced Libby she was stupid and ugly. He kept up a daily barrage of criticism: her clothes were too tight, her hair a mess and her legs ugly and fat. When he died, a weight lifted from Libby's shoulders.

She recognised, with hindsight, how Trevor had controlled everything she did. Once he'd gone, Libby vowed to take charge of her own future, and wasted no time in leaving London for Exham on Sea. As soon as she arrived in town, she set about building a new life making cakes and chocolates.

When she'd uncovered Trevor's involvement in the series of financial frauds Max was investigating, Libby was mortified.

'Talking of Trevor,' Max said, 'which is a subject we try to avoid, I've got a meeting in London soon, to pull together the threads of money laundering in Leeds.' Libby snorted.

'What?'

'Sorry. Laundry. Threads. You know. It seemed funny for a moment.' She swallowed. 'I get nervous when we talk about Trevor.'

'There's no need for you to feel bad. Your husband had a

portfolio of houses bought with funny money. You didn't. You've done nothing illegal. Be patient a while longer. I'm hoping we can wind the whole business up soon.'

'The sooner the better.' Libby had an idea. 'I need some fresh air. D'you fancy a walk? Let's pick up Shipley from Marina and go out to the cliffs at High Down.'

8

HIGH DOWN

Shipley's high pitched yelp echoed from inside Marina's house. As the door opened, the springer spaniel bounded out, whining with excitement, nails clattering on the wood floor. Libby grabbed his collar and guided him back into the house. Marina seemed ill at ease, with flushed cheeks and untidy hair. 'Are you all right?' Libby asked.

'Fine, I'm fine.' Someone coughed inside the house, and Libby had to bite her cheeks to keep from laughing. That cough didn't belong to Henry Sellworthy.

'Is it an awkward time?' Libby's tone was innocent. Her friend appeared to be conducting the affair in her own home, right under her husband's nose.

Marina's eyes flashed, but she beckoned Libby to come inside. 'Actually, Chester's here. We're going over a few business details.'

Business? Libby shrugged. It was nothing to do with her. 'I won't come in. I'm wearing wellies, ready for a walk on High Down. We're taking Bear and I thought Shipley might like to come.'

'We?' Marina peered round Libby.

Max stuck his head out of the Land Rover and waved. 'Hi, Marina. Fancy a run?'

'No, thank you.' Her voice crackled with ice. She raised an eyebrow at Libby and murmured, 'You two spend a lot of time together, these days. Still, you're a free woman, now Trevor's gone.'

Libby started. 'You sound as though you knew my husband? Had you met?'

Marina waved a hand vaguely. 'Oh, just the once. You were on holiday in the area, I believe, and Trevor took a few hours to discuss business with Chester – some boring insurance details about damage to one of Pritchard's business premises. I think he said you took the children to a matinee at the Hippodrome.'

'Yes, Trevor worked on the Pritchards' account.' She remembered that day, halfway through their holiday in Exham. Ali had begged for them all to go to Bristol, to the ballet, but Trevor refused. He said he couldn't bear to sit through an afternoon of dancing, but he'd take them all out to dinner as compensation.

Marina had never mentioned knowing Trevor. That was odd, but perhaps she didn't want Libby to know more about her involvement with Chesterton Wendlebury. That seemed to be far more than just a business relationship.

Lately, Libby had discovered her husband had hidden some rather unsavoury business connections from her, but Marina would know nothing about all that.

She smiled at her friend. She wouldn't discuss her relationship with Max. That would give Marina even more ammunition for tittle-tattle. 'What about it, Shipley? Ready for a walk?'

At the magic words, a frenzy of excitement sent Shipley scurrying to the back of the house to find his lead.

Marina followed, a cloud of perfume drifting in her wake. Libby recognised the scent. *Poison;* a heady, glamorous perfume. Marina produced her parting remark. 'You know it's going to rain, don't you?'

Shipley dragged Libby out to the Land Rover, Bear barked a greeting, the spaniel piled in the back, Libby jumped in the front and Max drove off, squealing the tires to make Marina roll her eyes.

'There's something going on between Marina and Chesterton Wendlebury,' Libby said. 'Do you think she's about to leave Henry?'

'And deprive herself of his pension? Not likely.'

'Wendlebury's a rich man. He could look after her.'

Max shot an odd look in her direction. 'Rich on paper. He makes a good job of being the local squire, I grant you, but I've a feeling things aren't all they seem.'

'I've never quite trusted him,' Libby confessed, 'and he seems to have been one of Trevor's rather shady contacts.' Libby had looked into a house her husband owned in Leeds, and found he bought it on behalf of Pritchards.

'You don't trust anyone.' Max was brisk.

'Not surprising, since my husband turned out to be involved in some dubious deals.' Libby stole a sideways glance at Max. What did he mean, she didn't trust anyone?

'Don't look so worried.' He said. 'In our business, it doesn't hurt to be cautious.'

'Our business?'

'Private investigation. Come on, Libby, we've talked about it before. You've got a nose for things that don't add up and a logical brain. I've been trained in undercover financial research. I'm not suggesting you ditch the cakes and chocolate. You've got a great business going there, and we're never going to make a fortune as private eyes, but we're good partners.'

Libby's heart pumped so fast she thought Max would hear it over the rumble of the engine. She took a deep breath. He meant business partners, of course. It was Mandy's fault Libby felt so unsettled. She'd suggested he cared, just because they went to the exhibition in his posh new Jaguar.

Libby pulled a map out of the pocket of the car door and pretended to study the route to High Down, while she let her flaming cheeks cool. 'Let me think about it, Max. The chocolate business is just beginning to take off, and I've asked Mandy to do a proper apprenticeship. When that's going well, maybe...'

'Let's face it,' he went on, 'we're already working together. Why not make it official? You know, business cards, a website and a bit of mouth to mouth advertising. That's all I'm suggesting.'

'But what happens if we're in the middle of an investigation, and you suddenly disappear to South America for work? How can I trust you, when you keep things from me?' Max turned and stared.

Libby grabbed the wheel. 'Look where you're going.'

'I'm not the one who ran their car into the ditch.'

'I've only done it once. Don't change the subject. The point is, how can I work with a partner who takes off without a word and never tells me where he's going?'

Max let the silence draw on. When he spoke again, he sounded thoughtful. 'I suppose you've got a point, but I won't be doing consultancy work for ever.'

Libby swallowed hard, battling to keep her breathing

steady as Max pulled through a gate and drove along a rutted path towards the cliffs. As the Land Rover drew to a halt, Bear and Shipley whined and drooled with excitement. Max jumped out, threw open the doors and shooed the dogs onto the Downs, where the first few drops of rain heralded Marina's promised rainstorm.

* * *

The rain drove hard across High Down, but neither of the dogs cared a jot. Libby pulled up the hood of her new parka, zipped the collar and strode on, enjoying the rain against her face. In London, she'd always carried an umbrella, terrified of a sudden storm causing her unruly hair to frizz, but she'd learned to love a good downpour.

To her surprise, Max took her arm. 'Sorry if I upset you,' he murmured.

'You didn't,' she lied, startled.

He squeezed her arm. 'Come on, let's look round the old fort.'

For half an hour, they explored the ruined buildings. Shipley raced in and out of the wartime pillbox while Bear investigated interesting holes in the ground and chased imaginary rabbits.

'The rain's getting worse,' Max pointed out. 'Maybe we should go. Am I really invited to this sticky chicken dinner tonight, or have I blown my chances?'

A sudden burst of barking interrupted him. Bear hovered at the edge of the cliff.

'Can you smell another rabbit?' Libby waded through muddy puddles on the path. As she reached Bear's vantage point, Shipley appeared behind her, keen to see what Bear was doing. He brushed past Libby, just as she raised a foot to step over another puddle.

Caught off balance, she tripped and fell, rolling down the steep slope, scrabbling to clutch at tufts of grass and wild-flower stems.

'Libby!' Max was too far away to help as Libby slid over the edge of the cliff. After a long moment, she landed with a thud that squeezed every ounce of air from her lungs. Her head connected with something hard. *So that's what it means to see stars.*

For a moment, lights swirled in front of her eyes before darkness descended.

* * *

She opened her eyes. A wide ledge further down the cliff face had broken her fall. Max was at the cliff edge, looking down, horror etched on every line of his face.

'Libby,' he called. 'Can you hear me? Are you OK?'

Libby tried to lift her right hand but it wouldn't move. Her wrist seemed to twist at an odd angle and it ached. She tried her left hand, relieved to find it uninjured. She used it to wave.

Max called, 'I'm on my way. I'll get a rope from the car.'

'No, don't come. You'll fall too.'

As she shouted, Bear jumped down from the top of the cliff and licked Libby's face. 'Get off, Bear. I'm quite all right.'

She lifted her head and discovered she wasn't quite all right. Her head hurt.

Moving as little as possible, she stole a glance over the ledge and shivered at the drop. She'd been close to falling the full height of the cliff. Bear stood between Libby and the drop and she pulled his warm body closer. 'You're a clever old dog. I'm glad you're here.'

'Hold tight.' Max was back. 'I've tied the rope to a tree. I'm coming down.' Seconds later, he joined her on the ledge. 'I'm getting too old for this.' He held out the end of the rope. 'Now, tie it round your waist, in case you slip. It'll stop you falling further.'

Libby fumbled, trying to tie a knot with one shaky hand. Max's fingers were warm on hers as he took the rope. 'Here, let me do it. I was a boy scout, you know. Knots are my thing.'

He secured the rope around Libby's waist. 'That's a bowline, I believe. I hope you're impressed.' He slid an arm round her shoulders. 'What's the matter with your hand?'

'I hurt my wrist.'

'Anything else?'

'A bit of a headache. Nothing to worry about.'

Side by side, they looked up at the climb. 'Can you make it, or should I ring for the coastguard?'

'Don't you dare. I don't want my picture in the paper.'

'You're as white as a sheet. Is your wrist broken?'

'Only a sprain, I think.' Libby cradled her right hand with her left. 'It only hurts if I move it.'

'I suggest you don't move it.'

With Max's arm round her shoulders, keeping her safe, Libby felt light headed. Overcome with relief at not falling to her death, she giggled and found she couldn't stop. Even Max was infected, his shoulders shaking with laughter. Bear remained on the ledge, patient, waiting for his two foolish humans to calm down, while Shipley scampered back and forth at the top of the cliff, thrilled by so much excitement, barking at the top of his lungs.

Max made his hands into a cup for Libby's foot and

hoisted her to his shoulders. Her head reached a little above the lip of the cliff. 'Right,' Max said. 'On three.'

He placed both hands firmly on her bottom and gave a mighty shove that sent her up and over the top, clinging on with her good hand as she scrambled, one knee following the other, onto the grass above.

Bear leaped up, making easy work of the jump. Max heaved himself up on the rope and joined Libby where she lay on her back.

'Take me home,' she begged. 'I think I've had enough fresh air for one day.'

9

STICKY SPICED CHICKEN

Miss Bakewell's stolen photographs decorated one wall of Libby's living room. Mandy, Max and Libby, her wrist tightly bandaged, scrutinised each picture in turn.

'We know these were taken by John Williams,' Libby said, 'but why did Miss Bakewell try to steal them?'

Mandy walked down the line, head on one side. 'The same people keep cropping up. Look, there's a couple of, like, hippies, I guess. All droopy moustaches and afro hair. These must be their girlfriends.' She squealed. 'Wow. Sick clothes.'

'You can talk.' Libby gestured at Mandy's latest tattoo, a lurid design representing a skull with angel's wings. 'I hope that's not permanent, by the way.'

Mandy tossed her head. 'I'm not daft.'

Libby returned to the photos. 'Caftans, tight purple loons and flowery shirts with enormous sleeves were high fashion in the sixties, Mandy. You know, Carnaby Street, the Rolling Stones, miniskirts the first time round...'

'Yeah. I've seen the retro stuff, like, a million times. The

Beatles, Sergeant Pepper, Hari Krishna, psychedelic drugs, frizzy hair...'

'No proper hair straighteners in those days. Girls used steam irons on their hair, so most of the time it was pretty much as nature intended.'

Max, tired of their discussion of sixties culture, studied a photo at the end of the row. It showed a girl wearing a tiny skirt and a wide-brimmed hat. 'If I'm not very much mistaken, that's our Jemima Bakewell, in her youth.'

'Never.' Libby leaned close and squinted. 'Are you sure? I mean, look at all that lovely brown hair. I suppose, if you picture that face with short grey hair and a pair of spectacles, it could be her.'

Mandy sniffed. 'You said Miss Bakewell needed make-up and a decent haircut. She looks cool in the photo.'

'Deteriorated over the years,' Libby sighed. 'Happens to us all, as you'll find out soon enough, Mandy.'

Bear lay on his back, wriggling, demanding attention. With his three favourite humans in the room at the same time, surely at least one could talk to him. Mandy gave in, squatted down and scratched his stomach while Max and Libby focused on the photos. Max sucked his teeth. 'I'm almost certain it's Miss Bakewell. See that mole on her cheek?'

He was right. The girl laughing into the camera had the teacher's mole and Libby recognised that square jaw. 'How old d'you think she was when the photo was taken? Nineteen or twenty?'

'About that, I'd guess. Let me do the sums.' Max paused. 'Yes, she must be over sixty now. I'd say that's about right.'

'It looks like she had a boyfriend. That one in the pink

shirt has his arm round her. I wonder why she didn't admit to being in the picture.'

Interested, Mandy strolled back to the photos. 'Hey,' she shouted. Bear grunted, lurched to his feet and pushed his head under her arm. 'Get away, Bear. I wasn't talking to you. Look, Mrs F, she's wearing the amber beads.'

Max thumped Mandy's back. 'So she is. Well spotted. Maybe that's why she took the photos; so no one could see her with the stolen necklace.'

'Or perhaps she didn't want to be recognised. I think we need to find out more about these people; who they are and what they know about the necklace.'

Libby gasped. 'I've just realised. You see the girl behind the others? The one with long black curls half way down her back? She looks like the child on the top of the Tor.'

'Pretty girl,' said Max, 'but there were thousands of pretty girls with hot pants and long black hair in the sixties. She could be anyone.'

Libby compared the modern photo of the child with the old picture of Miss Bakewell and her companions. 'They look exactly like each other. Same hair, similar noses, and their smiles are identical. They must be related.'

'Maybe. Miss Bakewell will know, but will she tell the truth?' Max began with the first photo and pointed at each in turn. 'These people are probably all local. The photographs are taken in several different places, all near here. There's the Tor, and this one,' he said, pointing, 'shows the beach in Exham. Look, there's the lighthouse. And that's the Knoll, just outside town.'

Mandy took up the thread. 'So, they were all here together. Could they have been on holiday?'

'No, I don't reckon that's it. If that were the case, all the snapshots would be taken within a few days or weeks, but if you look carefully, you can see they're spread out across a year or more.'

His finger moved from one picture to the next. 'Here, the trees are bare, photographed in winter, but this one's taken in the summer. The trees are in leaf, there are flowers in the hedgerows and the girls are wearing thin dresses.' He hummed as he thought. 'Yes, I reckon they're students.'

'Why?'

'For one thing, they're all about the same age but they're too old to be school kids. We've agreed they look maybe nineteen or twenty. So, we've got a group of young people together for long periods of time.'

'You're right.' Mandy punched Max's shoulder, getting her revenge. 'They're all students at the same University.'

Libby added, 'Miss Bakewell was reading Classics, so I wouldn't mind betting they were at Bristol University. They award degrees in Greek and Latin.' She held up her undamaged hand in self-defence. 'And if either of you thumps me on the back, I'll empty my wine on your head. My arm's still aching.' Excitement carried her along. 'It's a starting point, at least. Would anyone at the University remember students from those days?'

Max was humming again. 'Where do you keep old newspapers?'

'In the rack, over there.' Libby pointed behind the sofa. 'Why?'

He dragged out a muddle of magazine fliers and old papers and Libby winced. Time to throw a few things out. The cottage had needed a spring clean for weeks.

Max shuffled the pile, flicking through pages, tossing them aside in a swelling flood of paper on the floor. 'Ah.

Thought he looked familiar.' He folded a recent copy of the Bristol Gazette into a neat square and held it next to one of the photos. 'Look.'

Libby narrowed her eyes, trying to see a likeness. 'You're right,' she agreed. 'The boy standing next to Miss Bakewell in the photo looks like the man in the newspaper. Only much younger. Who is he?'

'A Professor Malcolm Perivale.' Apparently, he presented a paper to the Bristol Antiquarians on radiocarbon dating of bronze artefacts.' Max's eyes gleamed. 'I've seen him on television a few times. One of those arrogant, know-it-all experts who wear three piece suits and cravats. He's an archaeologist, but I suspect it's a good while since he got his own hands dirty.'

'And what's more,' Libby read from the paper. 'He's worked at the University for years. I think we should pay him a visit as soon as possible. He might be able to tell us more about these students and I bet he knows all about the necklace.'

'That's all very well,' Mandy complained, 'but you promised us sticky spiced chicken for dinner, Steve will be here in a minute and I'm starving.'

Libby waved her bandaged wrist in the air and Mandy groaned. 'I'd better start the rice.'

* * *

Late next morning, Frank, the owner of Brown's bakery and now Libby's partner in the chocolate business, loaded boxes into her Citroen. 'Thanks for offering to deliver the cake.'

Libby hovered. 'Take care. The icing's still soft.'

Frank pointed at her arm. 'Can you manage?'

'No problem. It doesn't even hurt any more, and the headache disappeared after a good night's sleep. I feel a fraud wearing this bandage on my wrist. Anyway, I'm glad to help. We can't leave a customer without a cake for her son's birthday party. I hope she got the ice cream organised.'

A frantic late-night phone call, from the harassed, forgetful parent of a five year old with his heart set on a Spiderman cake, led to a rapid flurry of design and icing in the bakery.

'Good job we weren't too busy. I'll get this over to – er...' Libby consulted the scrap of paper Frank had thrust into her hand. 'To little Ernest. Ouch. Who calls their child Ernest?'

'Think your rust bucket will make it?' Frank leaned in at the car window. 'Sounds a bit rough.'

'It always sounds rough. Alan Jenkins at the garage keeps it going for me. Mind you,' Libby let in the clutch with a loud screech, 'he keeps trying to sell me a new one. I think there are at least a few thousand miles left in this old thing.'

With a wave, she drove off on the mission of mercy.

Ernest's mother, hair escaping from an elastic band on the top of her head, tiny infant in one arm and smelly nappy in the other hand, looked as exhausted as only a mother with young children can. Libby juggled the cake one handed into the kitchen and made a space on the table, elbowing aside a jumble of socks, Babygros, muslin squares and vests.

The trip to Bristol gave Libby time to call on Professor Malcolm Perivale, the man in Miss Bakewell's stolen photos. Max was free to accompany her, and he'd suggested they have lunch at a restaurant in Bristol before visiting the professor. Libby tugged at her pencil skirt, hoping it wasn't too short, conscious of her mother's half remembered warnings about mutton dressed as lamb.

A schoolboy on a scooter sped around the corner, almost under her wheels, and Libby slammed on the brakes. After that, she concentrated on the road, blocking thoughts of Max from her mind.

Squeezing the car into one of the last spaces at Bristol Harbourside, she walked across the bridge, a stiff little breeze blowing hair in her eyes. Max, unusually smart in a suit and tie, waved from a table for two in the window of the restaurant. Had he dressed to impress Libby, or the professor?

Libby smoothed a lock of hair behind an ear, fingered a gold chain that hung round her neck, and took a deep breath. 'Have you been waiting long?'

'Only five minutes. I'm mixing business and pleasure. I had an appointment with a firm of auditors in Queen Square.' That explained the suit. 'Pritchards is their client.'

Pritchards. The company with Chesterton Wendlebury on the board; the one Trevor had dealings with. 'Are they as shady as we suspected?'

A waitress brought plates of food. 'I've ordered tapas, hope that's all right?'

'Lovely.' Libby ran an eye over dishes of chorizo, tortilla and seafood. 'Calamari? Terrific. Haven't had squid for ages.' She piled it onto her plate.

'Thought you'd like it. Can't bear the stuff, myself, so I'm sticking to roast peppers and ham.'

'Did the auditors tell you anything interesting about Pritchards, or are they bound to secrecy by client privilege?'

'I have ways of making companies talk.'

Libby spluttered. 'Strong arm stuff? No, I don't believe it.' Max was tall, trim and looked fit, but no match for gym bunnies in their thirties.

'Much too old for that. My leverage is more in the nature

of a financial threat, if you know what I mean. Looking at the firm's tax situation, for example. Amazing how willing companies are to help, once I suggest that. You'd be surprised how many financial wizards neglect their own records.'

'I'd better keep the chocolate accounts straight, then.'

'Or bribe me with the product.' Max served garlicky shrimp to them both. 'This is good, whatever it is, though we'd better not breathe too hard on the professor. Anyway, Pritchards have a pretty complex set up. Off-shore accounts, a series of complicated financial instruments and a lot of buying and selling of shares among board members. Not illegal, unless it's used to manipulate prices on the stock market.'

'And Chesterton Wendlebury's been doing that?'

'He's certainly an active board member.'

Libby hesitated, not sure she wanted to ask the next question. 'What about Trevor? You said his name was on some documents you found. How was he involved with Pritchards?'

Max wiped sauce from his chin. 'He dealt with their insurance, all above board and open for scrutiny, but I'm afraid he was also in on some of the murkier deals.' Libby kept her eyes on her fork, moving squid from one side of the plate to the other. When she thought about Trevor and his criminal past, her stomach churned. What would she find out next? She laid her fork down, unable to eat any more.

Max changed the subject. 'Mandy seems happy. Growing up, do you think?'

Libby forced her whirling thoughts back from Trevor to her lodger. 'Steve's influence, I suspect. They spend a lot of time together. There's a gig tonight with his band. I sometimes get the impression Steve's not entirely committed to being a Goth, though, which is probably a good thing.'

'It's tough being a teenage boy, no matter how easy it looks.'

Libby glanced up. 'That sounded as though it came from the heart.'

Max smiled, but his eyes were serious. 'I wish I'd known you when we were young.'

Thrown off balance, heart racing, Libby couldn't think of a single thing to say. She waited, to see if he'd explain. Did he mean he cared about her? Was he asking for more than friendship?

Max said no more, but went on eating, avoiding her eye. Libby, suddenly tired of uncertainties, of second guessing Max's motives and wondering what he was thinking, downed a gulp of wine and plucked up every scrap of courage.

'Max, never mind Mandy and Steve.' She swallowed. 'Don't you think it's time you and I decided whether we're having a relationship?'

There, she'd said it. She clenched her hands tight under the table, so tense she could barely catch her breath, and waited.

Silence dragged on until she thought she might scream. At last, Max raised his head to look at Libby's face, unsmiling. 'Don't ask me to answer that, Libby. Not yet.'

10

PROFESSOR

Max might as well have punched her in the stomach. *I'm not going to cry.* Slowly, she unclenched her fists, looking everywhere except at him. 'It – it doesn't matter. I thought – you know – I wanted to be sure.' She took a deep breath that made her head swim. 'I was going to say we should keep things strictly business. I don't think either of us is looking for any sort of – er – arrangement.'

She was talking too fast, struggling to hide the hurt. She shrugged into her coat. 'It's time for us to meet the professor.'

Max busied himself with the bill. 'Your car or mine?'

Libby glanced at her wine glass. How much wine had she swallowed? 'Better be yours.'

'Look, Libby, let me explain—'

'There's nothing to explain. Nothing at all. Let's get going.'

The ride to the professor's house seemed interminable, the atmosphere in the car claustrophobic. Libby clenched her arms tight to her sides, pressing her knees against the passenger door, terrified Max might touch her leg. She couldn't bear him to think she'd engineered a contact.

In her head, she replayed the scene in the restaurant, each iteration more depressing than the last. She'd exposed her feelings for nothing. Max shared none of them. She shot a glance at his profile. A cheek muscle twitched, but his eyes stayed on the road.

Well, Libby could live without Max. What was it she'd said to the children, breaking the news of her move to Exham? 'I'm starting a new life. I'm going to be independent. I can make my own living.' She'd meant it, too. She didn't need a new man.

Max yanked hard on the handbrake as they arrived, climbed out of the car and walked to the professor's house. He didn't even come round to open Libby's door.

The professor appeared on the threshold of his house before they reached the halfway point on the path. His shapeless brown jacket had leather patches on the arms. Perhaps he bought it when he reached the starry heights of professorship in an attempt to look the part. Under normal circumstances, Libby would have shared a glance with Max, but today she couldn't bear to look at him.

Instead, she focused on the professor, picking up an overwhelming impression of an absent minded academic, a kind of Einstein look-alike. The man's wire-framed glasses teetered halfway up his forehead. Tufts of wispy hair stood out like an electrified white halo.

'Come in, come in,' he boomed, waving the visitors along a corridor to his study.

Stacks of students' work overflowed every chair. A globe stood in a prominent spot on a side table next to a sherry decanter, and in one corner, a glass cabinet displayed misshapen pieces of pottery and metal. Libby peeked inside, noticing chunks of iron with sharpened ends, a lump of greenish glass and something that looked like a primitive saw.

'I see you're admiring my artefacts,' the professor said, prolonging the word, emphasising every syllable, a technique most likely developed for the benefit of sleepy students. 'They're from the Glastonbury Lake Village. Over 2,000 years old. Can you imagine that?'

Libby and Max sat apart, awkward on a lumpy sofa, separated by a gap that felt as wide as Exham beach. They refused sherry, biscuits and coffee.

'So,' the professor said. 'How can I help you? Is it about the new excavations? You don't look much like the usual amateur archaeologists. No dirt under your nails.' His smile exposed a gap between the front teeth.

'We wanted to ask you about John Williams. He was at University with you.'

The smile faded. 'Haven't seen him for years. Heard he topped himself. Read it in the papers. The man was a waste of space. Huh.'

He downed a glass of sherry in one gulp and poured another. 'Sure you won't?' He waved the glass. Not the man's first drink of the day, judging by the bulbous nose and red cheeks. Libby turned towards Max, remembered they weren't speaking and looked down at her hands.

Max said, 'Some of his photographs were in a local exhibition. Jemima Bakewell was there.'

The professor frowned. 'Was she, by George? Shouldn't have been.' His mouth snapped shut, as though he'd said more than he should.

What did he mean by that? Libby leaned forward, elbows on her knees. The man was half drunk. She intended to take advantage of the fact and find out everything she could. 'Tell me about Jemima Bakewell and John Williams and the others. You were friends, weren't you?'

'Used to be. Not any more. Had a falling out, you know, over some stupid business, back when we were young. Huh. Something to do with Jemima's beads. She lost 'em, accused us of stealing the things.' The professor waved a hand. 'Can't remember the sordid details. Far too long ago. Went our separate ways. Haven't seen 'em since then.'

'Those beads. Miss Bakewell said she found them.'

'Maybe she did. They're fine examples of Iron Age amber. We were just students, then.' His laugh turned into a cough. 'Seen more beads than I could shake a stick at since. Nothing like the first time, though. Beauties, they were.' The professor wiped his face on a large blue handkerchief. 'Hot, today. Must be a storm coming.'

'When did you last see Miss Bakewell?'

He folded the handkerchief into a neat square and tucked it with care into his jacket pocket. 'Not since we were students.'

Max raised an eyebrow. 'But you only live a few miles apart. You must have bumped in to each other at conferences or similar. I mean, she studies the Classics, you're an archaeologist...'

The professor's ruddy face deepened to an unhealthy purple. 'You calling me a liar? Huh!'

Max's lip twitched. He'd scored a hit. 'And the beads?'

The professor's eyelids flickered. 'Those beads. Yes.' Libby could hardly keep a straight face at the sudden grunts and exclamations. Maybe they were involuntary, like a twitch. His students must have fun with them. 'Made of amber. Know anything about amber?'

Sensing a lecture, Libby interrupted, 'I'm sure you know all the myths surrounding the beads.'

'Myths? I don't deal in myths, young lady.' The glare would silence a roomful of the rowdiest undergraduates. 'Stuff and nonsense. The beads are mentioned in the records. From the grave of a high status woman, one would imagine. Possibly stolen by vandals. Yes. Grave robbery's a taboo, you know. Always was. Some nonsense about the beads being cursed. Huh! Made up in recent years. Glastonbury's the place for myths and legends. King Arthur, lot of tosh. Good for tourism, that's all. Huh.'

'Have you been to Glastonbury lately?'

'Not since the last excavation, three, four years ago. Place is full of tourists, these days.'

Max asked, 'Where were you two days ago?'

'Me? What day was it now? Tuesday? Huh! Yes. Spent the morning in a tutorial with a student, then lunch with colleagues. Someone's leaving do. And, now, I have work, so if you'll excuse me...'

* * *

The professor poured more sherry into a crystal glass and let Libby and Max find their own way out. 'Take me back to my car,' Libby demanded.

'You've had far too much wine. I'll drive you home, and when you get a free day, we'll come back to get your car.'

Another silent drive, then, and Libby wouldn't be first to speak. After a few miles, Max broke the oppressive silence. 'What did you make of our professor? Huh!'

Libby refused to smile at the imitation.

He went on, 'I don't think he could help the twitches, but

he's a pompous old fool and he didn't want to tell us anything. He's in the clear for John Williams' death, anyway. His student can put him in Bristol on the morning John Williams died.'

Libby said nothing.

Max tried again. 'Reading between the professor's lines, they made some pact never to meet again. What could have shaken them so much?'

'No idea.'

'Do you know, I think I'd like to pay another visit to our professor.'

Libby said, 'You'll have to go on your own. I'm going to the history society meeting tomorrow.'

'I'll come up on the train, then, and bring your car back.'

Libby just shrugged. She wasn't going to thank him. She never wanted to see the man again.

Max's new Jaguar drew up at her house. A lump formed in Libby's throat as Max killed the engine. 'Libby, you caught me off guard at lunch.'

'I didn't mean to embarrass you.' Libby's voice quivered.

'You deserve an explanation—'

'No need.' She had to get out of the car, right away.

Max put a hand on her arm. 'I should give you a proper answer to your question.'

'No.' She pushed him away, shoved the car door open and swung her legs out. 'No explanations, no answers. We're partners. And friends, I suppose. That's all. It's good to know where we stand.' She strode away, refusing to look back, determined Max should not see the tears that coursed down her cheeks.

11

EXHAM HISTORY SOCIETY

Next day, Libby spent far too long composing questions for the history society meeting. Her car still in Bristol, she arrived late, hampered by the need to walk with Bear's lead in one hand and a bag containing cake tins in the other. Marina opened the door, scarlet and pink scarves flying, silver bracelets clanking. 'Libby, darling, how's your wrist? And did you remember to bring the cake?'

Libby let Bear off the lead. 'Hope you don't mind Bear coming. Max is on his way to Bristol to – er – talk to an old colleague, so he left Bear with me.'

'Bear can stay in the back room. Shipley's always pleased to see him.' Marina's house, a substantial, brick built Georgian mansion, included several rooms at the rear. These, built in the days when servants were commonplace, had once served as sculleries and dairies. Now, they were perfect for dogs.

Shipley greeted Bear in Marina's back cloakroom, barking and running in circles, full of unhinged excitement. Libby sometimes wondered if the spaniel could be heading for a stroke.

The drawing room, far more elegant than the servants' quarters, buzzed with gossip. Samantha Watson stopped talking in mid-sentence as Libby entered and wrinkled her nose.

Marina's stage whisper must have been audible to everyone. 'Chief Inspector Arnold rang Samantha with the news.' Samantha, having divorced her ne'er-do-well husband, Ned, was engaged to Chief Inspector Arnold, Joe's boss.

'I'm sorry,' Libby confessed. 'I've no idea what you're talking about. What news?'

'Well,' Samantha sipped from a delicate bone china teacup, one little finger held aloft with a daintiness Libby hadn't seen since she was a child at her mother's tea parties. 'The Chief Inspector told me about the explosion.'

The woman's smile could have frozen waves on Exham beach. 'He said it had something to do with a schoolteacher. Marina says you were talking to the woman at the photographic exhibition, Lizzy.'

Libby's heart lurched. She ignored the deliberate mispronunciation of her name. 'If there's something you think I should know, I'd be grateful if you'd tell me.'

'Oh, the police will talk to you soon enough, I'm sure. The Chief Inspector says everywhere you go, trouble follows.'

Libby sighed. 'Samantha, I have no idea what you're talking about. Has something happened to Miss Bakewell?'

Samantha slapped her cup so hard onto its saucer, the contents slopped onto Marina's marble topped table. She pointed a manicured finger at Libby. 'I knew you'd be involved. I wish people would mind their own business instead of poking around in local affairs...'

'Do calm down, Samantha,' Marina broke in. 'I'm sure Libby knows nothing about the explosion.'

Libby lost patience. 'For heaven's sake, tell me what you're talking about. What explosion, and why do you think I'm involved?'

'Well, darling, you and Max Ramshore were at the photography exhibition together, talking to that Miss Bakewell.'

'Why shouldn't I have been there? You were there, too, Marina.'

'No reason at all. I'm just explaining. According to Samantha, the inspector told her—'

'Chief Inspector,' Samantha put in.

Marina sighed. 'Chief Inspector Arnold said Miss Bakewell has been involved in an accident.'

'I'm sorry to hear that.' An accident?

The back of Libby's neck prickled. What was that nonsense about the beads and a curse? 'What kind of accident are you talking about?'

Marina was enjoying the limelight. 'Apparently, she went to see some professor. Perivale, that was the name. After she left his house, there was some sort of explosion.'

Professor Perivale's house? Libby's throat felt tight. She whispered. 'Was anyone hurt?'

'That's all we know.'

Libby's hands were clenched tight in her lap, the knuckles white. Her nails forced themselves into the palms. She stood up. 'Doesn't anyone know any more?'

Someone said, 'We might catch the local news, if we're quick,' and Marina switched on the vast television. Libby bit her lip, trying to think, but there was only one idea in her head. What if Max was there? He planned to visit the professor today. He could be hurt, or even dead.

A local reporter stood in front of a row of tall Victorian houses that had a jagged edged gap, like a missing tooth, in the centre. Libby recognised the street she'd visited yesterday.

'Police say one person has been taken to hospital, but no one else was in the house,' intoned the journalist. 'Neighbours tell us the property belongs to a Professor Perivale from Bristol University. It's believed he may be the injured man. We have no further news at this time.'

Not Max. The words hammered in Libby's head. *Max isn't dead.*

'Are you all right, Libby?' Marina's face creased with anxiety. 'You're white as a sheet.'

'I'm fine.' Libby's phone rang. She fumbled the buttons with shaking fingers as the name flashed up on the screen. *Max.* 'I have to take this.'

She stumbled to her feet and ran to the hall, as Samantha remarked, 'Really, some people are so *over-dramatic.*'

'Max, are you OK? I saw the news...'

'You've heard about the explosion, then. Don't worry, I'm fine. Miss Bakewell's pretty shaken, though. I'm about to drive her home.'

'What was she doing there? And what about the professor?'

'He's gone to hospital, but the neighbours say he was awake and talking while they put him in the ambulance.'

'Did you speak to him?'

'No, unfortunately, the explosion came a moment before I arrived. Miss Bakewell had just left. I'm hoping the shock will make her a little more forthcoming about the photographs. Could you meet us at her house in Wells? We'll be there in less than an hour. I want to find out what she was doing at the professor's house, and I think it would be better if you were there. Will you come?'

Libby looked at the phone. Max sounded stressed. No wonder. 'Yes, of course. I'll get a taxi. Lilly's Cabs are always happy to carry dogs. Max, what do you think happened?'

His voice was grim. 'I don't know, but the professor could have died. It's a coincidence, don't you think?'

Libby shivered. She dropped her phone in a pocket. The history society would have to wait. When she took a step, her legs shook so much she could hardly walk, and she sank down on to the stairs.

The adrenaline of fear ebbed away, leaving her exhausted, and she let her head drop between her knees until the faintness passed. She was still mad at Max, but at least he wasn't dead.

12

CATRIONA

Jemima Bakewell kept a bottle of whisky in a corner cupboard in her kitchen. It took Libby only a few minutes to track it down and pour a big slug into a cup of tea, add six lumps of sugar and carry it through to the tiny sitting room, where Bear, bribed by treats, lay curled in a corner.

The retired schoolteacher pulled a plaid blanket tight round her shoulders and sipped. 'I knew something like this would happen. It's all coming horribly true.'

She looked thirty years older than last time Libby saw her.

The room was stuffed with mementos from Miss Bakewell's travels. Busts of Greek philosophers jostled with photographs showing the teacher in various locations. Libby studied them while the woman drank her tea. In one picture, Miss Bakewell wore a sun hat and waved a trowel, surrounded by the open trenches of an archaeological dig. Another showed her walking in the Greek islands, while in another she was with a group of middle-aged ladies wearing flowery skirts and cardigans, enjoying a bottle of red wine under azure skies.

Books cluttered every spare inch of space in the room. A Latin dictionary and a well-thumbed copy of the Aeneid leaned against a leather bound version of the poems of Catullus. It was clear Miss Bakewell loved her subject.

Max remained silent, letting Miss Bakewell recover from the shock of the explosion at the professor's house. He raised an eyebrow at Libby, and she nodded.

He said, 'I think it's time you told us the truth, Miss Bakewell, don't you?'

Taken aback by the sharp tone, the woman licked her lips, eyes larger than ever behind the tortoiseshell spectacles.

Max persisted. 'Tell us what you mean. What's coming true?'

The ex-teacher's lip trembled. 'The curse. I thought it was all nonsense, but it isn't. It's catching up with us.'

Libby leaned forward. '*Us?* Who do you mean by *us*?'

The woman's eyes flickered between Libby and Max, seeking sympathy, but Max's face was stony. She wasn't getting away with evasions this time. Her shoulders slumped. 'It's the beads. They're causing it.'

'What rubbish.' Max snorted. 'They're old and possibly valuable, but that's all.'

Libby held out a hand. 'Wait, Max. Let's hear what she has to say.'

The woman's hands trembled, tea spilling on her tweed skirt. 'It's all in the paper.' She took a newspaper from the table. 'Here it is.'

Libby recognised the picture. 'It's that photograph from the excavation, Max. The one you emailed to me.' She took it from Miss Bakewell's shaking fingers and read aloud. *Beads from Glastonbury Lake Village discovered near Deer Leap Stones.*

She frowned. 'I've heard that name, somewhere.'

Miss Bakewell had stopped trembling. The light of an educator shone in her eyes. 'The Deer Leap stones are a pair of ancient standing stones, said to mark the entrance to a tunnel leading to Glastonbury Tor, eight miles away.'

'According to the newspaper,' Libby was scanning the story, 'a man called Roger Johnson was out for a walk last week when he found an amber bead beside the stones. Being a local man, he knew about the archaeological digs and the stories about a tunnel and contacted the newspaper. They're going to have the amber dated.' She looked up from the paper. 'Here's a picture of the bead. What do you think, Max? Is it one of ours?'

Miss Bakewell removed her glasses, breathed on the lenses and scrubbed at them with a scrap of handkerchief. 'A warning,' she whispered. 'That's what it is. From all those years ago.'

Goose-bumps prickled the skin of Libby's arms, but Max snorted. 'Come on. There must be millions of amber beads lying around in jewellery boxes across the country. Amber's not a precious stone and anyone could have dropped it. I bet it's nothing to do with the necklace, anyway,'

Libby cleared her throat. He was right. With any luck, Max hadn't noticed her moment of foolish panic. She said, 'We all know John Williams didn't die because of some magic curse. I heard what you said at the exhibition, Miss Bakewell, when you saw the photographs. It wasn't the beads that bothered you, it was someone you saw in the picture; a friend. You said a name; Catriona. Later, you said, 'It's not her, after all.' What did you mean? Don't you think it's time you told us what happened to this Catriona?'

Miss Bakewell's hand flew to her chest. Colour leached

out of her face, leaving her pale, eyes staring. Libby pushed her advantage. 'We're not leaving until you explain.'

The woman seemed to shrink into her chair as she began to talk. 'I knew Catriona well, many years ago, when we were young. It was a shock, seeing the child in the photograph. She looked so like Catriona. You see, Catriona died.'

Libby gulped. 'How did she die?'

The woman shrugged. 'It was an accident at a party. She fell out of a window. She was on drugs, you see. After all, it was the sixties.'

* * *

Libby and Bear ran after Max as he hurried down the path. The shock of thinking he might be dead had overcome the anger and shame she'd felt when he turned her down. Seeing him safe in Miss Bakewell's house, her heart had leapt. That told Libby everything she needed to know. She was falling for him. Even if Max never returned her feelings, she couldn't bear to lose him from her life. She'd been a fool, doing her best to drive him away, because he'd asked for more time.

She wouldn't make that mistake again. 'Wait for me, Max.'

He turned and smiled, and Libby's heart lurched. It was hard to hide her feelings, now she understood them, but she had to try. 'How much of that did you believe?' There, that sounded sufficiently matter of fact.

'Hardly any. She's trying to pull the wool over our eyes with all that 'curse of the beads' malarkey. Misdirect us.'

Libby nodded. 'I believe Catriona's death is important. When Miss Bakewell saw the girl in the photo and mistook her for the woman who'd died, back in the sixties, she was terrified.'

Libby paused, one hand on the door of the Land Rover. 'It's difficult, sifting through to find out what's true. We don't even know if more beads were really found at Deer Leap. Anyone could tell the press a trumped-up story.'

'Including Miss Bakewell.'

As they fastened their seat belts, Libby pondered. 'No, I don't think she did it. She was genuinely scared.'

'You know what I think?' Max put the key in the ignition. 'I think she's got a thing going for the professor. That's why she's so upset about the explosion. It might have nothing to do with the amber beads.' He turned. 'Libby, are you listening?'

Libby swallowed. 'Sorry.' Her voice shook. She hadn't intended this to happen. She cleared her throat.

'What's the matter?'

If only he'd stop looking at me like that, as if he cares. 'Nothing.'

'Come on. Tell me.'

A sob rose in Libby's throat. She muttered. 'She's not the only one who thought someone died.'

'What?' Two vertical lines appeared between his eyes. 'Oh. You mean...'

Libby sniffed hard, struggling to keep the tears at bay. 'Yes.' She couldn't stop her voice squeaking. 'When I heard about the explosion, I thought you'd been killed.'

'Oh, Libby.' His arms slid round Libby's back, pulling her close. 'I should have realised.'

Her face pressed against his shoulder, his woody scent filling her head. Her voice muffled by his jacket, she muttered, 'The people at the history meeting were ghouls, wondering if anyone died, while all I could think about was – was you.'

Max looked into her eyes. 'I'm so sorry, Libby,' he

murmured, and for once there was no hint of sarcasm in his voice or face. 'I didn't think...'

Libby scrubbed her eyes with the back of her hand.

Max smoothed a lock of hair behind her ear. 'I should have realised you'd be upset. I would have been, if it were you.'

'Really?' She tried a laugh. 'I think that's the nicest thing you've ever said.'

'Is it?' The frown was back. 'Then, I should be ashamed of myself. You're a wonderful person, Libby Forest.'

'If that's the beginning of a 'you're too good for me' speech, you can shut up, right now. I'm not a teenager.' The corners of his mouth twitched. 'It's not funny.'

'No.' Max fixed his gaze on the windscreen. The smile had disappeared. 'It's not.' He started the engine. 'I'll drop you off at my place to pick up your car. Miss Bakewell and I called in there to leave it. I couldn't go another mile with my knees wedged against my chin.' He grinned and Libby relaxed. Max was safe and they were friends again. She could take some time to deal with the other problems in her life.

13

TREVOR

That evening, Libby roamed the house, searching for any distraction from the questions hammering in her head. She flicked through every channel on television, dropped the remote control in disgust, and started the latest Diane Saxon novel. She read the first chapter twice. With a groan, she snapped the book shut. She hadn't taken in a single word.

It was Trevor's fault. Libby managed not to think about Jemima Bakewell and the beads, and with a supreme effort of will, she could even force Max Ramshore out of her mind, but she couldn't stop thoughts of Trevor. Every time she remembered her husband and the financial mess he'd left behind, her stomach heaved with anxiety. She'd never rest until she knew the full story of his crimes.

She headed to the study. Fuzzy lay stretched across the computer keyboard, tail dangling in front of the desk drawer. Libby gave her a nudge. 'Shift over, will you?' The cat stared, unmoving, through slitted eyes. Libby pushed harder. 'Come on, you silly animal.'

Fuzzy stretched, sighed, and turned round twice. Libby

seized her chance to grab the folder containing Trevor's papers from the drawer, before the cat settled down in exactly the same position as before.

Two cups of coffee later, Libby had read and re-read every word of the documents in the folder; a portfolio of houses, bought with money from criminal activities. All the houses had mortgages due to be paid off in five years' time.

One question kept pounding in her head. Why five years?

She flipped through the documents one final time. For heaven's sake, why hadn't she noticed it before? *Call yourself an investigator?* Libby had spoken aloud. Fuzzy stirred, stretched, and went back to sleep.

The letter about the first mortgage was dated six years ago. Trevor died last year.

She took a shaky breath. Was there the slightest chance Trevor's death had not been from a heart attack?

She shook her head. She was over-dramatising – seeing crime everywhere.

But she'd been involved in two murders since arriving in Exham, even before John Williams died. Both of those had looked, at first glance, like accidents or suicides.

What if Trevor's death was another murder?

* * *

'Mrs F? Shouldn't you be in bed at this time of night?' Libby was making bread, taking out her feelings on the dough.

She registered Mandy's flushed face, smudged lipstick and bright eyes, and thumped the dough harder. 'Looks like you've had fun.'

'What's wrong?' Mandy spooned instant coffee into a mug.

'Won't make you one. You look wired already. You know it's after midnight?'

Libby grunted, pounded the bread into shape, turned it into a tin and dumped it in the oven. 'If that doesn't rise, I'm giving up and moving back to London.'

'Anything I can do?'

Libby swept a cloth over the counter with unnecessary force. 'It's just life.'

'I know. Life sucks.' Mandy rescued a jug of milk. Libby flung the cloth into the sink and flopped onto a stool, head resting on her hands.

'Want to talk?'

'Give me a minute.' It wasn't fair to burden Mandy with her problems. Libby wiped her sleeve across both eyes, blew her nose, and forced a smile on her face. 'Sorry. I was having a moment. About my husband.' Mandy deserved more than that. 'And Max, actually.'

'Men. What are they like?'

Libby managed a watery smile. She wished she could tell Mandy the truth. Her husband was a crook, she suspected he hadn't died of a heart attack after all, and Max had turned down her offer of a relationship. Things couldn't really get worse.

She let her breath out in a long sigh. Mandy had enough problems in her own family. She'd moved in with Libby to escape them and it wasn't fair to dump the landlady's woes on the lodger. 'Cheer me up. Tell me about Steve.'

Mandy's face melted into that dreamy expression only first true love could conjure. The gig had been wonderful, Steve had been amazing, and the audience had been phenomenal. Mandy's enthusiasm, pink cheeks and ear-to-ear grin lifted Libby's mood an inch or two from the mire of gloom. So what if Max didn't share her feelings? Who cared if Trevor hadn't died of natural causes? The world was still turning.

Libby yawned and forced a smile. 'I'm truly happy you had such a good evening. Sorry to be grumpy. Hope I didn't spoil things.'

'You go to bed. I'll take the bread out when it's cooked. Everything will look better in the morning.'

Tears welled in Libby's eyes. Somehow, she and Mandy had reversed their roles. 'I'm sure it will,' she mumbled, like a tired child. Her life was a mess. She didn't want to think about it any more. Far better to keep her mind busy with the murder on the Tor. She thought back to her morning walk on the Tor. Bear had seemed ill, and she'd taken him to Tanya, the vet.

While she was waiting, and the receptionist regaling her with Glastonbury myths, she'd looked at the posters on the walls.

Tanya's framed certificate had been there, in pride of place. Her degree had come from Bristol University, and Libby had smiled. It seemed local people rarely left the South West. Not surprising, really. Apart from the beauty of the region, it boasted one of England's top universities.

Jemima Bakewell had studied there. Libby lay back on the sofa and closed her eyes. If only she could remember the date on Tanya's certificate. Had she, too, been a contemporary of Catriona, and the professor?

14

TANYA

Bear tugged on the lead, dragging Libby through the door of the vet's surgery. Tanya Ross reached for a pack of worming tablets. The dog reared on his hind legs, placed a pair of heavy front paws on her shoulders and licked the vet's face.

Libby tugged his collar. 'Get down, Bear.'

He dropped to all fours as Tanya wiped drool from her cheek. 'I haven't had a hug like that all day.' She eyed Libby. 'There's not much wrong with him today, so how can I help you?'

'I wanted to have a word with you about Jemima Bakewell.'

Tanya's eyes slid away. 'I'm sorry. Who did you say? Bakewell? Like the tarts?' Tension in the vet's voice killed the lame joke.

'I think you know her. Weren't you at University together?' The vet was motionless, as though holding her breath. 'With Jemima Bakewell and Professor Perivale? Bristol in the sixties?'

Libby waved at the certificate on the wall. 'According to that, you were contemporaries.'

Tanya Ross swallowed. 'So what if we were? I haven't seen either of them for years.' She made a show of looking at her watch. 'Now, the receptionist will be back soon, and I've got appointments, so I'll have to ask you to leave.'

'Oh, no. You're not getting rid of me that easily. People have died.'

'Is that any of your business? You don't know them. You've only—'

Libby cut her off with a sigh. 'I know, I've only lived in the area for a short while. If I had a pound for every time one of you locals told me that, I'd be living in one of those houses by the golf course.'

The ghost of a smile spread over Tanya's face. She pushed past Libby. 'Come into my room.' Bear sniffed at Tanya's pockets and the vet brought out a handful of dog treats. She beckoned Libby to follow and opened a door marked *Private*, where racks of professional journals climbed the walls and a computer covered most of the surface of a small desk.

The two women perched on small brown tub chairs, on opposite sides of a cheap, deal coffee table. A textbook lay open on the desk. Libby averted her eyes from a lurid diagram of the lungs and heart of some unknown animal. Tanya snapped the book shut. 'Coffee?'

Libby shook her head. 'Information.'

'I don't see why I should tell you anything.'

'You won't put me off by saying, 'It's none of your business.' I was there, up on the Tor with no one else around except a child, and just after I left, John Williams' body was dumped with a plastic bag round his head. That makes it my business.' Libby remembered every detail. 'That poor child could have found it, and the thought of that makes my blood boil. So, don't tell me to walk away. I'm determined to find out what's been going on. If you know something, you'd better tell me.'

Libby paused, waited and added, 'For Catriona's sake.'

The shot hit home and the vet's mouth dropped open. 'What do you know about Catriona?'

'I know she was your friend. There was a group of you, all at University together. Catriona was one of that group and she died at a party.' The vet shifted, crossing and uncrossing her legs. 'Were you there, the night Catriona died?'

Tanya chewed her lip, her eyes on the table, focused on the closed veterinary textbook. She murmured, 'None of us was in the room when Catriona fell out of the window. We were all downstairs.'

'That's what Miss Bakewell said.' Was that a tiny sigh of relief? Libby let it go, for the moment. If the vet thought she'd side-stepped a difficult question, she'd be likely to open up and tell Libby more than she intended. 'Tell me about Catriona.'

Tanya looked up from the book on the table. Her eyes were very bright. 'She was beautiful. She cared about people. If you had a problem, she'd always listen – really listen.'

Briefly, a smile lit the woman's face, then faded. 'We shared a house, Jemima, Catriona and me, and while we were there, I was happier than I'd ever been in my life. My own home was a place where we kept a stiff upper lip and spoke when we were spoken to. I came to University to escape, and I found Catriona.'

Tanya pressed a balled-up tissue to her eyes. 'I'm sorry. I haven't talked about it for so long.'

Libby, careful not to shatter the woman's mood, kept her voice low. 'You found Catriona and...?'

The vet drew a shaky breath. 'Everything was fine until that night.'

'What night? What happened?'

'It was the May Ball. We were all there. I wore a long, velvet dress. Navy blue. Catriona said it matched my eyes. She had a red top with enormous sleeves. She looked wonderful; like a queen. Even Jemima seemed pretty, that night, but the two of them had far too much to drink and they had a fight over that stupid necklace...' The vet fumbled in her pocket for a new tissue.

'The beads belonged to Jemima, didn't they?'

Tanya's lip curled. 'Malcolm Perivale gave them to her. She said she found them but no one believed her. Malcolm stole the necklace from some dig he was working on in Glastonbury and gave them to her. They were going out together, you see. What he saw in her, no one could understand.'

'What happened to the beads, that night?'

The vet shrugged and stood up. Her voice rang with spite. 'Oh, it was just a storm in a teacup at first but it ended in disaster. Jemima accused Catriona of taking the necklace; as if Catriona would steal things. Or, maybe it was the other way round. It was so long ago; I can't remember exactly. Anyway, they had a quarrel.'

She shrugged. 'It was hot, and the music was loud. Catriona went upstairs to cool down. The next thing we knew, she'd fallen out of the window.'

'She fell? You mean...'

'No one saw her fall.' Tanya's eyes were narrow slits, 'but someone found her on the pavement.'

She shuddered. 'We all ran out to see. There was a huge

pool of blood on the paving stones and Catriona was dead. Her skull was crushed by the fall, you see.'

Libby let the vet sit in silence for a moment, reliving that night, before she asked, 'Had Catriona taken LSD?'

Tanya threw her hands in the air. 'Catriona tried everything. She said LSD made her think she'd died and gone to heaven. She saw multi-coloured angels and flowers and heard music. Psychedelic. That's what we called it, in those days.'

'And taking LSD makes people believe they can fly.'

The vet nodded. 'We were such fools.'

15

DEER LEAP

'Weather doesn't look too good.' Mandy leaned from the kitchen window, eyes on a system of grey clouds scudding across the sky. 'Still, Glastonbury isn't Snowdonia.'

'We won't need climbing boots but we'd better wear waterproofs,' Libby agreed. Mandy was silent, staring at her landlady's hands. She'd taken to watching Libby like an anxious guardian angel since the midnight baking episode. It was touching and infuriating at the same time.

Libby looked down. A dozen expensive chocolate wrappers, bought for the batch of Jumbles chocolates, lay under her fingers, shredded into tiny pieces. She tossed the ruined gold foil in the bin. No need to take her feelings about Trevor out on her work.

The first item on the day's agenda was a visit to the Deer Leap stones. Max decreed it was a wild goose chase. He was probably right, but Libby refused to ignore even the most unlikely clue and he'd agreed to come along.

Bear, at least, was enthusiastic. His head on Mandy's lap, he spent the drive to the Mendip Hills panting, mouth agape.

Jumping from the car, he led the way up the path to the stones with tail aloft, sniffing the grass as though on the trail of some truly sensational scent, but when they arrived, he refused to go anywhere near the stones.

Rain clouds hung low, hiding the distant summit of the Tor. Libby pulled her jacket close, shivering from more than the cold. Bear snuffled her leg and she touched him, gently, behind the ears.

'You remember it, too, don't you?' Libby whispered. 'That morning on the Tor. It feels like that, here. I don't like it, either.'

They stood in the field and gazed round, disappointed. 'No sign of a tunnel,' Max pointed out. 'Not that it's at all likely. If it existed, someone would have found it.'

Mandy remained upbeat. 'The Deer Leap stones are here, anyway.' Two upright lumps of rock, set ten yards or so apart, stood alone in the field. 'They're like a piece of Stonehenge.'

'It shows we're in the right place.' Max threw a stick for the dog, but he ignored it, sticking close to Libby.

'Bear doesn't like it here,' Mandy pointed out. 'Maybe there really is a tunnel underground, full of ghosts, and he can sense it.'

'Nonsense.' In an attempt to throw off the gloom that weighed on her shoulders, Libby set off across the field and marched round the boundary, swinging her arms, inspecting the hedges.

Mandy and Max followed her example and spread out, searching every blade of grass.

'We're not going to find anything,' Mandy said at last, 'and I'm getting cold in this wind. Shall we give up?'

Max was on the other side of the field, bending low in a corner, peering at the ground. He beckoned. Suddenly excited, Libby and Mandy ran to join him. 'Have you found something?'

He straightened up, holding out one hand. 'A bead.' It was covered in mud, but Max rubbed away the dirt, uncovering the glow of a reddish-yellow stone.

Mandy breathed, 'It's amber.'

'Now, there's a coincidence.' Max turned the stone in his hand. 'An amber bead, just where we thought it would be.'

Mandy squeaked. 'So, it's all true? There's a tunnel under here? Someone came through from the Tor and dropped the bead and…' She stopped, deflated by her companions' expressions. 'It's all nonsense, isn't it?'

Max grunted. 'Afraid so, Mandy.'

'But look at Bear. Why's he so miserable?'

Max watched the dog. 'Bear relies on his sense of smell. What if he's caught the scent of someone he knows instinctively he can't trust?'

Mandy breathed. 'The murderer?'

Max scratched his chin. 'Someone who left the bead for us to find, is leading us up the garden path, and is probably the killer. The question is, who?'

Libby pulled off her hat and let the wind catch her hair. 'Do you think Miss Bakewell had anything to do with it? I don't trust her.'

Max was nodding. 'I think another interview with our retired schoolteacher is called for, don't you, to find out why she sent us all on this wild goose chase?'

Libby agreed. 'If you ask me, she talks about the amber beads just a little too much, as though she's trying to make us think about them instead of something else. I think she's trying deflection – a sort of sleight of hand. It's making me suspicious.'

'Whatever we decide to do, can we please get away from this place? I'm freezing.' Mandy's face was pinched with cold.

'Let's find a cafe in Glastonbury, get warmed up and have a walk up the Tor,' said Max.

* * *

Half an hour later, stomachs full of scones and jam from a cafe near Glastonbury Abbey, they emerged from the trees at the base of the Tor and trudged up the hill.

'Cheer up,' Mandy said. The cream tea had given her a second wind.

Max walked by Libby, close, but not touching. She kept her gaze averted, like a nervous schoolchild. 'Maybe it's the weather,' she muttered. 'All these dramatic thunder clouds. I think we're in for a soaking.' They were halfway up the hill now and the clouds were gathering fast. 'Do you think we should go back? It's going to rain.'

'Not now,' Mandy pleaded. 'I'm in the mood to see a ghost or two.'

Libby's cry cut her off. 'There she is.' She pointed up the hill where the top of St Michael's Tower disappeared into black clouds.

Max took her arm. 'There's no one there.'

'I saw her.' Libby pulled away. 'Didn't you? She was there – the little girl.' She whirled round. 'And it's no good making faces at Mandy behind my back as if I'm crazy. I saw her, I tell you.'

The first heavy drops of rain began.

'Well,' said Max, 'Whatever you saw, we need to get up to the Tower now, if we're going. We can shelter there. In any case, I don't think we'll make it back down again without getting soaked. In for a penny, in for a pound, as my mother used to say.'

His long legs soon took him ahead. Bear jogged at his side and Mandy did her best to keep up, panting hard. Libby brought up the rear. 'I saw her. I did, and she must be real – if I'd seen a ghost, Bear wouldn't be trotting up so cheerfully. You know he senses things.'

'Hey, I believe you,' Max called back. 'You saw something that wasn't a ghost.'

'I saw the little girl.' They were almost at the top. Rain sliced into Libby's face as she covered the last few yards to the shelter of the Tower. She found Max, Mandy and Bear in the arch at the entrance.

Inside one corner of the Tower, crouched by a stone bench, the child's big eyes stared from a pink raincoat, wet black curls escaping from the furry hood.

'Hello, again,' Libby said. The child stayed still, except for her eyes. They flickered from the adults to the doorway and back. She was poised, ready to run.

Bear trotted over, tongue lolling. The child stretched out a hand and touched his ear. He stood quietly, letting her pet his head.

Libby took a step forward. 'Does your mother know you're here?' The little girl took no notice. Couldn't she talk?

Max murmured in Libby's ear. 'I've got an idea. Let me talk to her.' He pointed to the dog. 'This is Bear. He'd like to know your name.'

The child squatted down, her lips close to Bear's ear and whispered. Libby had to strain to hear.

'Katy,' the child said.

Max went on, 'Bear wants to know if Mummy's here with

you, Katy.' The girl stroked Bear's head but said nothing more. 'Or Daddy?'

The child pointed down the hill. The wind had dropped and the rain subsided to a steady drizzle. A figure emerged from the trees. The child waved, and it waved back.

'Shall we go and talk to him? Bear will come too.'

She nodded.

The man that met the little procession halfway up the hill looked about forty, despite the long blonde dreadlocks tied at the back of his head. A hole in one elbow and a couple of missing buttons spoiled what must once have been a good leather jacket. 'Af'ernoon,' he nodded.

Max said, 'Is this your daughter? Shouldn't she be at school?'

The man ignored the question. 'Talked to you, did she?'

Libby said, 'Not us. To Bear – the dog.'

'Ah. She'll talk to animals, will Katy. Not to people, though.'

'Why not?'

He pulled at his goatee beard as though deciding whether to answer. 'She don't like people much.'

'Fair enough.' Max nodded and walked on, a hand on Libby's elbow.

'Why did you drag me away? We should have asked a few more questions,' she hissed as soon as they were out of earshot.

'None of our business, is it? Katy's with her father. She's perfectly safe.'

'I wonder why she won't talk. Do you think there's something wrong with her?'

Max shook his head. 'Some children can't bring themselves to talk out loud. Especially to grownups; they feel overwhelmed. Animals are less demanding or scary.'

Libby thought back to her first meeting with the little girl. 'I wonder where her father was last time I saw her. Down in the mist, I suppose. I let my imagination run away with me that day. I was almost ready to believe in fairies.'

'Wait.' The man called. 'Aren't you that detective woman. The one that was in the papers when the singer died?'

Max murmured, 'You're famous.'

Libby ignored him. 'Yes, that's me? Why?'

'Maybe you can help us. We've lost something, you see. Something that matters to Katy. We need to find it.'

'Is that why Katy's on the Tor?'

He nodded. 'She runs away, that's the trouble. Any chance she gets, she runs up here, looking for it.'

Libby had a moment of inspiration. 'The necklace?'

The man laughed. 'Fancy you knowing that. She's attached to those old beads. Been in the family for forty years or more.'

Libby, spirits rising, reached into her bag and fumbled with the zip. 'Here it is.'

She held up the necklace. She'd polished the beads until they gleamed and threaded them on a length of stout leather. 'The wire was broken. I expect that's how she lost them.'

Katy's father took the beads, running them through his fingers. 'Katy,' he shouted. 'Get over 'ere.'

The child saw the beads and held out a grubby hand. Her father dropped the necklace on her palm. A grin spread over the child's face, colour flooded her cheeks and she looked, suddenly, just like any other happy little girl.

'Thank the nice lady,' said her father.

The child's smile died. She inspected her feet.

'Actually,' Libby said, 'it's Bear you have to thank. If it hadn't been for him, I wouldn't have found the beads.'

Katy sank on to her knees and threw her arms round the dog's neck.

'Thank you, Bear,' she whispered.

16

TRUFFLES

'You've got some explaining to do.' Libby had hammered on Jemima Bakewell's door until the woman came running. Libby's face burned with fury. 'All that nonsense about beads and legends.'

Jemima Bakewell held the door ajar. 'I suppose you'd better come in.'

'It's about time you started telling the truth.' Libby refused to sit, choosing instead to stand by the window, so she could see every twitch of Miss Bakewell's face. 'Who is Katy, how do you know her, why does she have your beads, and why didn't you tell me the truth from the beginning?'

Miss Bakewell perched on the edge of the sofa. 'What do you know about Katy?'

'We went up the Tor and she was there again, looking for the beads. We met her father.'

Miss Bakewell snorted. 'He's a useless article, that man. Always been a cup short of a tea service. Even at school.' She rolled her eyes. 'I taught him once. Nothing stayed in that head. Had to be kind to him, though, given...' she stopped.

'It's no good, Miss Bakewell.' Libby was stern. 'You won't get away with half answers, not this time. Nor talking about ancient history or myths and legends. I need the truth.'

'No.' The woman suddenly stopped twisting her hands. She folded her arms. 'What's past is past.'

'But John Williams died,' Libby shouted. 'Have you forgotten? Don't you care?'

Miss Bakewell's face crumpled. 'Of course, I care, but there's nothing more I can do.'

'You can tell us the truth.'

The woman strode across the room and threw the door open. 'I can't tell you anything. Now, please leave my house and don't come back.'

* * *

Libby met Max on the beach. He'd phoned, sounding uncertain, to suggest they walk the dogs together. 'Are we still partners?'

'Of course, we are, but we're no farther forward.' She tried to sound neutral. 'Miss Bakewell called my bluff, just when I thought she was about to tell me everything.'

Max was thoughtful. 'She knows who killed John Williams and she knows why.' He walked faster. 'Come on. I think best when I'm moving. Let's find some sticks for the dogs.'

The sun was back, there were no signs of yesterday's rain clouds, and the beach was thronged with visitors enjoying the heat.

Libby pulled off her jacket and a sweater as her spirits rose. 'This is proper summer weather.'

'Now, let's have a look at the facts,' Max suggested. 'Come

on, Libby, this is what you do best. Sort out the truth from all this misdirection.'

'Misdirection.' Yes, that was the problem. Someone had been orchestrating events to throw Libby off the scent. 'It's like a magic show,' Libby said, trying to untangle her thoughts. 'We need to keep the facts separate from the special effects.'

She used Shipley's stick to write numbers in the sand. 'Number one fact; the death of John Williams on the Tor. That really happened. That day was a muddle because after I was caught in the mist, I met Katy on her own, then found the beads. Bear was chilled and unhappy, and I panicked, thinking he was ill. I can see things more clearly, now. The beads are 2,000 years old, but the myths around them are just stories. The beads belonged to Katy – or, at least, she had them in her possession.'

Max put in, 'How did she come by them in the first place?'

'Her father said they'd been in the family a long time. Forty years. Miss Bakewell had them first.'

'Right, that's one question we'll have to answer. How did the beads get from our teacher to Katy? We'll need to find that out. But, going back to the facts...'

Max drew the number two, then threw the stick for Shipley to chase. 'Miss Bakewell, Tanya Ross and the professor all admit they knew each other, plus Catriona and John Williams.'

Libby nodded. She looked around for another stick but found nothing. She used a finger to draw in the sand, instead. 'Fact number three. The body was found on the Tor, the day before the exhibition. John Williams was killed because someone wanted to stop the exhibition.'

Max nodded. 'That didn't work, and Miss Bakewell stole the photos. Fact number four.'

'Don't forget number five, the explosion on the day Miss Bakewell went to see the professor. That's another coincidence. A lot of them about, aren't there?'

They looked at each other. Libby was the first to speak again. 'Things don't look too good for Jemima Bakewell. She's involved in everything. No wonder she won't talk to me any more.'

'But we still don't understand what else links all our facts together. If Miss Bakewell's been going around killing people, there must be some sort of a reason.'

'Unless she's just a nut case.'

* * *

The doorbell rang. 'Mandy, can you get it?' Libby called, forgetting Mandy was out. She cursed, shouted, 'Just a minute,' and elbowed the tap. Tempering chocolate helped her think, but it was a messy business. She was still drying her hands as she opened the door. 'Miss Bakewell?'

'Can I come in?'

'I suppose so.' When would Libby remember to use the safety chain? She ushered the teacher to the sitting room, wondering how to tell if her visitor had any sort of a weapon in that familiar brown handbag.

'How did you get my address?'

'Oh, dear me, you're quite famous, Mrs Forest. Everyone knows you live at Hope Cottage. It was in the paper when you solved the murder on the beach.'

Libby swallowed. She didn't like that idea at all.

Fuzzy, stretched on the sofa, opened one eye but to Libby's surprise, she stayed where she was.

'What a lovely animal.' Miss Bakewell held out a hand. Fuzzy sniffed at the fingers and allowed the newcomer to stroke her cheek. 'I've always had cats, you know, until a few months ago when poor Sebastian had to be put down.'

Fuzzy seemed to trust the woman. Weren't cats supposed to have a sixth sense? Maybe Fuzzy lost hers by spending too much time asleep in the airing cupboard. Libby felt torn between sympathy for this lonely woman and frustration with all her stories. 'Do you eat chocolate?'

Her visitor beamed.

Libby piled a tray with coffee, cream, and a plate of chocolate mis-shapes from the kitchen, seizing the opportunity to send a text to Max.

Get here now. Miss B's here – I think she's about to confess.

No need to tell Max about the hairs standing on the back of Libby's neck, like a warning not to trust anyone.

Cheeks pink with delight, Miss Bakewell considered, fingers hovering over odd shaped coffee creams and squashed strawberry shortcakes before settling on a wonky white chocolate truffle. 'You sell these in the bakery in Exham, don't you? I bought a box recently. For a friend, of course.'

She wagged a finger. 'Now, just a word of warning. Don't let that dog of yours anywhere near chocolate. It's poison to dogs, you know.'

'I did know, actually.' Had the woman come to confess or give unwanted advice?

Libby cut to the chase. 'I hope you're here to tell me what's been going on.'

Miss Bakewell, taken by surprise, swallowed the last of the truffle with an audible gulp. 'Oh.' She recovered. 'Very well. I think you and your friend, Mr Ramshore, may have jumped to the wrong conclusions.'

'Do you?' Libby kept her voice non-committal.

'Yes, you see, when you asked me about little Katy, I didn't tell you everything.'

'As far as I remember, you didn't tell us anything useful.'

'You and that friend of yours – Max, isn't it – were very kind, after that dreadful explosion, so I decided you should know the truth.'

Libby held out the plate and Miss Bakewell selected another chocolate.

'Let me guess,' Libby prompted. 'We know you were one of the group of friends at University with John Williams and Professor Perivale. You visited the professor even though you'd kept away from each other for so many years. You wanted to know if he had the beads, didn't you? You're obsessed by them. Did you cause the explosion?'

Miss Bakewell sat ramrod straight. Two pink spots appeared on her cheeks. 'No, no, you've got it all wrong. I wouldn't do a thing like that. I'll be frank. I went to see Malcolm, as you say, to beg for the beads. You see, nothing's been right in my life since I lost them. Nothing.'

The pink flush deepened to purple. The teacher's lips suddenly curled. 'They were mine.'

The doorbell rang. Miss Bakewell clamped her lips together and Libby winced.

Max's eyes sparkled. 'Am I in time?'

'Your timing couldn't be worse,' Libby hissed as she let him in. 'She was just about to spill the beans. Don't upset her.'

She returned to Miss Bakewell and offered an encouraging smile. 'You can tell Mr Ramshore the truth. We're partners.'

The teacher looked at Max as though he were an insect in a bowl of cereal. 'Very well, if you insist. Where was I?'

'Let's go back a bit. Explain what happened at University.'

'There were several of us. All friends together. It was the sixties – well before your time. I'm afraid we experimented with some rather inappropriate substances.'

Max chuckled. 'The generation that invented sex.'

Libby glared, but the teacher ignored him. 'There were five of us in all.'

Libby counted them off. 'You and the professor, John Williams and Catriona. That's four, plus Tanya, the vet.'

'Catriona,' said Max. 'You recognised them in the photograph you stole.'

Miss Bakewell's lips trembled. 'I thought it would all come out if people saw the pictures. It was so long ago. When I read about the exhibition in the local news, I couldn't sleep. How could John show everyone? Why couldn't he leave well alone?'

'Show everyone what?'

'The pictures of us all – of Catriona.'

Libby nodded. 'It was all about Catriona, wasn't it?'

Miss Bakewell paused, blinking. 'I wonder if I could perhaps have another chocolate. And a glass of water?'

Libby fought an urge to grab the woman by the throat and shake her. She raised a hand, warning Max not to interrupt, fetched water and offered more chocolates. Miss Bakewell sucked a salted caramel, making it last, as Libby forced herself to count to a hundred.

She reached ninety and the wait was finally over. 'John put photographs of Catriona in the exhibition, and I had to hide them. I couldn't let anyone recognise her because – because she looked exactly like that child.'

'Katy,' said Libby. She smiled, realising her intuition had been correct. 'I think Catriona was Katy's grandmother.'

Miss Bakewell heaved a sigh. 'The likeness is unmistakable.'

Max said. 'Which of you killed Catriona?'

Miss Bakewell gasped. 'I – we didn't. She fell – it was an accident – we were at a party. I told you, it was the sixties. She'd taken something – LSD, I suppose. She went upstairs to find her coat and she fell.'

Libby leaned forward, trying to read the teacher's face. 'That's not the whole truth, is it? What really happened?'

Miss Bakewell's lip curled. 'You have to understand. Catriona was always wild. She looked lovely, of course. Her face was quite exquisite, so of course everyone adored her.' The words dripped with sarcasm. 'When Catriona was around, the rest of us faded into the background. She outshone us all in every way, and what's more, she knew it and used it.'

She glared. 'Catriona was a mean, spiteful cat. She won her place at University by flirting in the interview; the interviewers were all men, of course. She wanted to be an architect, like her father. He died when she was very young. She shouldn't have been at a University like Bristol. She couldn't cope with the work and she was jealous of those of us who could. There was nothing Catriona liked more than spoiling things for the rest of us – especially me. Of course, all the men worshipped her.'

'Including the professor?'

'He wasn't a professor then. I met him first, before Catriona, and we were a couple. I thought we'd get married, and...'

She took a bite from a chocolate, swallowing hard. 'Catriona set out to take Malcolm away from me. She was always there, in between him and me, looking pretty and fluttering those long eyelashes.

'Of course, she succeeded. She stole my fiancé from me.' She took a long, shuddering breath. 'Men are so superficial.' She spat out the last words, with a venomous look at Max.

Max started, as though about to speak, but changed his mind and let Miss Bakewell continue. 'When she managed to get her hooks into Malcolm, Catriona set her sights on my beads. She had to have them, just because I loved them.'

She banged her fist on the arm of the chair. 'They were all I had left of – of Malcolm and me. He'd taken them from the dig, just for me, but Catriona persuaded him to give them to her. He threatened to tell the University authorities I'd stolen the beads if I didn't hand them over.'

Tears tracked down Miss Bakewell's cheeks. She whispered, 'How could he be so cruel? I did nothing wrong. It was Catriona's fault. She made him hate me.'

Max leaned back; eyes half closed. 'You must realise you've given yourself the perfect motive for killing Catriona.'

17

CHOCOLATE AND WHISKY

It took liberal doses of chocolate and whisky to calm Miss Bakewell. At last she departed, leaving Libby and Max confused. 'It's no good,' Libby yawned. 'My head's spinning and I can't think any more today.'

'No,' Max said. 'You're right. We'll talk again tomorrow.'

Libby spent an hour in the kitchen, piping flourishes on chocolates destined for Jumbles, pleased to finish the batch. The chocolate turned her stomach a little. It reminded her too vividly of Miss Bakewell, filling her face with sweets as she vented her hatred of Catriona. Her feelings had run deep. It was perfectly possible that in a burst of fury, she'd killed Catriona. If the evening had been hot, like today, Catriona may have stood by the open window or even perched on the windowsill. A single push could have tipped her out.

John Williams was another matter. Miss Bakewell was nowhere near strong enough to force a plastic bag over a grown man's head or carry his dead weight up the hill. Perhaps Libby was wrong and the man really had killed himself; the police investigation appeared to have gone quiet.

If you were going to end it all, the summit of Glastonbury Tor was as suitable a place as any.

Libby cleaned the kitchen until every inch sparkled. She was too tired to bake, although she had to finish the Jumbles order soon. She needed a bath, to wash away the smell of chocolate. She'd lie in warm bubbles, let her mind wander, and hope her subconscious would sort out the interlocking strands of recent events.

Upstairs, the airing cupboard door was ajar as usual. Fuzzy liked to lie, full stretch, on the best towels, shedding orange fur that resisted every attempt at removal, but she wasn't there now. Libby called her name, but nothing happened. No surprise there. Fuzzy never came when she was called.

Libby dropped the plug in the bath and turned on the taps, at full tilt, squeezing in half a bottle of ridiculously expensive bubble lotion. The water level rose, and she prepared to step in, trying to ignore the faint anxiety tugging at her. When did she last see Fuzzy?

It was no use. She turned off the tap, slid a dressing gown round her shoulders and perched on the edge of the bathtub, thinking. After Miss Bakewell left, the cat refused to eat the bowl of cat food Libby offered; had sashayed, tail aloft, through the cat flap and disappeared. Libby hadn't seen her since.

Fuzzy liked to stretch out on top of the computer in the study. Libby looked there, found no sign of her and moved on to the bedroom. Fuzzy was nowhere to be seen. Libby ran downstairs, half expecting Fuzzy to trip her up. She searched the house from top to bottom, even upending the kitchen bin in case Fuzzy had taken it into her head to sleep in there. The creature had chosen far worse places in the past but wasn't there today. Maybe the garage?

On hands and knees, Libby crawled around the Citroen, peering under the body at the mysterious underside. What on earth were all those pipes for? She searched every inch of the garage, poking in empty cardboard boxes, peeking inside a roll of carpet and opening the doors of an old cupboard left over from the kitchen renovation.

When there was nowhere else to search, she returned to the house, grabbed a box of dry cat food and walked round the garden, shaking the box and calling. It was crazy to feel so anxious. Cats look after themselves. Everyone knows that, and Fuzzy was more independent than most. It was just nerves, that was the problem. Libby wished Mandy were here. There was no one more down to earth than her Goth lodger.

The sun remained high in the sky throughout the evening, for midsummer was only a few days away. The house was hot, and stuffy. Maybe she should stop worrying about the cat and take that bath, after all.

The water steamed gently, cooling in the tub. Libby turned to close the door and hesitated. Suddenly nervous, she didn't want to be alone and cut off behind a locked door, but she certainly wasn't about to take a bath with the door unlatched. She leaned over, grabbed the plug and, as the water drained away, stepped in and took a quick shower. The noise of the water drowned out all noise. She wouldn't hear Fuzzy.

She grabbed a towel, rubbed until she was dry, and dressed in jeans and a jumper. She wouldn't relax until that cat came home. 'Fuzzy. Fuzzy, where are you? Come on, you stupid cat. Stop playing games.'

Was Libby going to have to make some of those 'Have you

seen my cat?' notices to fix to the lampposts? She was fast turning into an old cat lady.

* * *

Libby slipped on a pair of wellies. She'd take a final look through the nearby lanes, before she gave up. She left the rows of houses behind, turning across a main road to a tree lined footpath that led onto the water meadows. *When I get my hands on that cat...*

'Meow.' The noise came from deep inside a hedgerow.

Libby swept aside layers of foliage and found a marmalade tail. She knelt down, following the tail along the fluffy, bedraggled body, to Fuzzy's head. 'Hey, there,' she whispered.

Fuzzy meowed again, the noise pitiful.

'What's happened to you?' One of Fuzzy's hind legs stuck out at an angle. 'Was it a dog?' Fuzzy had a habit of teasing dogs, staying just out of their reach, driving the animals wild. This time she might have got too close, or met a fitter, cleverer animal.

Libby slipped off her light summer jacket and eased it around the cat's body. Fuzzy purred. 'That's right. I'm trying to help.'

She carried the cat, wrapped in her coat, back to the cottage and rang the vet's number, expecting to hear a recorded message. Instead, Tanya Ross answered, voice muffled as though eating. Libby shot a glance at her watch. It was definitely out of office hours.

'I'm so sorry to bother you,' she began, and heard a sigh on the other end, 'But my cat's had an accident. I think she's broken her leg.'

The vet paused, probably swallowing a mouthful of dinner. 'Where are you?' Libby gave her address. 'Oh, you're so near. I'm not really open in the evenings but I don't mind, just this once. Come around here.'

The cat's wicker carrier lived in the boot of Libby's faithful purple Citroen. She eased Fuzzy inside and fitted it into the front passenger seat, securing it with the seatbelt. Fuzzy seemed very tiny, huddled against the side of the basket.

Libby begged the car, 'Please start.' It was becoming more and more eccentric with every passing month, but today, the Citroen was on its best behaviour. Sliding into gear with unusual care, Libby drove to the vet's practice in town. 'This is so kind,' she murmured. 'I know it's late.'

'No trouble.'

Libby forced a smile. 'Is it serious?'

The vet was gentle with Fuzzy, stroking the cat's head as she examined the leg. 'You'll have to leave her with me. It looks like a fracture and if I'm right, she'll need surgery. I'll have to give her a general anaesthetic.'

Fuzzy's eyes were huge, her gaze soulful. 'Whatever she needs.'

At least Tanya Ross sounded hopeful. Libby's heart rate settled.

'How did it happen?'

'I don't really know. She might have been run over, I suppose, though she's a pretty wily animal. She usually keeps well out of the way of traffic. We lived in London for years.'

Tanya's head came up, her eyes boring into Libby's. 'You've had a spell of bad luck. Your dog was ill, up on the hill, then you fell over the cliff, and now this. Maybe you should take a little more care.'

Libby swallowed, the prickles of fear she'd felt that first

morning on the Tor, returning. 'How did you know about my fall?'

'News gets around.' The vet's eyes gleamed, pale in the bright overhead strip lights of the surgery. Libby concentrated on keeping her breath slow and steady.

The vet went on, 'I hear you've met that funny little girl that runs around on the Tor. She should be in school. I don't know what her father's thinking.'

'She's very odd. She wouldn't talk to me. All she would do was whisper to the dog.'

Tanya's head shot up. 'She spoke to him. Really? Does her father know?'

'He said it's only people that frighten her. Why? Is there something wrong?'

The vet looked down. 'She's a strange little thing. Born too close to the Tor, that's the story, one midsummer night. Folk see lights dancing around the summit at that time of year, you know.'

Libby groaned. 'Look, I've had enough of local ghost stories. Mysterious lights. Beads that bring bad luck. It's a load of nonsense that you and Miss Bakewell use to throw me off the scent whenever I get close to the truth.'

Colour had drained from the vet's face.

Libby was right, then. 'Miss Bakewell told me about Catriona's death.'

As Tanya Ross gaped, Libby went on, 'You were one of that little group of friends and rivals, all at University together, as I suspected. John Williams used to take photographs of you all and his exhibition brought those days back.

'You must have been horrified when you heard about his retrospective exhibition. Miss Bakewell went along and her fears were confirmed. She took some of the photographs, to keep them secret. For a while, I misunderstood. I thought her concerns were around the necklace – who it belonged to, and where it was found. I was wrong. It wasn't seeing the necklace that gave her such a fright. It was the likeness between Catriona and little Katy.'

She paused, watching Tanya closely. 'The link between Catriona and Katy is at the bottom of all this. Come now, Tanya. Things are serious. John Williams is dead and the professor was nearly killed in an explosion. I think you know what's going on.'

The vet licked her lips and swallowed. Her eyes were on the door, as if she hoped someone would interrupt, but Libby wasn't going to stop. 'Jemima Bakewell hated Catriona, but you didn't. You loved her and you were jealous because she was with Malcolm Perivale. Did you quarrel with her that night because you couldn't have her for yourself?'

Tanya Ross filled a syringe from a bottle. When she turned back, her colour was high and her chin thrust out, as though she'd made up her mind. 'Hold your cat steady,' she commanded. 'I'll tell you the story – at least, the parts I know.'

She slipped the needle into the fur around Fuzzy's neck, but the cat hardly stirred. 'Much of what you say is right; I did love Catriona but I knew she didn't really care for me. Even I could see she was spoiled – too attractive for her own good, but envious of other people's happiness. I wasn't surprised when she set her heart on Malcolm. He was with Jemima and so Catriona wanted him. She liked everything to turn out the way she planned.'

The vet gave a little, sad laugh. 'She wanted to be an architect and she managed to talk her way into a place at one of the best universities in the country. She wanted Malcolm Perivale and it was the easiest thing in the world for her to take him from Jemima. She should have been happy, but...'

She looked straight at Libby. 'She had a secret. She told me about it. She trusted me, because she knew how I felt about her, even though she didn't return my feelings.'

The sadness in Tanya's face reminded Libby of Jemima. 'Catriona needed men like she needed air to breathe. She couldn't help herself – she fell in love with one man after another. She could tell me, because I was no threat. I never cared for men. She felt safe, confiding in me, and she told me about all her conquests. I begged her to be careful, but she wouldn't listen. The university doctor prescribed the contraceptive pill for her, but she often forgot to take it.'

Tanya stroked Fluffy. The cat's eyes closed, her breathing getting deeper. 'Catriona used to say, 'It'll be fine, don't fuss,' but of course, the inevitable happened. She fell pregnant and she was distraught. She could hardly believe such a thing would happen to her. She imagined all her dreams of a future career disappearing if she left university to bring up the baby.'

Tanya avoided Libby's eyes. 'She gave him up for adoption. She couldn't bear to let anything stand in the way of her future.'

'Not even her own child?' Try as she might, Libby found it impossible to hide her shock.

Tanya's eyes met Libby's, hard and bright with unshed tears. 'Don't you dare judge her. Things were different, in those days. It broke Catriona's heart to give away her son.'

The vet gulped and dashed a hand over her eyes. 'When she fell from the window that night, she dropped the necklace – the amber beads she'd fought Jemima to keep. I ran outside when we heard the noise of her fall – that dreadful sound. I saw the necklace on the pavement, by her head, and I picked it up. No one noticed, they were all too busy watching Catriona's blood seep all over the pavement.'

She blew her nose. 'The necklace was her only legacy to her child. I would have liked to keep it, but I knew her son should have it, so I passed it to the couple who adopted Sam. I knew that's what Catriona would have wanted. Sam's new parents kept it for him and he passed it on to his daughter, Katy.'

So, that was how the little girl came by the beads. 'Did Jemima Bakewell know about the pregnancy?'

The vet shrugged. 'I don't know; we never mentioned it, and Catriona disappeared for six months to have the baby. The story was, she was working for an architect – some of the courses included practical placements, so the other students believed her. She thought everything would be all right. There was no need for her to die.'

'No need…' Libby stopped in mid-sentence. Slowly, the pieces of the jigsaw fell into place in her mind. 'I can think of a very good reason why someone thought Catriona needed to die. And there's someone else in danger, right now.'

18

JEMIMA

Max's Jaguar squealed to a halt outside the vet's surgery. Libby jumped inside, pulling on her jacket. Adrenalin pumped through her body.

Max's hands were light on the wheel. 'Good of you to call. Mind telling me why you need to get to Miss Bakewell in such a hurry? I left Bear behind – he wasn't happy with me. He thinks he's missing a treat.'

Libby was silent, leaning forward, straining to see the lanes in the dark. 'Can't you go any faster?'

'We're there.' She was out of the car and running up the path before Max had pulled on the handbrake.

He shouted, 'Come back, you idiot.'

She pounded the door with her right hand, left thumb hard on the bell, but no one came. She jabbed the letter box open, shouting. 'Jemima. Miss Bakewell. Let me in.'

Slowly, the door inched open, jamming on the chain. The ex-schoolteacher's eyes peered round the door. Her mouth trembled. 'You can't come in.'

'Open the door, Jemima.' The teacher shook her head. 'You can't…' she whispered. 'I'm busy.'

Libby raised her voice. 'The police are on their way. They'll be here in a moment.'

The door slammed shut. Max said, 'Stay here.'

To a backdrop of wailing sirens and flashing lights, he took off at a run, trampled over flowerbeds, cursing as he crashed into a rubbish bin. He leapt over a side gate and disappeared around the back of the house.

'Stay where you are, Mrs F.' Joe Ramshore jumped from the first police car as it squealed to a halt, lights flashing, and followed his father. A young detective constable circled round the other side of the house.

With a rattle, the front door flew open. Libby pushed past a terrified Jemima Bakewell and ran through the building, emerging at the back, just in time to see Max in the garden, rolling on the grass. His opponent was aiming ineffectual punches at his face as Joe arrived and, in seconds, the man was in handcuffs.

Max brushed mud from his trousers. 'Well, Professor, don't you think it's time to give in? You're really too old for this sort of thing.'

* * *

Mandy will be furious to have missed the fun. She'd been putting in extra hours at the bakery, saving for a holiday in Cornwall with Steve before he left for college.

Libby made tea, once more adding a dash of whisky to Miss Bakewell's cup. After a moment's thought, she added a bigger dash to her own.

Miss Bakewell fussed in cupboards, looking for chocolate

hobnobs, as though Libby and Max were ordinary visitors invited into her home for a chat.

Max was stern. 'Time to explain yourself, Miss Bakewell. And let's drop all the ancient 'curse of the beads' flim-flam.'

Libby giggled, elation making her foolish. *Flim-flam?*

Max shot her a warning glance and she subsided onto a chair. 'Yes, you'd better come clean. We know what's been going on.'

Miss Bakewell picked at a thread hanging from her tweed skirt. 'I suppose the story has to come out now.' The woman's self-possession was astonishing. The professor had been close behind as she opened the door, a kitchen knife in his hand. She'd been in terrible danger, yet she was quite calm.

Libby shuddered to think what might have happened if she and Max hadn't arrived. 'Is there anyone who'll come and look after you?'

Miss Bakewell shrugged. 'I'm used to being alone.'

'You've been in love with the professor all these years, haven't you?'

The elderly spinster let out a long sigh. 'We had so much in common, Malcolm and I. I knew him first, at university. My mistake was introducing him to Catriona. He fell in love with her and made me give the necklace back to him. She wanted it so badly, you see. Malcolm said he'd tell the authorities I stole the beads if I didn't hand them back.'

The man was a monster. 'What really happened at the party? We've heard so many different versions.'

'It was the sixties, so there was drink everywhere, and drugs. Catriona was drunk and high, and Malcolm danced with me.' Her face lit up at the memory, then her lips quivered, 'I was so happy, thinking he'd come back to me, but later I realised he only did it to make Catriona jealous.'

She gulped her tea and held out the cup. 'I think I need a refill.'

As Libby obliged, she went on, 'I'm afraid the details are a bit blurry. I'd had too much to drink, and the Professor and I...' An ugly blush disfigured the teacher's face. 'He took me upstairs to – you know.'

Libby smiled sympathetically as the blush deepened. 'Anyway, Catriona burst in, screeching like a crazy woman. They had a fight, right there in the bedroom, and Catriona screamed at Malcolm, saying it was his fault she'd had to give away her baby and she'd tell everyone he was the father.'

A sudden flash of spite lit Miss Bakewell's face. 'You can imagine what that did to the professor. He was on the way to a great career at the university. He'd be ruined if people found out. He lost his temper and ran at her. She backed away, against the window. It was open. You see, I told you, she fell out of the window.'

Max broke in, 'But she didn't fall, did she? The professor pushed her.'

Miss Bakewell's hands fluttered round her neck, as though feeling the invisible beads. 'I never knew, not for sure. Our little group stuck together after it happened. Malcolm was the cleverest of us all. He was going to do great things and we were his friends. He couldn't have the truth about Catriona's baby getting out. It would ruin any chance of employment at the university, back in those days. He insisted Catriona's fall was an accident.'

Libby said, 'But you all knew. I think you're still lying to us. You guessed the truth about Catriona's absence that summer, you found out about the baby, and you told Malcolm Perivale. You thought he'd break up with her and come back to you, but you were wrong. You underestimated the cold-blooded ambition of the man. He wouldn't let anything get in the way of his career, and he couldn't trust Catriona to keep the baby quiet. Who knows, she might even have talked about getting her child back. He couldn't take the chance. We'll never know whether he pushed Catriona to her death, or she lost her balance and fell, but either way, it let him off the hook.' Libby shuddered. 'With Catriona out of the way and the child safely adopted, the professor got away without a stain on his character.'

'We made a pact not to meet again, but I couldn't forget him. I put him on a pedestal. In my eyes, no one could measure up to him.' Miss Bakewell sounded desolate. 'I wasted my life dreaming of someone who never existed.' She sighed. 'At least I can see the truth now.'

Libby's heart went out to her, but she had one more question. 'Did you plant the single amber bead in the field?'

'I'm afraid I did. I thought another strand to the myths about Glastonbury Tor would muddy the waters enough to make you forget about the professor.'

Max folded his arms. 'He deserves to pay for what he did, although I'm not sure the police have enough evidence to convict him of John William's murder. At the moment, they're questioning him about the explosion. But why did he start killing people now, after so many years?'

Libby said, 'It was the photographic exhibition. The professor killed John to stop it, afraid there would be photos of Catriona. He didn't want people to remember Catriona's death, or discover she had his child. Deluded, pompous man, all he cared about was his reputation.'

Miss Bakewell's head wagged. 'That's right. I suppose he lured John up to the top of the Tor with some story about the old days. He's strong, the professor, and John was so small and slight. All Malcolm had to do was trip John up, get the plastic bag over his head and sit on him until he died. But then the exhibition went ahead, anyway. That Chesterton Wendlebury wouldn't waste the money his company spent on setting it up. He said it was a tribute to John.' Her eyes flashed. 'I went to see the photographs, not even thinking about Catriona, but when I saw that familiar face, I panicked. There she was – Catriona. Except, as you discovered, it wasn't Catriona at all, but her granddaughter. The photograph brought those days back to me, and I think I went a little crazy.'

Libby said, 'Why wouldn't you open the door to me?'

Miss Bakewell took a bite from the last biscuit. 'Malcolm was inside my house. I'd let him in, thinking he was coming back to me at last, but instead, he threatened me. When you knocked on the door, he stood behind me, hissing in my ear that he'd kill you if you came inside. He was so angry, I was terrified.'

Libby said, 'You put yourself in danger to stop him hurting me?' Who'd have thought Miss Bakewell had such courage.

'I'm getting on – it doesn't matter what happens to me, but you're still young.'

Libby frowned. 'I don't know how I can thank you.'

'Why, Mr Ramshore's already returned the favour. Let's call it even.' Miss Bakewell smiled, a genuine, wide smile. 'And perhaps you could invite me along to the Exham History Society one day, to talk about the ancient history of Somerset. It would give me such pleasure – I've missed teaching, so very much.'

* * *

Back in the car, Libby shivered. 'She's a little odd, but very brave. She probably saved my life.'

'The professor was cleaning up his mess and she was next on the list.'

'Poor soul. Keeping the flame of love alive for so long, and for a ruthless killer like the professor. We should keep in touch with her. She seems so lonely.'

Libby thought about the child; the grandchild of foolish, selfish Catriona and the cold, calculating professor. What an ancestry. 'Do you think Katy will ever talk properly?'

Max grinned, a little sheepishly. 'I told her father I'd take Bear over to see her, now and then. Well, quite often, really. Sam reckons she's already taken the first steps to recovery from whatever they call it – elective mutism, I believe. And if she's got the beads, she won't keep running away to look for them on the Tor.'

'The Tor. All that nonsense about the beads bringing bad luck. It's just another story to add to all the others.' Libby laughed. 'Funny, how easy it is to start believing in the supernatural, when all the time there was an explanation for everything that happened.'

Max drew to a halt. 'Libby,' he said. 'I know you're angry with me about Trevor. I'm sorry I didn't tell you everything. I wanted to be sure.' His arm slid round her shoulders. 'I should have trusted you.'

'Yes, you should.' Libby longed to lean her head on his shoulder. His arm was so comforting. She took a long breath. 'I think I can forgive you, Max, but not quite yet. You see, I trusted Trevor for all those years, but he was making a fool of me. I have to sort things out in my own mind. Did he love me? Was he a wicked man, or just a silly, weak one who controlled me because he couldn't control himself? I can't decide, and it's driving me mad. I need the full story.'

19

SHARK

The sun was already beating down on Exham when Libby woke two days later; perfect weather for a run on the beach with Shipley.

First, she checked on Fuzzy. She'd returned from the vet wearing a heavy plaster on her leg, but otherwise back to normal. Scorning the padded basket and blanket Libby had set up, she'd spent most of yesterday sleeping along the back of the sofa, descending only to nibble special treats from the dish Libby had situated close by, and to use the carefully positioned litter tray.

Pleased to see Fuzzy almost back to normal, Libby thought it safe to leave her and take Shipley for a run on the beach.

She heard his frenzied bark as she approached the house. Marina took longer than usual to open the door, and at first sight, looked flustered. Her hair stuck out at wild angles and the top of her frilly blouse drooped, unfastened.

'You'd better come in,' she murmured, blushing and fiddling with the floppy bow.

'I came to take Shipley for a run...'

In the doorway of the living room, Chesterton Wendlebury beamed. 'My dear lady. Have you come to help Marina prepare for her book club?' His voice boomed.

Libby shook her head. 'Dog walking.'

'Ah. Do you have the redoubtable Bear with you?'

'He's at home with Max.' Finding the man here was a surprise, but Libby wasn't going to waste the opportunity. 'Mr Wendlebury.' She took a slow breath. 'I believe you might have known my husband.'

'Oh? What makes you think that?' His voice purred.

'Trevor – that's my husband – brought us all here for a holiday a few years ago. He had business in the area and spent almost every day driving off to meetings with clients.'

Wendlebury inclined his head in a vague non-committal gesture.

Libby ploughed on. 'After that holiday, my husband changed. I know that, around that time, he became involved in shady business deals.'

'Ah.' Wendlebury crossed one leg over the other. 'I recognise the influence of Mr Ramshore on your information. I've often wondered about him. A banker, taking early retirement, making frequent trips abroad.'

He smiled, showing large, tombstone teeth. *Like a shark.* 'Oh, yes, Mrs Forest, I've made it my business to check up on him; a financial wizard with a burning desire to interfere where he has no business.'

He broke off as Marina arrived with a tray of coffee. 'Marina, Mrs Forest and I were talking over old times. I expect, like most people in town, you thought she was new to the area?'

Marina gave an easy laugh. 'Plenty of summer visitors

come back here to retire. Not that you've been taking it easy. You're always busy with something.' She adjusted the scarves at her neck, settling back onto her pale sofa.

'Did you know my husband, Marina?'

Marina glanced at Wendlebury, and away. 'We met once or twice. He came here a few times, without you and the children. On business, of course.'

Libby's next question was drowned by a crash that echoed through the house and brought Marina to her feet. 'Shipley,' she shouted. 'That dog. What mess has he made, now?'

Libby took Shipley off her hands as soon as she could and walked for over an hour on the beach, her head full of unanswered questions about Trevor's activities.

* * *

Next day, Libby leaned on Max's doorbell. *Come on. Wake up.* Her eyes were gritty from a night tossing and turning, puzzling over the connection between Wendlebury and Trevor. Flashes of memory from that first visit to Exham left her astonished she could have been so stupid. The children were still young then, and money tight, but Trevor hadn't wanted Libby to work.

'We need you at home to look after us,' he insisted, and Libby, wanting to be a good wife for the man she loved, took his words as signs of affection. She'd stayed at home, worrying about her husband. He spent hours alone in his study, and when he came out, he could be distracted and offhand.

Libby decided he was working too hard and suggested a holiday. 'The English seaside. Buckets and spades for the kids, fish and chips for dinner.'

Trevor grinned and the lines of worry faded. 'One of my clients, Pritchards, has a head office on Exmoor. We could stay at the seaside in Exham on Sea. Let's combine business and pleasure for a week.' That was how they came to visit Exham. It was all her fault. How could she have forgotten?

Maybe she'd deliberately wiped it from her memory, because after that week, Trevor grew more distant, angry and unkind, and more critical of his wife. He spent long hours in the office or on business trips, his hair turned grey and he drank heavily, but Libby never dared speak of it. She watched, helpless, from the side-lines as her loving husband gradually disappeared, to be replaced by a cold, angry stranger.

If only she'd stood up to Trevor, tried to find out what was going on, maybe she could have made a difference. She shuddered. What if she'd discovered his criminal dealings? What could a wife do – shop him to the police? Or, could she have put a stop to it all? She'd never know, but one thing was certain. She'd let no one make a fool of her again. That's why she was here, on Max's doorstep, at a crazy early hour; to discover the truth about him.

The door opened. 'Whatever time do you think this is?' Max's hair stood in spikes on top of his head. In dressing gown and bare feet, rubbing fingers over early-morning beard stubble, he squinted at Libby. 'This had better be an emergency.'

She pushed past. 'I want an explanation from you, Max Ramshore.'

'Can I make coffee, first?'

'Answers first, then coffee.'

'That serious?' He led the way to the study, his private sanctum. Part of Libby registered the gesture. Maybe she'd get some honesty, for once.

She pushed a pile of documents at him and waited, foot tapping, taut with anxiety, as he fumbled in his desk for reading glasses before scanning the first page.

'We've already talked about these.' He sounded perfectly reasonable. 'We know your husband had a portfolio of houses, bought with money from criminal activities.' He shot a glance at Libby. 'Trevor was just the admin man.' Libby waved a hand, impatient. This was old news.

She grabbed the pile of papers so agitated, she could hardly get her tongue round the words. 'What if Trevor's death wasn't an accident? He had a sudden heart attack. Not uncommon, I know, in a middle-aged man who drank and smoked and took no exercise, so how hard did the pathologist look for another cause of death? How did Trevor really die?'

Max leaned forward and took Libby's hands. 'You said it yourself. Your husband was a middle-aged man under a huge amount of stress. Why would you imagine he died from anything but a heart attack?'

Libby snatched her hands away and stared at Max, wondering what she was really seeing. Her voice was hard. 'Trevor had links to Exham on Sea. We came here when the children were young, and around that time, Trevor changed. He became a different person. He'd been kind and loving when we first married.' Tears slid down her cheeks. 'I know he loved me, once. Over the years, he became more controlling; telling me I was stupid, stopping me from seeing friends. It was gradual, and I didn't realise it was happening until he'd turned me into some sort of door mat. But I can see, now, that person wasn't the real Trevor. Maybe he was just weak. He got into bad company, couldn't find the way out of the mess he was in, and the result was terrible stress.' She could barely speak, for tears. 'If only he'd told me the truth, we could have sorted it all out.'

'Even if it meant prison?'

Libby wiped the tears away with the back of her hand. 'Even then. He should have trusted me. I could have helped, somehow.' Max walked to the window and back. Libby let the silence grow, but as each second ticked past, the knot in her chest tightened until every breath hurt and she couldn't stand it any longer. She whispered. 'Did – did you know about Trevor? Tell me, Max. Stop pretending.' When he turned, his face told the truth. 'You did. You knew what my husband was up to. You knew about the money and the properties from the start.'

Her fingers shook. Trevor's paper slid from her grasp scattering on the floor. 'You knew who I was, before I even arrived in Exham.' Every moment with Max flashed through Libby's mind. That first meeting, when he'd walked past her house, taking Bear for exercise. Why had he chosen to go that way when he could be on the beach or in the fields? Later that same day, he'd come into the bakery as if by accident and whisked Libby away for coffee. She shook her head, trying to clear it, letting in the stark truth. 'You've been watching me ever since I arrived in Exham.'

He put a hand on her arm, but she shook it off, spitting out bitter words. 'I understand, Max. I can see it all, now. You thought I was one of Trevor's – what should I call it – accomplices? You got close to me, deliberately, so I'd lead you to my husband's ill-gotten gains. And all the time I thought – I hoped...' She clenched her jaw, refusing to cry. 'Just tell me one thing, Max. How did Trevor die? Did you, or one of your shady friends, kill him?'

There. She'd said it. The shocking words were out. Her head was spinning, her heart thudding, blood hammering in her ears. She feared she was about to faint. Max gripped her arm, fingers digging in to her flesh. His eyes, usually so blue, glowed dark in a white face. 'Is that what you think? Do you honestly believe I'm a killer?'

Libby gulped. 'I – I don't want you to be.' She forced the words through dry lips.

Max let his hands drop. 'I had nothing to do with Trevor's death, although I can't blame you if you don't believe me.' With gentle fingers, he took one of Libby's hands. 'I'll tell you the truth. You're right about some of it. I did know who you were when you moved to Exham. I thought you'd come to tidy up Trevor's loose ends and my job was to stop you. I was looking for the mastermind behind the whole criminal conspiracy, and I needed to get close to you, so you could lead me there.'

Libby pulled her hand away. Her throat burned. 'You followed me.'

'You didn't notice a thing until I made the mistake of walking Bear too close to your house one morning and he got into a scrap with Fuzzy.'

'Which Fuzzy won.'

'She did. That cat's as feisty as her owner. Believe me, Libby, I soon realised you had nothing to do with your husband's crimes.'

'Am I supposed to be grateful?' Her fingers itched to slap his face. It would serve him right. 'Anyway, what made you decide I was innocent?'

'You were happy to get involved in police business. If you'd been a real criminal, you'd have let the authorities deal with the body under the lighthouse. I could see you were one of two things. Either you were a criminal and hopelessly incompetent, or you were innocent and nosy.'

She let that pass. 'So that's why you were keen to work with me. To see if I was what I seemed to be.'

He nodded. 'When I realised the truth, I was – well...' He fell silent. 'I'm sorry.'

'Sorry? Is that supposed to make it all right? You lied to me. And all the time I thought...' She shook her head, trying to clear it, struggling to think. What would she have done in Max's shoes? She didn't have to think for long before recognising the answer. She'd investigate, of course, as he'd done.

Max had known she was innocent since last autumn's murder at the lighthouse. She'd been no more use to him in his hunt for the person at the top of the criminal tree, but nevertheless, he'd stayed by her side, ready to help, watching out for her. She whispered, 'In Bristol, I asked if we had a relationship...'

Max slid one arm round her shoulders and pulled her close. 'I was cruel. You took me by surprise. I'd taken so much care to keep my distance, trying to pretend I wasn't falling for you. I never imagined you gave a fig for me. I thought it was all one way. In Bristol, I panicked and had a few second thoughts. What if I'd got it wrong and you were Trevor's accomplice, after all? Maybe, because I wanted you to be innocent, I was making a big mistake.' He grimaced. 'I'm not much good at relationships. Never have been. I couldn't believe my luck, that I stood a chance of getting this one right. So, I blew it all.'

'You should have trusted me.'

'I know. I was a fool. But I want to put it on the record,

now. I've cared about you the whole time, Libby Forest, from the moment you first shouted abuse at me in the street. I'd love you, even if you were a master criminal.'

20

FRENCH TOAST

'Well, that was worth waiting for.' Max's kiss lasted a long time, until Bear, whose humans had spent far too long ignoring him, finished all the food in his dish, gobbled a few titbits left on the table, and came looking for action. He arrived on the sofa, all over-sized paws and wet nose, forcing Max and Libby apart. Which was just as well, Libby decided, as she had a hundred questions to ask.

Max grabbed the dog by his collar and led him away. 'He lives in the back place. Used to be a gun room, I suppose, when the squire lived here, but Bear's learned to open the door. I'm going to have to change the lock.'

As Max filled the dog's water bowl, Libby made tea and French toast and laid down a few ground rules. 'I'm not standing for any more secrets. I lived half my married life in the dark. If we're going to – you know.' She knew she was blushing. 'If we're going to be together, I need to trust you. You have to tell me everything you know about Trevor.'

'Fair enough, I suppose. Trouble is, I've got used to being secretive. It's a habit, these days. Let me try to put it all in order.' He chewed in silence for a moment. 'I'll start at the beginning. I was called in as part of an investigation into Trevor's insurance company because there seemed to be some creative accounting going on. I'm afraid Trevor wasn't a very efficient fraudster.' Libby winced, bracing herself for the worst. 'HMRC picked it up first and passed it on. My job then was to re-audit the finances.'

Libby nodded. 'The tax people never miss a trick, do they?'

'We could see Trevor was a weak link. He came down to Exham several times, after that first visit with you and the family, and that made us curious. I wasn't living here at that time. You and I didn't meet.' He stopped talking, his eyes on Libby. She knew what he was thinking because Libby was wondering as well. What would have happened if the two of them had met, back then?

He looked away and the spell broke. 'He had plenty of insurance customers here but all the paperwork seemed above board. I realised someone around here was running things. That's when I moved back. I had the perfect cover because I grew up in Exham. Local people trust me and I was the best one to untangle the relationships in the area. Families are so closely woven. Everyone is somebody's aunt, or step-brother, or second cousin twice removed, and they all look out for each other.'

'It's rather lovely, in a way,' Libby put in. 'Families are sometimes all you have.' She thought of Ali, on the other side of the world, sending lengthy emails each week, and Robert, planning to bring his girlfriend home. She was almost sure he'd be announcing their engagement.

She bit into her toast. Max looked so serious, his brows almost meeting. Libby had to pick up her coffee cup to keep from stroking his hair. 'I found a reference to property in Leeds and we sent one of our men up there to rent it, under cover.'

'Your friend Cal James and his wife. The ones living in Trevor's house.'

'Yes. Well, the wife was Cal's idea – part of the cover story. What is it?' He frowned. 'What's so funny?'

'Cover stories, laundering money, Mr Big in the Exham area. Who would have thought it in a quiet seaside town like this? It's hard to believe.'

Max's lips curved but the smile didn't reach his eyes. 'Unfortunately, it's true. We're very close to catching the person at the top of the tree but I don't want you any further involved.'

'Why not? You can't be afraid anyone's going to shoot me, are you?'

This time, Max didn't even try to smile. 'That's exactly what I'm afraid of. You're too good an investigator. That'll be fine when we're operating as Ramshore and Forest, Investigators at Large, but it might put you in danger with Trevor's masters.'

'Forest and Ramshore, you mean.'

The smile reappeared. 'Whatever. I want you to be safe, Libby. We're close to finishing this business but don't forget, the criminals have been watching you, as I was. Will you promise to be careful and stop poking your nose in everywhere when I'm not around?'

Libby sighed. 'I suppose I'd better come clean.' She told Max about the visit to Marina's house. 'Chesterton Wendlebury was there. I think they're having some sort of a liaison. In her own home.' She stopped, thinking about Marina's husband, Henry. Did he really have no idea what was going on? 'I'm convinced Chesterton Wendlebury's behind it all, though I don't have any evidence.'

'You really don't like that man, do you?'

She shivered. 'His eyes are too close together.' Max was silent.

Libby narrowed her eyes. 'What aren't you telling me? I thought we were being honest with each other.'

His sigh was heavy. 'It's not so much Wendlebury, as his company.'

'Pritchards.' Libby was triumphant. 'I knew it.'

'Most of their business is above board. Cut-throat, of course, but that's how they make money.'

'They tried to buy out the bakery for pennies when it had to shut.'

'As I said, that's business, but they were also running local gangs of petty criminals; the vehicle ringers and cannabis growers. The police closed most down but they let a few continue so they could gather more evidence. Joe's been part of the team working on that; he's known what I've been doing all along.'

'And that's why you two kept up the pretence of not speaking.'

'Some of that was genuine. I was a pretty bad father. But we rub along most of the time.'

Libby drained the last drops from her mug. 'I'm still puzzled by Trevor taking out mortgages on his houses. Seems odd to me.

It's all part of the scam, laundering money and covering his tracks.'

'How exactly did it work?'

'His criminal contacts put money into his bank accounts – he had several you never knew about, and he bought the houses using a mix of that tainted cash and short-term bank mortgages. He thought his bosses wouldn't check on him – they have dozens of properties all over the country. He foolishly gambled on them taking their eyes off him.

'The gang handed the tenants of Trevor's properties enough cash to cover the rent. That way, more dirty money changed hands and became legitimate. But Trevor thought he could hold on to the properties for five years, until the mortgage terms expired, then sell them under his own name and keep the proceeds.

At the same time, he used his job as an insurance agent to organise inflated payments for repairs that were then carried out at a fraction of the price, while he kept the difference. Unfortunately for Trevor, he didn't understand how ruthless his contacts could be – or that they were checking up on him all the time.'

'He was trying to double-cross the bosses but they found out?'

'His insurance activities put them at risk. Once they suspected he was syphoning money off for himself, they looked more closely and saw the danger. If the authorities followed the same trail, the entire money laundering empire could unravel, so they got rid of the weak link. Unfortunately, the weak link was Trevor.'

Libby drew a long breath. 'So, they had him killed.'

21

LEMON CAKE

Beryl, a long-term member of the Exham History Society, sat in a corner of Marina's room dressed in her favourite shade of brown, sipping Earl Grey tea. Her cup rattled in its saucer, her fingers trembling with excitement. She was about to present her paper to the group.

The First Post Office in Exham had been opened by Beryl's great grandfather, and she'd been waiting a long time for the opportunity to tell the tale.

She had high hopes of today's meeting. True, it had been convened to celebrate the end of the great Glastonbury Tor murder mystery and the part in the story played by the historic amber beads. Jemima Bakewell, currently eating biscuits and chatting with a couple of society members, was giving the main talk, but surely there would be a few moments at the end to fill?

'I wouldn't get your hopes up,' Libby whispered, as Detective Sergeant Joe Ramshore and his father, Max, arrived together, looking awkward and uncomfortable as they perched on two of Marina's antique chairs.

'Have more cake, darling.' Marina offered Beryl a slice of Libby's acclaimed whisky and lemon cake. 'It'll settle your nerves.'

All the society regulars had come for this special meeting. Even Samantha Watson found time in her important schedule to attend. She held one of Marina's bone china cups in her left hand, little finger raised, over-sized engagement ring on prominent display. She was due to marry Chief Inspector Arnold in three months.

George Edwards gave his wife's apologies. She'd sprained her ankle. Libby suspected George's wife's ailments were an excuse; after every meeting, he took home a large doggy bag of cake.

Chesterton Wendlebury arrived with a flourish, heaved his bulk into the largest, most comfortable armchair, and beamed round the room. 'So kind of you to invite me. I'm agog to hear more of Mrs Forest's adventures.'

'Well, if we're all here,' began Angela Miles, one of the society's founder members, 'I'll ask Libby to tell us about the latest events on Glastonbury Tor.'

The society listened, enthralled, as Libby told the sad story of Catriona's murder, so far in the past. 'It was hard to get at the truth, after so long. People remember the same event in different ways, even in the best of circumstances. In this case, our university students from the sixties were ashamed of things they'd done or said. Each of them tried to distance themselves from the truth. They couldn't even agree on the character of Catriona, their friend. Was she beautiful and kind, or greedy and selfish? Why did she hand her child over to adoptive parents; for the sake of appearances, or her career, or to keep the professor's love? We'll never know, for sure, but her death led directly to the death of John Williams so many years later.'

No one interrupted, even as she took a gulp of tea. 'Professor Perivale was confident he'd escaped punishment for pushing Catriona out of the window. I don't believe he was capable of love. He was driven by a desperate need to maintain his reputation.

'Imagine how such an arrogant, self-absorbed man felt when he heard about a retrospective exhibition of his old colleague's work. Those photographs could stir up memories of Catriona's death and put the professor's reputation at risk. He couldn't allow that. He'd managed to commit the perfect crime once, so he was confident he could do it again. Without a second thought, he killed John Williams.'

Joe took up the story. 'The professor blackmailed a failing student into giving him an alibi for the time of the murder and setting off an explosion in his own house. As he hoped, that threw everyone off the scent. He used a fertiliser based explosive, following instructions from the internet. We found them in his browsing history.'

Max grinned. 'He underestimated the force of the blast and landed up in hospital. He wasn't as clever as he thought but he did succeed in throwing us off the scent for a while.'

Joe finished the tale. 'We interviewed the professor's student, who soon realised a failing grade was preferable to a conviction as an accessory to murder. He admitted there had been no tutorial that morning and the professor's alibi for the time of John Williams' murder fell apart. He's safely in custody now, condescending to the police officers and convinced he's still cleverer than the rest of us.'

As the story ended, Marina poured more tea. 'Today, we're also welcoming Miss Jemima Bakewell to our society. She'd going to tell us a little of the prehistory of the area. Let's give her a warm welcome.'

The society clapped politely and Jemima launched into her lecture on the Iron Age. She'd borrowed Katy's necklace from Catriona's son, Sam, for the occasion, and the society members were enthralled by the chance to see and touch a 2,000 year old artefact.

'Luckily for us,' Jemima finished, 'the necklace contains no precious metal, so Sam and Katy can keep it safe. We've registered it with the Portable Antiquities Scheme and Katy can pass it on to the Museum of Somerset, in Taunton, when she's older. In the meantime, they have one bead already on display – the one Libby found at Deer Leap.'

She took off her spectacles and polished them vigorously. She'd already confessed her part in the Deer Leap escapade to Libby. 'I wanted to protect Malcolm, so I tried to add another myth to the mix. Silly, I know – I was panicking.'

As Jemima finished, Beryl reached into her handbag, groping for her own speech, but Libby held up a hand. 'Sorry, Beryl, there's something important I have to say.'

Out of Libby's line of sight, someone coughed. Marina offered cake. 'Another story, darling? Do be quick, the cake's almost finished.'

'This one's personal. When my husband brought me to Exham, many years ago, I had no idea he was setting up contacts with local criminals. For years, local vehicle ringing and cannabis businesses filtered money through Trevor. Max spent months tracking financial deals and all the trails led back here, to Exham.'

She looked from one face to another, searching for signs of guilt. 'One company in particular make money buying up properties cheaply.'

Someone murmured, 'Pritchards.'

'Exactly. We've all heard they stop at nothing to ruin small businesses. Max had a look at their affairs.'

Marina rubbed her hands together. 'Ooh, Libby, this is too exciting.'

Samantha Watson set her cup in its saucer. 'I'm quite sure the police are far better placed to uncover this – what shall I call it – nest of thieves, than an amateur sleuth like you. I suggest you leave everything to them and stop poking your nose in where it isn't wanted.'

Joe intervened. 'Detective Chief Inspector Arnold is well aware of the situation, I can assure you, Mrs Watson. I have his full authority.'

Samantha tossed her head. 'Then, I suggest you do your job and catch the criminal.'

'That's exactly what I'm here to do.' Someone gasped. 'But I'd like Mrs Forest to finish the story.'

Libby cleared her throat. 'I wondered who Trevor knew in Exham, and two people were at the top of the list.' She turned to Chesterton Wendlebury. 'You admitted to being on the board of Pritchards, and I've bumped into you in some strange places over the past year; at the county show, riding with Marina on the Levels.'

Wendlebury smiled, the shark teeth prominent. 'My dear lady, if your friend Max has investigated my business affairs, you must know they're completely in order.'

Max was smiling. 'I've read every budget and report you've had your hands on, Wendlebury. You've done a great job. I couldn't locate a single suspicious account or strange payment. No, it isn't you at the top of the tree. You provide cover for someone far cleverer.'

Libby said, 'I'm afraid it's someone who's always been at

the centre of things in Exham. Someone who knows everyone in town and lives a wealthy, innocent life. Someone who made friends with me as soon as I arrived in the town, knew all about my husband's business affairs, and wanted to keep a very close eye on me.'

She examined each face. Only one pair of eyes looked away.

'In fact, the genius at the top of the whole pyramid of crime is our generous host and town busybody, Marina Stallworthy, aided and abetted by her quiet, hen-pecked husband, Henry.'

* * *

The shock of Marina Stallworthy's arrest reverberated through Exham for weeks. The community lost interest in the murder on the Tor, as the townspeople realised they'd never quite trusted Marina, and always suspected there was something odd about the inoffensive Henry.

'Marina made sure I knew all about her fictitious affair with Chesterton Wendlebury,' Libby admitted, lying on Max's sofa, Bear at her feet. 'She knew I'd tell you about it. Like everyone else, I hardly gave Henry a thought.'

'They made the perfect criminal couple,' Max agreed. 'Marina at the centre of the community, watching and manipulating, while Henry, almost unnoticed, directed operations through his old client, Wendlebury. I don't believe Wendlebury ever understood what was going on. Underneath the country gentleman act, there's precious little intelligence. Marina was at the centre of a complicated web. It will be a long time before they come to trial.'

'Will you be involved?'

'I'll be giving evidence, with the greatest of pleasure.'

A shiver travelled up Libby's spine. 'We still don't know whether Trevor's death was an accident, or murder. He was cremated, so we'll probably never be sure unless Marina or Henry decides to tell us. I'm afraid they're not likely to do that.'

Max drew her head on to his shoulder. 'Can you live with that? Not knowing for sure?'

'I shall have to. At least, there are good things to look forward to. My son emailed me this week and he's coming home, bringing his girlfriend. I'm almost sure there's a wedding on the horizon and I'll be busy making the biggest, grandest cake Exham's ever seen.'

Max fetched a bottle of champagne and popped it open. Libby said, 'We ought to drink a toast: to cake, chocolates and our partnership, Ramshore and Forest, Private Investigators.'

Max's raised glass sparkled with condensation. 'I'll drink to that, with just one proviso. Let's toast our real future. Here's to you and me: Libby and Max.'

MURDER AT THE CATHEDRAL

AN EXHAM-ON-SEA MYSTERY

1

CATHEDRAL CAFÉ

Libby Forest and the enormous sheepdog, Bear, climbed the steep street to Wells Cathedral. With no cats to chase, Bear turned his attention to the human passers-by and tried to plant a slobbery, doggy kiss on each face. Libby's cheeks flamed with embarrassment as she steered the animal through Penniless Porch, the archway leading to the green lawn in front of the cathedral. 'I almost wish I hadn't agreed to look after you. The sooner Max gets home and takes you back, the better.' No need to tell Bear how much she loved having him with her as she visited the beauty spots of Somerset.

The duo of walkers paused at last, Libby's eyes drawn to the statues carved on the building's stunning West Front. She raised a warning finger at the wriggling dog. 'You're on your best behaviour.' The last thing she needed was a spat with Louis, the cathedral cat, and there was nothing Bear enjoyed more than chasing cats. He made an exception only for Fuzzy, Libby's aloof marmalade cat, who'd turned out to be Bear's soulmate. The pair liked curling up together in as small a space as possible and dozing the hours away.

They navigated the spiral stairs to the café without incident and Libby poked her head round the door. Conversations buzzed amid enticing smells of cake and spice, but Libby was immune to food. Cakes and chocolates were her business, and she spent most days mixing and tasting, surrounded by sugar. On a rare free morning she stuck to coffee.

She spotted Angela Miles at once. Immaculate grey locks teased into a neat French Pleat, pearl earrings dangling from tiny ears, her friend raised a leather-gloved hand in welcome. Libby tugged at her thatch of damp brown hair. She should have visited the hairdresser weeks ago.

Pulling a dog treat from the jumble in a pocket of her parka, she bribed Bear to lie down under the table. Angela stirred a steaming cup of coffee. 'So, your son's getting married in the cathedral? How wonderful.'

'Isn't it? His fiancée, Sarah, has family connections; her mother grew up two streets away. Even so, they were lucky to find a vacant date for the wedding. The cathedral gets booked up in the summer, but there's a cancellation in June. At least the weather will be warmer. I'm tired of winter…'

Angela's attention had drifted. Libby, intrigued, followed the direction of her friend's gaze. A familiar figure occupied a table in the corner with her back to the room. Even at a distance, the back-combed haystack of black hair was unmistakable. Libby would recognise Mandy, her lodger and apprentice, anywhere.

She rose to wave. 'Hey, Mandy…'

Angela tugged her arm. 'Shh. Don't interrupt. Mandy hasn't seen us and she's having a row with Steve.'

That young man, Angela's nephew and Mandy's boyfriend, sported spiky, dyed-black hair and a tight t-shirt. He banged a fork on the table. 'Suit yourself,' he snapped, face red and angry.

Libby's eyes met Angela's. 'We shouldn't eavesdrop.' They turned away, full of good intentions, trying to carry on a conversation, but the fight proved irresistible. At last, they gave themselves up to unashamed eavesdropping.

Steve's romance with Mandy had lasted almost a year, even surviving his move from Wells Cathedral School to study music at the Royal College of Music in London, but the relationship looked under strain, today.

Libby caught fragments of angry whispers. 'You could if you wanted to,' Steve hissed.

Mandy wailed, 'You don't even try to understand…'

To Libby's disappointment, she missed the rest and, succumbing to guilt, dragged her attention back to the reason she and Angela had arranged to meet. From the depths of her bag she retrieved sketches for the bride's wedding dress, samples of lace, and lists of guests. 'She hasn't made her mind up yet, so people can see the sketches – apart from Robert, of course. Sarah tells me it's unlucky for the groom to see the dress before the wedding.'

Angela settled a pair of reading glasses on her nose, leaned both elbows on the table and examined the plans, cooing with approval. 'What a gorgeous dress. I love a fishtail, don't you? Sarah will look stunning.'

She sat back. 'Now, tell me about the cake. That's your department, isn't it? What are you going to make? Sponge cake? Fruit? How many tiers? I bet you can't wait to start.'

Libby avoided her friend's eye. 'They want cheese.'

'Cheesecake? That's unusual, but I suppose you could make it look good—'

'Not cheesecake. Cheese. Three different varieties, all produced in Somerset. Cheddar, Brie and – er – Buffalo. One for each layer of the cake. Sarah's father's a dairy farmer.'

Angela's eyes opened wide. 'So, you won't be icing the biggest and best wedding cake in Somerset, after all?'

'No; and I had such plans...'

Their laughter died as Mandy's voice rose. 'Don't you dare call me a stupid child. I've got, like, a job, you know. I can't come running down to London every time you snap your fingers. Why don't you ask your friend, Alice. She'll be there in a second.'

A hush fell throughout the café, half embarrassed and half expectant. Mandy threw a handful of coins on the table and stamped out. Steve scrambled to his feet as if to give chase, but stopped, hesitated as though making his mind up, and flopped back into the chair.

Angela peered over the rim of her reading glasses, muttering under her breath, 'Follow her, Steve, you idiot,' but the young man sipped coffee, as though quite unaware he was the centre of attention. Only a spot of pink on each cheek gave the game away.

Angela sighed. 'That'll teach me to eavesdrop. I was hoping they'd stay together for good and maybe even get married. I know they're young, but they seemed so happy.'

Libby sorted the wedding plans into a pile. 'D'you think that's the end of the relationship? Perhaps they're not as well suited as we thought.' Mandy had seemed to be on cloud nine recently. 'It's a shame, but they're still young. Living so far from each other must be a strain.'

She put her papers back in the bag. 'I remember Alice. I

met her one day at your house. Very glamorous and a musician, like Steve.' She shrugged. 'Maybe she's a better match for him, but I'm sorry for Mandy. It seems her heart's about to be broken.'

Angela rearranged packets of sugar in the flower-painted china container. 'Look at us, worrying about Steve and Mandy as if they're our children.'

'Mandy's almost a third child to me, now Ali and Robert have grown up and left home. She's tidier around the house than they ever were, though.'

Angela looked thoughtful. 'I never had children of my own. Didn't think I had maternal instincts until Steve's motorbike accident. That hit me for six.'

'You were like a tiger with her cub,' Libby recalled, 'and you spent every day at the hospital until you were certain he'd recover.'

Angela laughed. 'I suppose you never stop wanting to look after them, do you? No matter how old they are.'

The excitement died away, the café returned to its normal state of soporific calm, and Bear rested his head on Libby's lap, eyes pleading for treats. As she tickled his favourite spot, just behind a front leg, Angela's phone rang.

She made an apologetic face. 'Sorry, do you mind if I take it? It's the verger. I expect he's calling about my shift this afternoon.' Angela worked in the cathedral as a volunteer guide.

She answered the phone with a cheery 'Hello,' but a second later, the smile froze on her face. Colour drained from both cheeks, leaving Angela looking pale and shocked. Her lips moved, but no sound came. Her eyes flickered.

Libby put out a hand, afraid her friend was about to faint, but Angela recovered enough to talk. 'Are you sure? It can't be true – I mean – it was only yesterday…'

Her hand shook and the phone fell, spinning and rattling, onto the floor.

'Is everything OK?' Libby bit her lip at such crassness. What a stupid thing to say when it was blindingly obvious things were very far from OK.

Angela was mumbling, shaking her head. 'It's dreadful. I can't believe it…' She gasped for air.

Libby squeezed her elbow. 'Breathe out, now. Slowly.' Angela shuddered, regaining control. 'That's better. Now, tell me. What's happened?'

'It's Giles – Giles Temple – he's been working at the cathedral library.' Libby had never met Mr Temple, but Angela had spoken of him once or twice. Whenever she mentioned his name, her cheeks turned a delicate shade of pink.

'What about him?'

'He's – he's had an accident.'

'Is it serious?'

Angela nodded, lips quivering. 'Very. I'm afraid he's dead.'

2

LIBRARIAN

'Is your friend ill?' One of the women serving at the counter hurried across the room, sympathy in her eyes.

'She's had a nasty shock.' Libby avoided going into details. Soon enough, everyone working in the cathedral would know about Giles Temple's death.

'Well, she'd better have a cup of tea, that's my advice. It's the best remedy for shock. Poor Mrs Miles. I've seen her many time, working in the cathedral. Very kind, she is. Couldn't be nicer. No airs and graces, like some folks working at the cathedral.'

The woman bustled about, bringing a pot and cups on a tray. Libby, with superhuman self-control, asked no questions of Angela as she poured tea, added milk and several spoons of sugar, and waited until her friend drank every drop.

As Angela settled the empty cup back in its saucer, hands still shaking, a touch of colour returned to her cheeks. The threat of a fainting fit gradually receded, and Libby gave way to curiosity. 'Now, give me the facts. What happened?'

'The librarian found Giles this morning when he opened the room. He'd been—' Angela swallowed and finished in a rush, 'He'd been strangled. With a chain.'

'Strangled? You mean, accidentally?' Not another suspicious death in Somerset, surely. 'What do you mean by a chain? Some sort of necklace?'

Angela shook her head, as though trying to clear it. 'No, it's a chained library, you see. The chains are attached to valuable books and bolted to the shelves to prevent anyone wandering off with a priceless volume. So many books in the library are irreplaceable.'

Her high-pitched laugh sounded dangerously close to hysteria.

Libby concentrated, determined not to miss a single word as Angela explained. 'There are keys, you see. One locks the gate to the library, and another attaches each chain to a book.'

Tears glittered in Angela's eyes. Libby, horrified as she was, couldn't help a familiar spasm of excitement in her stomach. She felt it at the beginning of each of her amateur investigations, and every time she'd succeeded in uncovering the criminal. 'And one of the chains was used to strangle the victim?' Libby winced as the shocking image took shape in her head.

'Apparently. It happened last night. Giles was working late; he often did...' Angela picked at a tissue, pulling it to shreds.

Libby sipped the dregs of cold tea left in her cup, trying to make sense of the information. 'Are all the books chained?'

'Only those from before the eighteenth century.' Talking about the details of the library arrangements had a calming effect on Angela, so Libby let her talk. At least her teeth had stopped chattering. 'You know, early copies of the King James version of the Bible, illuminated manuscripts from the sixteenth century, books of maps, translations of religious books into different languages. All that sort of thing…'

Angela screwed the remains of the tissue into a ball, looked around for somewhere to put it, opened her handbag and dropped it inside.

'Which book did the chain in question come from?'

Angela blinked. 'I've no idea. Does it matter? Giles was a historian, so I expect the book was part of his research.'

'I bet Chief Inspector Arnold will be holding a press conference,' Libby murmured. 'Nothing he likes more than seeing his name in the papers and his face on the screen, and the national press will love this story. In fact, it's probably on the internet already.' Libby fell silent but her pulse raced. Another suspicious death in Somerset!

'There's more.' Angela fiddled with the strap of her bag.

'Go on.'

'They found something else. An object at – at the scene.'

'Come again?'

'A knitted scarf.'

Libby puffed air through her lips. 'Anything special about it?'

Angela's gaze faltered. She avoided Libby's face and focused on her own clenched hands, where the knuckles gleamed white. At last, she took a shaky breath and whispered, 'Hand-knitted in orange wool.'

Libby opened her mouth but closed it again. Was a hand-knitted scarf significant? It was winter after all. Everyone wore scarves and hats. On the other hand, how often did a man willingly wear a hand-knitted garment, especially a bright orange one? Most males never learned to knit, though a few did, of course. Fishermen; they were famous for it. And hadn't one Archbishop of Canterbury knitted jumpers? Still, he was the exception, rather than the rule. Most men wore hand-knitting only when the garment was made by a wife, girlfriend, or mother. In other words, a present, and one they felt duty bound to use.

Angela's reaction struck Libby as odd. Still pale and distressed, she seemed suddenly embarrassed. Could it be that Giles Temple's scarf was not a present from his wife? If her suspicion was right, it suggested a whole area of enquiry.

'Come on,' Libby said, keeping her tone gentle, for Angela was still pale and distressed. 'You can tell me. You know something about this scarf, don't you? Where did it come from?'

Angela looked Libby in the eye, suddenly defiant. 'We've been making scarves at the Knitters' Guild. Scarves, hats and gloves, but mostly, knitted squares. We're planning to yarn-bomb Wells, but it's a secret. We don't want everyone in town to know about it. It would spoil the surprise.'

'Yarnbombing? What on earth...' Libby tapped a finger against her teeth, struggling to recall an article she'd read. 'Yarnbombing. Wait. Don't tell me. I know I've heard of it.' Angela managed a weak smile while Libby pondered.

The penny dropped. 'Got it.' Libby said. 'You drape lamp-posts and trees with knitted things.'

'Brightly coloured knitting, yes. It's supposed to cheer everyone up, so we thought this was a good time of year to try it, before spring arrives. Folk feel miserable in February, and it feels as though it will never be warm again.

'And the Wells event is also meant to celebrate the completion of renovations at the cathedral.' Scaffolding had obscured the West Front of Wells Cathedral for many months.

'Had Giles Temple heard about your plans?'

'Oh, yes; as have most of the staff at the cathedral, but

they've been sworn to secrecy. Even the Dean's given it his blessing. Orange is one of the main colours we're using because it's bright.'

'It's not the only explanation,' Libby murmured, thinking aloud, 'but quite possibly, someone in the Guild knows Giles well and knitted a scarf for him.' She shot a sharp look at Angela, but her friend made no reply.

* * *

Angela, restored to calm, pronounced herself ready to leave the café, so the two friends and Bear clattered downstairs, the dog panting and waving his tail, already scenting exciting smells from the outside world.

Too late, Libby spotted a pile of books making its way up the stairs, apparently under its own steam. She tugged on the dog's lead. Bear skidded to a halt, but the man underneath the books panicked, tried to back away, lost his footing and grabbed at the handrail. The stack of books, magazines and documents exploded from his flailing arms and rocketed high in the air.

Libby watched, knuckles jammed against her mouth, as leather covered books thudded on the floor. A storm of loose papers followed, fluttering in ghastly slow motion to blanket the flagstones. Bear barked, delighted by the new game.

Angela shrieked. 'Dr Phillips, I'm so sorry…' She bent to retrieve a book, smoothing its Moroccan leather spine. Libby, mortified, shot a look at Bear that sent the animal's tail between his legs, and stooped to help.

'My books, my books,' the man stammered, breathlessly. 'What a day. Oh, my goodness me, what a terrible day.'

Angela examined the one in her hands. 'I don't think this one's damaged.'

The man stopped collecting paper long enough to glare at Libby through pebble spectacles. 'That dog of yours...'

'I know.' She was contrite. 'I'm sorry. He's a bit excited...' She stopped talking. Really, there was no excuse.

Angela intervened. 'Libby, this is Dr Phillips, the librarian.' Libby, far too flustered to listen properly, barely registered the words.

'We won't shake hands.' Dr Phillips drew bushy brows together, raising himself to his full height, the shiny top of a bald head barely reaching Libby's shoulder.

'I'm so very sorry,' Libby stammered. Bear wagged an enthusiastic tail, trying to attract this new friend's attention.

'Just move that animal out of the way and let me pass.'

The significance of the pile of books and Angela's introduction finally filtered into Libby's brain. 'You're the librarian?' One of the first people Libby would want to talk to, for Giles had died in Dr Phillips' domain.

'Of course. Who might you be? Wait...' He juggled books and pointed with a bony finger. 'I recognise that dog. Biggest in Somerset, I bet. It belongs to Max Ramshore, doesn't it? That makes you Mrs Forest, the lady who solves mysteries.'

'Call me Libby.'

He ignored that. 'Today is a very bad day.' His wagged a gloomy head. 'We've had a serious incident.'

'The verger told us about it.'

'It's a most dreadful business. Nothing like it has ever happened before. You can't go inside, you know. The police have removed the – er – body, but access to the cathedral is strictly limited. The whole area's smothered in 'Crime Scene Do Not Enter' tape. No doubt I'll find fingerprint chemicals on the books and they'll all be ruined.' The librarian's face crinkled with worry.

Bear, disappointed to find this new friend refused to play, whined and stared hopefully at the exit. Libby ignored him, keeping a tight hold on the lead. 'You found the body, I think, Dr Phillips?'

He nodded. 'Lying on the floor, he was. Face all purple, tongue hanging out. Oh, my, that tongue. What a sight...'

Libby shook her head to rid it of the image. 'Could it be an accident?'

The librarian pursed his lips. 'Planning to investigate, are you? Good idea. The police spend too much time giving out speeding tickets these days. It could be months before they find the murderer. You get on to it; speed things up, Mrs Forest, so we can get back to normal.'

He balanced books on the stair rail, scratching his head with one hand. 'Now, what did you ask? Oh, yes, was it an accident? Hmm. Funny sort of accident, strangled by a chain round the neck.' He chortled. 'Someone did him in, and that's a fact.'

'What about suicide?'

'You mean, could he have made a noose from the chain and hung himself?' The librarian's face wrinkled in thought. 'No, that wouldn't work. The ceiling's too high. He wouldn't be able to get up there, even if he climbed on the benches...'

'Was the chain attached to anything?'

'No. Just round his neck.' The man seemed to warm to his topic. 'I'll tell you a funny thing.'

'Yes?'

'The knitted scarf was wrapped round on top of the chain. Strange. D'you see? On top of the chain, not underneath.' He pursed his lips. 'Couldn't kill himself first, then wrap a scarf round his neck, could he?'

His expression brightened. 'At least there wasn't any blood. Don't want blood on that old oak floor; seventeenth century, you know. You'd never get the stain out...'

3

GILES TEMPLE

Libby brought Angela back to the cottage she shared with her apprentice, Mandy, and Fuzzy the marmalade cat. She couldn't leave her friend alone to brood.

They settled in the living room of Hope Cottage with Bear guarding the door. Until recently, the room had been functional and reasonably comfortable, but unexciting. Libby's priority had been her state-of-the-art kitchen, where she'd developed recipes and written the book that kick-started her new career in Exham on Sea.

At Christmas, her son had presented her with a book of Danish style called 'Hygge.' The idea of warmth, cosiness and a happy atmosphere had captivated Libby. She'd bought cushions and a fluffy rug, positioned candles in the empty fireplace and brought in stools made from tree trunks. She'd even considered investing in a solid fuel heater.

Bear approved of the changes and spent as much time as possible stretched across the rug, snoring. Even Fuzzy deigned to curl up on the soft, fleece cushions.

Perhaps the atmosphere would help Angela relax and

speak freely. Since leaving the cathedral café, she'd been unusually quiet. Even now, she remained tense, gripping the arm of the sofa with rigid fingers and biting her lips.

Libby brought hot chocolate. Angela gave a wan smile and ran a finger round the rim of her mug. 'It's been such a shock. You don't expect people you know to die like that – in a library, of all places.'

'That's true.' Libby tried to sound non-committal. *I'm not getting involved. Not this time. I'm too busy with Robert's wedding and my business, and everything else...*

She'd been setting up a private investigation service with Max Ramshore, who currently worked for one of the more secretive branches of government on financial business, but recently, she'd suffered an attack of second thoughts. Not long ago, she'd been a recently widowed newcomer in Exham, building a small but successful business. She hadn't wanted a relationship with Max or anyone else. They'd worked together on a couple of mysterious murder cases and she'd discovered Max's skills fitted well with her own.

Besides that, the man was undeniably attractive, with bright blue eyes, a sharp intellect and a huge fund of common sense. Somehow, their agreement to work together had led to a closer personal relationship.

She wondered if Max was expecting them to become an item – even to get married, and she was scared. Things were moving too fast.

Whenever Libby thought about Max her heart fluttered, but her head throbbed with questions. Would they tire of one another if they worked too closely together? Would a successful partnership mean she had to walk away from the cakes and chocolate business she'd struggled so hard to establish, just as it was taking off? What about Mandy? Libby couldn't let her apprentice down.

She needed a breathing space, with time to think and no crime investigations, while Max finished his current assignment. Any inquiry into this most recent suspicious death was best left to the police.

Nevertheless, Libby's curiosity continued to nag, insistent as an itch. Asking a few questions wouldn't commit her to anything. It wasn't real investigating, was it? Besides, judging from the way Angela gulped hot chocolate, she was deeply stressed and clearly needed to talk.

Libby gave in to the temptation to find out more. 'Why was Giles in Wells? Does he have a family?'

'His home's in Birmingham. He's – I mean, he was – married, with two children. They're grown up, now. He's been coming to Wells for a couple of days every week, working late into the night and travelling home as often as possible.' Angela shot a glance at Libby. 'He's nothing to do with Wells Cathedral. He's a history lecturer, studying texts from the sixteenth century and writing a book about old beliefs and superstitions...'

Her voice tailed away, but Libby hardly noticed. She'd stopped listening. The thought of Giles Temple's wife had sent a shiver down her spine. The police, probably on the way to Birmingham right now, would have to break the news to Mrs Temple. Libby pictured a cheerful woman opening a neat front door, her smile freezing on her face as the officer asked permission to come inside.

How quickly would realisation dawn? When would Mrs Temple understand she'd become a widow? Her husband had gone forever. He would not return home for dinner, that day or any other. She'd have to tell their children.

What would she do? Collapse on the floor, scream and shout, or hide her feelings with a clenched jaw and stiff upper lip until the police left and she could grieve in peace?

Libby blinked and forced her focus back to her friend. 'Giles was a lovely man,' Angela was saying. 'Gentle and kind. I can't imagine why anyone would want to kill him in such a horrid way; and in the cathedral, too.'

'It's certainly novel,' Libby mused. 'Strangled with a chain. That's a nasty way to go.'

Angela fingered the pearls in her necklace. 'Then, there's the scarf.'

'Now, that's interesting. I wish I could see it. I suppose Giles Temple wasn't a member of the Knitters' Guild?'

Her friend spluttered. 'Not likely. He was too old school. You know, women cook and knit, men work and think.' Angela's hand flew to her mouth. 'Oh dear, that doesn't sound kind at all. I don't mean he was a bully. I'm sure he couldn't have been. He was much too gentle.'

Her eyes met Libby's in a moment of shared understanding. Both had endured bullying husbands who liked to keep a wife in her place. A guilty-twinge reminded Libby she'd felt nothing but relief when Trevor, her own husband, died. But then, he'd been secretly money-laundering, so Libby had no need to feel guilty. Unfortunately, the habit died hard.

Angela pulled out her phone. 'How silly of me. I can show you a photo of Giles, taken in the library during a tour.' She flicked through screens on her phone, using a forefinger to swipe awkwardly from one picture to another. 'Here it is.'

She angled the phone towards Libby and the picture disappeared. Angela clicked her tongue. 'I'll never get used to this phone.'

Libby laughed, glad of the break in tension. 'Mandy never

goes anywhere without her mobile, but I can't get the hang of mine at all. I think you have to be young – preferably under thirty-five.' She crossed the room to sit on the sofa beside Angela, peering over her friend's shoulder as the picture returned.

Libby took in the details; rows of heavy, leather-bound books, neatly arranged on wooden shelves, their heavy chains dangling. Nearby, a small group of visitors peered into a glass display case. The camera had caught Giles Temple, one of two men in the group, with his mouth open. His hair was sparse, a rim of grey-speckled brown tufts worn a shade too long for Libby's taste. Round, tortoiseshell glasses hooked onto a pair of over-large ears.

'I'm afraid I took him by surprise,' Angela murmured.

'Who are the other people? Oh, that's the librarian.'

Angela pointed. 'The lady in the middle of the picture, next to Giles, is the Dean's wife, Amelia Weir. She works in the library once a week, as I do, but on different days. I don't know her well.'

Mrs Weir, much younger than Libby or Angela, stood very close to Giles Temple. Angela's voice had been sharp. Libby shot a glance at her face. Two angry furrows had appeared on her forehead. Could Amelia Weir and Angela both have had a soft spot for this Giles?

For now, Libby changed the subject. 'I think I need to know more about the Guild's yarnbombing.'

'There's a session this evening. Why don't you come along and meet the members?'

'I'll be there. I can't knit, but I'll bring cake.'

4

KNITTERS' GUILD

'What should I wear to a Knitters' Guild meeting?' Libby asked Bear. 'A knitted jumper's required, I suppose. Anyway, it's bound to be cold.' She'd been to history society meetings in the area before and learned to take warm clothes.

The dog gazed into her face; his eyes mournful. Libby frowned. 'Stop looking at me like that. You can't come.'

Three sweaters lay on the bed. The Arran cable tempted her, for the evening was chilly, but it made Libby look fat. 'I've been sampling too many chocolates, Bear. Time to take myself in hand. Tomorrow, maybe.'

She put the sweater back in the drawer. Fast losing patience, she grabbed a cheerful red and yellow striped jersey and shrugged it over her head. 'Will they know I didn't knit it myself?'

Bear lay on his back, inviting Libby to scratch his stomach, hoping to dissuade her from leaving him. 'Oh, very well. You can come as my guard dog. Just behave yourself and don't deposit dog hair all over the knitting.' Bear clattered towards the front door. Fuzzy the cat watched, envy glittering in her green eyes.

Fuzzy adored Bear. 'Sorry, you can't come with us, Fuzz, but I've left the door of the airing cupboard open. It's as warm as toast.' The airing cupboard was one of Fuzzy's cherished spots.

Libby emptied a can of the best wild red salmon into the cat's dish. Fuzzy pretended not to notice, but as soon as Libby closed the door, she'd gobble every scrap. Libby pulled on a woolly hat. 'Come on, Bear. Let's go.'

She felt a twinge of guilt. She spent so much time with Bear and Fuzzy these days that she'd given little thought to the dog she'd taken under her wing when she first arrived in Exham on Sea.

She'd been walking with Shipley, a friendly, excitable springer spaniel, when she came across a dead rock singer under Exham's unique, wooden legged lighthouse.

That encounter had begun her adventures in crime solving.

Poor Shipley had been abandoned when his owner, Marina, left the area, and currently lived with the vet. Maybe Libby could offer to walk him from time to time, as she used to.

Not tonight, though. The thought of the energetic Shipley at a Knitters' Guild meeting made her shudder. The wool would be chewed to pieces or tied in knots in no time.

The street was dark tonight. To make financial savings and reduce light pollution, Exham's town council had dimmed the streetlamps. As a result, stars glittered across a clear sky. The moon hung low, a shimmering crescent in crisp air. Libby inhaled the unmistakable scent of the ocean. The beach lay out of sight of her cottage, but it filled the air with the sharp smell of ozone.

She brushed gloved hands through a rosemary bush outside and inhaled. Few plants survived the salty winds that speckled and corroded every shiny brass number on Libby's front door, but rosemary and lavender flourished. They were her favourite herbs. She remembered a recipe she'd been developing; tea bread flavoured with rosemary. She'd planned to work on it tonight, but she was too intrigued by the Knitters' Guild to stay at home. Tea loaves could wait.

She shivered and loaded Bear into her purple Citroen, the car so small he overflowed across the whole back seat. If she hadn't quarrelled with Max before his current trip to London, she'd have borrowed the Land Rover.

They'd been arguing for weeks over silly things like Bear's tendency to dig up Libby's lawn, or whether Libby was unreasonable to beg her daughter to return home from her working holiday in South America for Christmas. Max advised leaving well alone, for Ali would come home when she was ready, but Libby wanted her family together. In the end, Robert and Sarah had stayed at Hope Cottage, Max had dropped in on Christmas Day and Libby had spent a tearful half-hour on the phone to Ali.

Max had been away for a few days, now, and Libby could see with clearer eyes. She suspected they were finding excuses for keeping their distance from each other, because both had endured unsuccessful marriages in the past.

Thinking of Max today, an ache of longing caught Libby by surprise. She missed him.

Determined not to be needy, she drove on through the darkness, meeting few other cars on such a chilly winter night. Anyone with good sense was at home, warm and cosy.

As she braked outside the tiny village hall where the knitters gathered, the door flew open and light, laughter and coffee smells spilled out.

Angela led her inside. 'Look, everyone, Libby's brought treats.'

'You'll soon get used to us,' bellowed a big-boned, hearty woman with a beaky nose, as she tucked into a slice of Dundee cake. Her voice boomed, deep and mannish. A single streak of bright green ran through a shock of wild grey hair. 'I'm June. Like the song: busting out all over.' She cackled.

Libby settled Bear in a corner with a huge chew, knowing he'd finish it in less than half an hour. The room was small and faintly oppressive. An electric fire hung awkwardly from the ceiling, throwing heat on the top of Libby's head while her feet remained chilled. 'How does this yarnbombing work, exactly?'

June hooted. 'It's art, you know. At any rate, it's a grand excuse to creep out in the middle of the night and tie things to lamp posts without being arrested. That's the truth of it. The fun starts the next day when folk see what we've done. Can't wait to see their faces. Tried it in Trivington a year ago. Just what Wells needs to liven it up.'

'Not that it needs livening up, of course.' Angela was always alert in case someone should be offended.

'Manner of speech, that's all. Livvy'll soon get used to me.'

'It's Libby, actually.'

June roared with laughter.

A plump, motherly woman poured tea from an old brown teapot. 'I don't do the bombing for fun, you know. I knit useful things, like hats and scarves. I'm Ruby, by the way. I shall hang my work on benches and people who need them can take them home. It helps the less fortunate. I call it 'giving back to society."

Another voice intervened. 'Do you remember that time we hung knitted underwear from the tower on Glastonbury Tor? The National Trust people were furious.'

Ruby glared but the other woman ignored her. Tiny and thin, she radiated energy. 'I'm Vera, by the way. Welcome to our group. You knit, of course?'

'I'm afraid not. Well, my mother taught me when I was small, but I haven't knitted for years.'

June swooped, green hair awry. 'Now's your chance to take it up again, then. Size ten needles and double knitting wool. That'll do the trick. You'll finish a square in no time.'

Plied with balls of every colour, Libby avoided orange and yellow, choosing instead the quietest colour available, royal blue. She settled on a wooden chair and allowed the plump mother figure, Ruby, to elbow June aside, cast on a row of stitches and hand them over.

Struggling with wool that stuck to her unpractised, fumbling fingers, Libby listened as the women talked. Silently, she repeated her vow not to investigate, although the knitters' unguarded thoughts would be fascinating. They were all connected with the cathedral, as volunteers, worshippers or friends of the clergy. As they chattered, needles flashed and balls of wool turned, like magic, into socks, scarves and hats.

News of the murder had spread like wildfire and everyone had a theory. June ran both hands through her hair until the green stripe stood on end, like an exotic parrot perched on top of her head. 'I reckon the Dean did it. Never liked the man. Always after money. Funds for clock renovation, contributions for new vestments. Can't say good morning without begging.'

'Poor man, it's his job, you know,' Angela soothed. 'He was very kind to me when my husband died.'

June grunted, bit the end off a strand of wool, threw a yellow square onto the table and cast on a fresh row of orange stitches.

Vera giggled. 'I don't want to speak ill of the dead, but that Mr Temple was a right one for the ladies.'

Libby felt Angela stiffen. 'How do you mean?' she asked, keeping her voice neutral.

Vera glanced round, nostrils flared, checking all eyes were on her. 'I saw him in The Swan with the Dean's wife.' She stopped knitting and hissed, in a loud stage whisper, 'I wouldn't be surprised if the Dean did it. You know—a crime of passion.'

5

CHIEF INSPECTOR ARNOLD

A stunned silence followed Vera's remark. Libby waited to see who'd speak first, shooting a surreptitious glance round her companions to judge their reactions. Angela's face turned puce red, her lips pressed tightly together. June's eyes bulged. *A frog. That's what she looks like. A great green frog.* Ruby poured tea. 'I think it's rather unkind to jump to conclusions. I've always had the greatest respect for our Dean. You should be ashamed of yourself, Vera.'

Vera shrugged, not the least bit ashamed. 'I speak as I find.'

'What exactly is that supposed to mean, Vera?' Angela's voice was sharp enough to slice a finger. Libby, eyes on her knitting, concealed a grin.

'I mean,' said Vera, 'that I can follow evidence just as well as our new, so-called member, here.' Scorn dripped from the words. 'Isn't it true you're a kind of amateur sleuth, Mrs Forest, and you're here to find out if one of us had anything to do with the murder?'

'What if she is?' Angela's eyes flashed. Libby thought she'd never seen her so furious. 'Libby has a wonderful track record of solving mysteries.'

'Well, she makes a good cake, I'd say that for her,' observed June, tucking in to a second slice. 'If she can find the killer, good on her, that's what I say.'

Libby put aside her square of dropped stitches, the wool grey from over-handling. 'You're quite right. I've been involved in other cases and I've had some luck, but I don't know the Dean or Mr Temple, or anyone else at the cathedral except Angela, and I'm not investigating. I trust the police.' She hesitated, exchanged a glance with Angela and decided not to mention the orange scarf.

Vera's eyes were wide. 'What if there's another murder. Is it likely, do you think?'

Libby shrugged. 'It happens. It depends on why Giles Temple was murdered, and who killed him.'

The motherly Ruby brushed crumbs from her bosom. 'In that case, we must find the murderer as soon as possible. I agree with June. I, for one, never liked that Dr Weir, the Dean. He's been here three years, and what's he done for the cathedral? Included a lot of silly new services for a bunch of noisy children, that's what.'

June wiped her mouth. 'Sooner they find the killer, the better. Come on, Vera, tell us a bit more. You saw Giles Temple meeting the Dean's wife. Were they having an affair?'

Vera hesitated, perhaps thinking better of her accusations. 'Dr Weir's wife is a historian. So was Giles Temple. I suppose they might have been comparing notes.' Bouncing back, she finished, 'But they seemed pretty friendly, if you ask me.'

A question was on the tip of Libby's tongue, but before

she could speak someone hammered on the door. Vera jumped, tea slopping from her cup as the door swung open. Libby recognised Chief Inspector Arnold and her heart sank. He made no secret of the fact he thought Libby a nuisance, even when she helped untangle a case. He'd been furious when she outdid the police and solved the murder at the lighthouse.

Uniform buttons glinting, he stepped inside and took a long, slow look round the room, enjoying the moment. His close-set eyes glittered. 'Sorry to disturb you, ladies.' The high-pitched voice grated on Libby's ears. 'I need a word with you. I expect you've heard about the incident at the cathedral.'

His gaze fell on Libby. 'Well, well.' He fingered his chin. 'Fancy meeting you here, Mrs Forest. Often turn up, don't you, when there's a crime? I'll be suspecting you're behind the murder, if you're not careful. Ha,ha.' The laugh was unconvincing, the small black eyes sharp. 'Trying to get one over on the police, I suppose.'

'Are we all suspects?' giggled Vera. 'How exciting.'

The chief inspector smiled through tight lips. 'There'll be time for that, later. We're just making preliminary inquiries at the moment. It's normal police procedure, nothing to be concerned about. I believe you all knew the deceased, Mr Giles Temple.' Heads nodded. 'What about you, Mrs Forest? Was he one of your acquaintances?'

Libby shook her head. 'I never met him.'

'And are you a member of the Knitters' Guild? I can't seem to find your name anywhere on this list.' He ran a long finger down a sheet of paper, his lips twitching. 'Or maybe you work in the cathedral?'

Libby tried not to squirm under the sarcasm. 'No, I was just…' She stopped.

'Quite. I suggest you get back to your chocolates and leave the police work to the professionals.' Libby turned to gather up the empty cake tin and call Bear to her side. The chief inspector used a finger and thumb to pick up the ragged, unfinished square she'd been working on. 'Not a professional knitter, I see.'

6

MAX

Libby curled her feet on the sofa and chewed a fingernail. Max had rung as arranged, soon after she arrived home, but their conversation had been difficult and unsatisfactory.

'I've cut down my consultancy work,' he reminded her, 'so at least one of us is committed to the future. Time to make your mind up, Libby. Are we a partnership, or not?'

'Don't hassle me. I need to think.'

'I don't know why you've suddenly developed cold feet. You usually jump headfirst into everything. once or twice you've almost got yourself killed as a result. No one could call you timid, so why are you being indecisive, now? Am I scary?'

A lump formed in Libby's throat. 'You're not at all scary, Max. Try to understand. I'm not only grappling with the implications of a private investigation business on my cakes and chocolates, although that's complicated enough. There's the other thing, too.'

'Us, you mean? Look we've talked about the future, and we're not in a hurry. It's not as though we're getting married.'

'No, but what are we doing. I mean, if we did, where

would we live? In your house? If we did that, what about my cottage? I can't just sell it. It's important to me and besides, I run the chocolate business from the kitchen. You see what I mean?'

Max sighed. 'It's not complicated at all. You're trying to think of problems. Be honest with me, Libby. We're partners, aren't we? We do well together. Why don't we take things further? Be real partners, not just in business?'

She gulped. What did Max really want? Was he proposing marriage? Out of the blue, like this? 'That's not fair. Not on the phone.'

There was a long silence. 'Max? Are you still there?' Libby's voice sounded very small.

'OK. I won't pin you down over the phone. Not about getting married, anyway. I suppose that's not fair.'

'Not very romantic,' she mumbled.

His laugh sounded rueful. 'No, I suppose not, but being away from you made me think.'

He cleared his throat. 'We don't need to commit. Not yet. But I won't wait for ever. When I get home in a couple of days, I'm going to set up the business. You can join me, or not. Up to you.'

Libby swallowed but the lump remained. 'Let's talk about it when you come home.'

'Meanwhile,' Max dropped the serious tone. 'Tell me about this murder you're determined not to investigate.'

Relieved to change the subject, Libby told him about the cathedral library and the orange scarf, her spirits lifting as he laughed at her description of the knitters. 'Angela's upset. She says this Giles Temple was just a friend, but I don't think she's telling me the whole truth.'

'And the police? Is Joe part of the inquiry?' Max's son, a

detective sergeant, had worked on several other murder investigations.

'I haven't spoken to him. Chief Inspector Arnold appeared at the Knitters' Guild, though, and sent me home. I could have slapped his smug face.'

'Turn the other cheek. You should hear the abuse I had from the company I visited today, when I questioned their shady accounts. Don't let Arnold intimidate you.'

'I won't. Anyway, I won't see him again. I'm not investigating, remember?'

'You should at least go back to another meeting. It's time you added knitting to your talents, and I could use a new sweater.'

Libby giggled. 'You can knit your own.'

'Did you discover any other keen knitters? Those who didn't attend the meeting.'

'Yes, Angela dropped a list of names through the letter box on her way home. They're planning a surprise for Wells, you see. A yarnbombing.'

Max chuckled. 'OK. I give up. What's a yarnbomb?'

Libby recited the details. 'It's due next week, on Tuesday, at dead of night.'

'Tuesday. Good, I'll be back by then. I wouldn't miss it for the world. By the way, some old colleagues have agreed to send some investigative work my way. That would give our business a boost.'

Max went on, 'And everyone in Somerset must have heard about Libby Forest, female sleuth, by now.'

'OK, you know I'm tempted to work with you, Max. Leave it for now. I don't want to give up my own business. Not yet, anyway.'

'You don't have to. Just cut back a little. Give Mandy more

to do and take on another assistant. Forget the cakes and stick with the chocolates.'

'I'll think about it.' Libby giggled.

'What is it?'

'I just realised the truth. You can't live without my chocolates.'

'Ah. You found me out.' His voice softened. 'I'm looking forward to coming home. Things will work out, you know. Oh, by the way, I'm bringing a colleague. An American.'

'Anyone I know?'

'No, but you'll love him, though not too much, I hope. He's younger than me.'

'I like the sound of him already. What's the occasion?'

'Some work he's doing.' Max's voice was vague. 'I thought I'd ask a few people round to meet him. His name's Reg Talbot, by the way. I thought, Robert and Sarah. You said they were planning to visit, to stay with her parents while they make wedding plans, read the banns and so forth. Mandy and Steve, of course.'

Libby took a deep breath. She'd mentioned Max to her son, Robert, but they hadn't met. This could be tricky. 'I don't know about Steve. He and Mandy had a falling out, and I'm not sure they're still an item. I'll check.'

'Cheer up. It'll be fun.' Libby's phone buzzed.

She had a text, from Angela.

I have to see you. Right now.

* * *

Angela had sounded desperate. The Citroen hurtled towards her house, squealing round corners as dread squeezed Libby's insides. Angela would only send such a message in dire circumstances.

She must have been watching from a window, for the door was already open when Libby ran up the path. 'What's the matter?'

'I'm so glad you're here. I don't know what to do.'

'Sit down, collect your thoughts and explain.'

Angela paced round her elegant, grey-painted room, moving expensive scented candles and straightening books in an already tidy bookcase. 'There's something I kept from you. I hoped it didn't matter, but it's been eating away at me.'

Libby thought for a moment, reviewing their conversation in the café. 'I had a feeling you weren't being entirely honest. It's the scarf, isn't it?' Her friend rubbed invisible specks of dirt from an over-mantle mirror, avoiding Libby's eyes. 'Did you give it to Giles Temple?'

Angela grabbed a tissue from a nearby box. 'It was a joke, just between the two of us. We laughed about the yarnbombing. You know, how tacky and bright it was going to be. Giles said no one would ever wear anything in those colours. Well, I couldn't resist knitting the brightest scarf I could and giving it to Giles. He promised to wear it. It was just a joke.' She dabbed at her eyes. 'What will the police think?'

Libby's brain clicked into gear. The presence of the scarf at the murder scene made Angela a prime suspect. She knew Giles was a married man, and she'd given him a gift she made herself. It looked suspicious, and Libby was sure, now, that the two of them had grown close. Libby groaned. She knew what was coming.

Angela said, 'Please, help me, Libby. I'm scared. You see, if the police know I spent a lot of time with Giles—' She winced, 'with him being married, they might think I had something to do with it. Revenge, if he was throwing me over, or something like that.'

Her cheeks glowed bright red. 'Find out who killed Giles. That's the only way I'll feel safe. You can't just leave it to the police. Everyone knows they're over-stretched. They'll find out about the scarf, decide I killed him and won't look for anyone else.'

Libby's head drooped as her hopes of a quiet life, with time to make decisions about the future, evaporated. Angela, normally so calm, looked terrified. Smudges of mascara ran into tiny lines around her eyes.

Libby rose and offered another tissue. 'I'll try to help, on one condition.'

'Anything.' Angela's face lit up. 'Anything at all.'

Libby hid a wry smile. Angela wasn't going to like her next words, but that was too bad. 'I can't help unless you swear you had nothing to do with Giles Temple's death.'

A flush covered Angela's face from neck to hairline. For a second, her eyes flashed anger. Slowly, she gained control. When she spoke, her voice grated, harsh and strained. 'I understand why you have to ask, Libby. I suppose you need to be sure. On my honour, I swear I didn't kill Giles Temple and I don't know who did.'

7

BAKERY

Libby spent the next morning with Mandy, working at the bakery. In the shop, she had no spare time to think of Max, or worry about Angela, or Giles Temple's murder. Mandy was unusually quiet. Libby supposed she was brooding about the quarrel with Steve.

Frank, the baker, had converted half the shop to a display space for chocolates, and his girth was expanding as a result. 'The wife's sending me out running every evening.' He heaved a sigh. 'I can resist bread and cakes, all except your squishy chocolate log...'

He centred a slice on a plate. 'But those chocs'll be the death of me. Still,' his long face lightened. 'My daily shuffle gets me out of the house for a bit of peace.'

He finished the last morsel and wiped his mouth. 'Delicious. Ah well. No peace for the wicked. They'll be coming in for their lunch time sandwiches, any minute now, wanting to talk about this affair over at the cathedral. I'll be off.'

Frank, unique in Exham on Sea, hated gossip. Mandy once suggested he'd been bullied in childhood. 'Impossible.

He's six feet tall with shoulders like bill-boards,' Libby objected.

'Maybe he grew after leaving school.' Frank made himself scarce whenever the door opened, leaving Libby, Mandy or one of his new part-timers in charge.

Along with bread, cakes and chocolates, the shop functioned as a branch of the local Exham grapevine, and sure enough, the shop soon buzzed with theories about the murder in the cathedral.

'I made a delivery there, just the day before he was found.' Gladys, the owner of the flower shop, panted with excitement. 'Imagine, it could have been me, lying dead on the floor.'

'Never been caught in a library, though, have you,' jeered one of the paper boys, paying for a pair of Belgian buns with a crumpled note, 'Have to be able to read.'

'I hope you won't be eating both those buns for your lunch,' Mandy snapped. 'All that sugar – you won't be able to walk. And don't lean your bike against the window. There's a sign there, you know. Maybe it's you who can't read.'

Libby shot a glance at Mandy. She was cranky today.

Gladys handed over a twenty pound note in payment for a waist-watching salad and glowered at the boy as she waited for change. 'Getting back to the cathedral. I was talking to the Bishop's wife, the other day. You know, the Bishop of Bath and Wells.'

She peeped under her lashes at the queue of customers, checking that they were listening and were suitably impressed. 'She told me the man who died, Giles something, was researching old stories from the past, about ghosts and the supernatural and such like. She said it wasn't a very suitable subject for a cathedral library, and I for one, agree.'

'Maybe it was a ghost that did him in,' suggested a young

man. New to Libby, he wore the estate agent uniform of short gelled hair, shiny pointed shoes and a vivid pink shirt. Exham was full of estate agents. House prices were rumoured to be due to rocket, now a new nuclear power station was being built nearby, at Hinckley Point.

The doorbell chimed and local solicitor, Samantha Watson, entered. Samantha, who was engaged to be married to the pompous Chief Inspector Arnold, disliked Libby as an interfering newcomer to Exham and only graced the bakery with her presence when she had a spicy police titbit to share.

'Pillow talk from her fiancé,' Max called it. Libby waited, expectant. Samantha's tips had been useful in the past, though Libby would die rather than admit it. The solicitor already thought far too well of herself.

She inspected Mandy from head to toe. 'What an original necklace, dear, and on such a heavy chain. A Celtic cross, isn't it? Did you know, the murderer used a chain to kill his victim in the cathedral library?'

Mandy rose to the bait before Libby could intervene. 'We did, as it happens.'

'Chief Inspector Arnold told me the chain was made of forged steel. Incredibly strong. But, that's not all...'

'Go on,' said Gladys, as Samantha produced a dramatic pause.

'Well, I'm not sure I ought to tell you. Police business, you know. In fact, I think perhaps I should wait. There's going to be a press conference in half an hour. I'll just say this – don't miss it. You'll hear something very interesting if you watch the local news.'

The paper boy tore off a slab of bun and spoke with his mouth full. 'That Inspector—'

'Chief Inspector,' Samantha corrected.

The boy licked his lips. 'Whatever. He'd better not come after our Dan.'

'Dan who?'

'My brother, Dan. He was at school with those lads who had a cannabis farm, and he reckons the cops are out to get him.'

Samantha looked smug. 'Those boys were lucky. They were given suspended sentences. Maybe your Dan should have been in court with them.' She glanced sideways at Libby. 'I worked on the case, you know.'

The boy wiped his mouth on a grubby sleeve, elbowed the door, and cycled away. Gladys huffed. 'Rude, that boy, like all his family. Thinks the world owes him a living.'

Samantha turned back to Mandy. 'Anyway, dear, perhaps you should rethink your jewellery. You don't want to be a suspect in a murder case, do you? It wouldn't be easy to persuade the judge to let you off lightly.'

8

PRESS CONFERENCE

Mandy served the remaining customers in tight-lipped silence, clearly upset by Samantha's remarks. The final customer, Mr Ali from the Indian restaurant, took an impossibly long time to choose a roll, settling at last on salmon and cucumber. A round, jovial man, he'd once confided in Libby how much he hated the 'English curry' his customers demanded. 'I wish I could serve some of the food my mother used to make, but it wouldn't go down well. Not enough spice, too many vegetables,' he'd sighed.

'Mrs Watson practically accused me.' Mandy burst out as the door closed.

'It's not you. She just likes winding people up,' Libby soothed. 'Ignore her.'

'Easy for you to say,' Mandy muttered, just loud enough for Libby to hear.

Better to ignore that. Mandy would cool down soon enough. Libby switched on the television in the back of the bakery as Frank returned. 'The press conference is about to start.'

Sure enough, Chief Inspector Arnold sat behind a long table, flanked by a female police constable on one side and Detective Sergeant Joe Ramshore, Max's son, on the other.

The police constable introduced Arnold, who nodded at the assembled body of local and national press. Arnold's face was composed, schooled into an ostentatious, solemn expression.

'Good afternoon, ladies and gentlemen. Thank you for attending on such short notice. I called this press conference to discuss the suspicious death of a man in the library of Wells Cathedral. The first forty-eight hours after a murder are vital.' He blinked as a press camera flashed. 'I expect anyone holding information that might help our inquiries to step forward.'

Mandy leaned closer to Libby. 'He can't help sounding up himself, can he?'

Libby said, 'He's not my favourite person. How he loves to be in front of the cameras.'

Glad to see some of her apprentice's good humour had returned, she focused on the TV. Now she'd promised Angela she'd make inquiries, she needed to know all the available facts.

Arnold performed well, she had to admit, with just the right amount of gravitas. Libby was impressed against her will. No wonder the man had risen so fast through the ranks. She pulled out a pen and scribbled in her newest notebook. The time of the victim's death had not been established, but the pathologist had identified a window of six hours, from the time Mr Temple spoke to the librarian at six o'clock in the evening, to midnight. Libby wrote, *Rigor mortis?*

'Did anyone notice Mr Temple near the cathedral after six

o'clock?' the chief inspector asked. 'We're keen to speak to the last person to see him.'

Mandy, scrubbing the counter, paused to chortle. 'That would be the killer, then. He was the last one to see the victim.'

'Shh. He's still talking.'

'The forensic pathologist suggests midnight is probably the latest possible time for the crime to have been committed. Anyone in the cathedral or the streets nearby, should come forward. We want to know if anyone entered the building or behaved suspiciously.'

The chief inspector spoke directly to the camera. 'Were you in Wells that night? Did you see anything strange? The police are waiting for your call.'

Libby murmured, 'They'll be swamped with statements. How many children board at Wells Cathedral School? I bet some were in town, and they'll all have bright ideas.'

The chief inspector added details. 'The last service at the cathedral, Evensong, finished around six o'clock. There was no concert in the building that night.'

'Don't expect many folks attended evening service in the middle of the week,' Frank pointed out. 'Not in winter.'

The chief inspector invited the press to ask questions, letting Joe Ramshore answer. 'Typical,' said Mandy. 'Everything left to his team while he claims the credit.'

Frank laughed. 'He's the boss.'

A journalist raised a hand, waited for a microphone to arrive and asked, 'Are there any significant clues as to the identity of the criminal, Chief Inspector Arnold?'

Arnold beamed at the journalist's use of his full title. 'We have several lines of enquiry, all of which will be pursued with the utmost diligence. However, I would like to bring one item to your attention. This was found near the body.'

With a flourish, he waved an arm. Libby squinted at the screen as he held up Angela's orange scarf.

As cameras flashed and whirred, Arnold explained, 'This is a hand-knitted scarf. Mr Temple was not an *aficionado* of the art and craft of knitting.' Scorn oozed from his voice.

Mandy muttered, 'An a*fici* – what?' Libby put a finger to her lips. She needed to hear every word.

'His wife does not recognise the scarf as belonging to herself or anyone she knows. She has never seen her late husband wear it. This item may be important, so we would like you to think carefully. Have you ever seen this scarf? If so, please make yourself known to the police.'

Joe gave the details of contact numbers for the incident room in Vicars Close, near the cathedral, and the press conference ended. Libby bit her lip. She must tell Joe of Angela's confession about her relationship with Giles Temple.

* * *

The phone rang before Libby could key in Joe's number. 'Hi, Mrs Forest? It's Joe here, Joe Ramshore.'

'That's a coincidence. I was about to ring you. By the way, Joe, I think it's time you called me Libby, like everyone else does. It can't be so hard, now you're talking to Max again.'

'Sorry. Libby. Look here, I can't speak for long. I'm just leaving the press conference.'

'I've been watching it.'

'Can I come over in the next day or so? There's something I want to run past you.'

'Well yes, of course. I need to speak to you, too. How about tomorrow morning, about nine?'

'Great, thanks. See you then.'

Libby frowned. 'That was weird. Joe wants to talk to me. I wonder what's happened.' There was a note of urgency in Joe's voice that unsettled Libby. Still, his visit would give her an opportunity to worm information out of him, once she'd shared Angela's confession.

Mandy polished the oven door until it sparkled. 'Don't forget you're taking me driving tonight.'

Libby stiffened. She'd forgotten that promise. Her heart sank, but she couldn't admit it. Not with Mandy in today's touchy mood.

Frank waved them away, 'It sounds like you two need to get off. I can manage the rest of the afternoon now the rush is over.'

Libby almost made it to the door before her phone rang again. 'Libby Forest here.'

'Oh, hello. You don't know me,' said a deep, plummy female voice with immaculate vowels, 'but I visited the vet today, and she recommended you.'

The vet? Libby thought hard, determined to remember the vet's name. 'Oh, yes, Tanya Ross. I know her.'

'She said you solve mysteries. I looked you up on the local news website and found you've been involved in a few little matters with some success, so I decided to give you a ring.'

She fell silent. Libby spoke cautiously, 'How can I help you?'

'It's my cat. He's disappeared into thin air. I'd like you to find him for me?'

'Your cat?'

Mandy's eyes were on stalks and Libby had to turn away to keep from bursting into laughter. 'I – er – I don't know.'

'I thought you were a private investigator,' the woman accused.

'No. Well – it's true I've inquired into a few things, but I've never dealt with lost animals. Except my own, of course...' Libby bit her tongue. Her first instinct was to refuse this case. She gave an exaggerated shrug and whispered to Mandy, 'What should I do?'

'Go for it, Mrs F.'

Perhaps unravelling a less stressful mystery might offer Libby perspective on the life of a private investigator. A lost cat couldn't be too difficult. Libby put on her best telephone voice and asserted herself. 'Maybe we should meet tomorrow.'

'Not until then?'

'I'm afraid not. Give me your details and I'll come at eleven. That's the earliest I can manage.'

'Oh, well, that's better than nothing, I suppose.' The woman gave her name.

'Marchant,' Libby repeated, making a note.

'Mrs.'

The call ended. Libby sighed. 'I must be crazy.'

Mandy leaned on the counter. 'I wonder why Joe wants to see you. I bet Chief Inspector Arnold won't listen to his ideas. By the way, while you were out yesterday, Jumbles sent us another big order. They need, like, twice as many chocolates as usual next week.'

Libby's legs wobbled and she sank onto a chair. 'This is impossible. There aren't enough hours in a day.'

'It's the price of success. Get used to it.'

'Is it? It feels exhausting. Will you visit Jumbles? Use all your charm and see how long they can give us.' The Jumbles account was the first one Mandy had negotiated alone.

She leaned over Libby's shoulder to read the address. 'Mrs Marchant. The Cedars. Wow, sounds posh. I bet you can charge her, like, a fortune. She must be rolling in dosh, and her cats are her babies. I think you've hit the big time.'

9

DRIVING LESSON

Mandy adjusted the driving seat in Libby's little purple Citroen and rattled the keys. Libby pulled her seatbelt tight. 'Tell me again, exactly how many lessons have you had?'

'Loads. The instructor said I need to practice, but I'm quite safe, honest.'

'Maybe I should drive us to the car park and start there...'

Mandy snorted, turned the key in the ignition and revved the engine. Libby shuddered as it howled. 'Oops. Sorry, Mrs F.'

She released the handbrake and the car lurched forward. 'Did you look behind?' Libby asked.

'Course. Nothing coming. Let's roll.'

The car moved sedately down the street, stopping neatly to turn at the T-junction, and Libby's clenched jaw began to relax. Mandy was perfectly competent. 'Were you trying to scare me, by any chance?'

Mandy giggled. 'Sorry, couldn't resist. Actually, my instructor's put me in for my test. It's in three weeks, but I need to practice parallel parking.'

Libby groaned. 'Definitely need to head for the car park, then, and I'm not sure I can help.'

'I know. You'd drive three times round town rather than reverse into a space.'

Half an hour later, Mandy had practiced the manoeuvre a dozen times. She drew to a halt facing the beach. 'Come on, then, out with it.'

Libby gulped, wrong footed. 'Out with what?'

'I saw you with Mrs Miles in the cathedral café when Steve and I quarrelled. I know you're dying to hear all about it. Why haven't you asked me?'

'I didn't want to interfere, but if you want to tell me about it, I'd like to help.' So, this was why Mandy suddenly needed driving practice; she wanted to talk. It was easier to share confidences in a car. Libby felt a warm glow. She valued Mandy's friendship.

'Well, we've split up. Steve keeps asking me to go to London at the weekend, but I don't see why I should.'

'Is it the expense?' Mandy's pay as an apprentice wasn't great, and the train to Paddington cost a fortune. 'You should be able to get a student discount, and…'

Mandy shook her head. 'It's not that. It's my clausta—thingy.'

Libby half turned in her seat. 'Your clausta— do you mean claustrophobia?'

Mandy nodded. 'I get it in the train. Or a coach.'

'And you haven't told Steve?'

'He'll think I'm pathetic. He wanted me to go to a concert and I said I would, but then I panicked and told him I was ill.'

'And he didn't believe you.'

'He thought I didn't want to go with him, and he took Alice, instead.'

'That's why you're suddenly so keen to take a driving test. You're planning to drive down to London?'

Mandy nodded. 'I'm fine in a car. I think it's all the other people on the train that cause the trouble. They seem so close, almost on top of me, so I can't breathe, and my tummy churns, and I feel all distant, as though I'm about to faint.'

'Mandy, you have to tell Steve the truth. He won't think any less of you.'

'Course he will. That Alice, she can do everything. She's going to be a violinist. She's already got an audition with an orchestra. She's got tons of A levels and so has Steve. And look at me. Just a chocolate-making apprenticeship.' Mandy sniffed. 'I don't mean to be rude about your business...'

'It's OK. I know what you mean.'

'When we argued, he looked at me like I was stupid.'

'Oh, Mandy. If I had a pound every time my husband made me feel foolish...' Libby's voice trailed away. She'd let Trevor call her stupid for years.

She looked across at Mandy's wet face. Her lodger wasn't going to suffer as she had; not if Libby had anything to do with it. 'If he insults you, he's not worth bothering with.'

'He didn't say it, exactly.' Mandy leapt to Steve's defence. 'I just know he's thinking it.'

Libby gave Mandy a hug. 'You daft thing. Don't imagine you know what someone else is thinking. Nobody can read minds. Now, let's do some more practice, you pass your test, and we'll think about how to get your hands on a little car. Maybe the business could manage something...'

Mandy rubbed her nose on her sleeve. 'You don't have to...'

'Let's get you through the driving test, first, shall we? We'll deal with the other stuff later. You could find someone to help you with the claustrophobia.'

Libby managed to sound calm, but she was worried. How long had Mandy been suffering from panic attacks? Did her mother, Elaine, now living quietly in Bristol after splitting with Mandy's violent father, know? Maybe Libby should call her. Or, was it none of her business?

She slumped back in her seat. Another problem to think about. Sometimes, it seemed solving murders was the least of her worries.

10

JOE

'Joe.' Max's son was on her doorstep on time the next morning, arm raised to pound on the door. 'You'd better come inside. It's freezing, out here.'

Libby pulled her dressing gown tight. She'd overslept, waking to the hammering on her front door. 'Couldn't you just ring the bell, like normal people do? Or is this an emergency?'

'Sorry. There's something I thought you'd like to know. I'm on my way to the station, so I can't stop.' Libby nodded, guessing he didn't want Chief Inspector Arnold to know he was calling on her.

She led him into the kitchen, flicking light switches as she went. 'Coffee? I need one before you tell me anything.'

Joe sniffed the air. Mandy must have fried bacon. 'What have you been cooking up?'

'Arsenic sandwiches,' Libby said. 'Want one?'

Joe snorted. 'Toast and Marmite would be good.'

Libby threw a couple of slices of bread in the machine. 'Watch that,' she ordered. 'It burns.'

Meekly, Joe oversaw toast while she fetched butter and Marmite. Settled comfortably at the counter, he explained. 'We've got a suspect for the murder.'

'My, that was quick. Chief Inspector Arnold will be impressed.'

'It's his suspect.'

Libby paused, and butter slid from the tip of her knife. 'By which you mean, I suppose, that he's got the wrong man?'

Joe nodded and glanced round the room, looking as guilty as if he expected his boss to appear. 'It's not a man…'

Libby interrupted. 'Let me guess. It's a member of the Knitters' Guild?'

Joe frowned. 'Not just any member. It's your friend, Angela Miles.'

Libby dabbed Marmite on toast, buying time to think. It hadn't taken long for the police to discover Angela's connection with Giles Temple.

She tried to smile. 'That's ridiculous.' Her voice was a squeak.

Joe shook his head. 'Not really. It's the scarf, you see. Mrs Miles told the police she made it for Giles Temple as a present.' Libby breathed out. Angela had done the right thing and gone to the authorities, saving Libby that unpleasant task. She could concentrate on proving her friend's innocence.

She jabbed a finger at Joe. 'And when Angela killed the victim, she made sure the scarf was round his neck so everyone would suspect her? That's crazy. It won't stand up in court. Any decent lawyer will make mincemeat of the idea.'

Joe grimaced. 'The chief inspector wants someone in custody as soon as possible. He needs a success to show the press.'

'The police won't find any real evidence, because Angela

didn't kill Giles Temple. You'll have to release her and then you'll look ridiculous.'

Joe nodded and Libby's breathing returned to normal. Joe knew Angela Miles, and he was a smart man. He wouldn't be easily misled. 'I'd rather stop that happening, but there's a lot of police time focused on establishing evidence against Mrs Miles rather than following other leads. I'd send my team out, but my hands are tied. I thought you might have spare time...'

'You mean, when I'm not struggling with orders for chocolates, planning Robert's wedding, sorting out Mandy's problems or finding lost cats?'

Joe held up his hands. 'Angela's your friend.'

Libby heaved a sigh and poured more coffee. 'Of course, I'll do what I can to help. Let's look at the facts. For one thing, Giles Temple was strangled. That would take some strength. I can't imagine the middle-aged ladies of the Guild overcoming a healthy man in a struggle.'

Joe was nodding. 'I agree. Go on. What else do you think?'

'I think the scarf was planted to lay suspicion on the Knitters' Guild, or on Angela herself. The members of the Guild are mad as a bag of ferrets, but I can't see them wanting to kill Giles Temple.'

She paused. After a moment's thought, she shrugged. Time to share Vera's gossip. 'There's one person who might merit a closer look. Have you met the Dean's wife?'

'Chief Inspector Arnold sent Filbert-Smythe, our new detective sergeant with a first class degree from a swanky university, to interview the Dean and Mrs Weir. We won't be getting anything useful from that; I can guarantee it.'

Joe rolled his eyes. Filbert-Smythe's Oxbridge accent had not endeared him to the local police force, but he'd impressed Chief Inspector Arnold. 'The lad will be fine, once he gets some experience and stops brown nosing the bosses,' was Joe's verdict.

Libby blew out her cheeks, thinking hard. Should she tell Joe the big secret? She made up her mind. She wanted him to share information, so she must do the same. 'The Guild have a big event coming up in Wells. It's supposed to be a secret, but I think you should know.'

Joe groaned. 'Not a Greenham Common-type protest – sitting down in the streets?'

Libby laughed. 'This is a celebration. Do you remember the scaffolding at the cathedral? It was there for months.' Joe nodded. 'Now the work on the West Front's finished, they're planning a celebration. I'll tell you about it if you promise not to whisper it to a soul.'

'Cross my heart, so long as there's no danger to the public. Go on, you can't stop now.'

'The Guild members plan to smother the centre of Wells with knitting. They'll hang scarves from lamp posts, leave hats and gloves on benches and wrap blankets round trees. It's called yarnbombing.'

'I've heard of it.'

'The bombs can be useful things, like mittens and ear warmers, and people are free to take them home. They'll leave silly stuff like toys and dolls as well, just for fun.'

'Do I need to request extra policing?'

'Well, they're not planning to do any damage and I can't imagine there'll be unmanageable crowds. Come along and see it. I imagine it'll be quite a sight.'

Joe's face was a picture. 'I wouldn't miss it for the world. In return, you'll help?'

Libby shrugged. 'I can't let Angela be a scapegoat, but you need to let me in on the evidence.' Joe hesitated. Libby rose, collecting cups and plates. 'If not, I can't help. You know I can be trusted to keep my mouth shut.'

Joe smiled. 'As a reward for breakfast, I'll tell you what I can. We don't have results from forensics yet, apart from the approximate time of death. Apparently, the heating in the library goes off at seven and it gets cold very fast up there, so it's only an approximation. The pathologist calls it an educated guess. Anyway, the best suggestion remains between six and midnight, as we said at the press conference.'

'What time does the library close?'

'Five o'clock.'

'Did Giles Temple have a key?'

'No. The bursar has one, I believe, and so does the verger.'

'Are researchers left alone with the books?'

'Occasionally. A volunteer often sits by the door.'

Joe had a glint in his eye. He tapped a finger on the countertop. 'Here's the thing I shouldn't be telling you. There's been another researcher working in the library this week. An American by the name of Reg Talbot.'

The name rang a bell. Libby closed her eyes for a moment as she struggled to remember.

Got it! Max's friend and colleague.

She said, 'That's been kept quiet. Not even the knitters mentioned it.'

'There's some sort of politics involved. I'll be in serious trouble if the boss finds out I told you, so keep it quiet, won't you? I think he's a contender, but the chief says we're to move on.'

Libby sucked her lower lip. 'I wonder why.'

'The thing is,' Joe went on, 'I've met him before. He works with Dad.'

Libby nodded. They were thinking along the same lines. 'So, there may be trouble at the cathedral?'

'Hard to say. It could be genuine research of some sort.'

'Like research into the Pilgrim Fathers? Has anyone interviewed this American?'

'I'm scheduled to speak to him later today.'

'I suppose I couldn't – I mean, can I watch from outside the room?'

Joe shook his head. 'Sorry, no clearance. But I'll tell you what I can, within the proper limits.'

'Not many Americans visit this part of the world. I suppose he'll be easy to recognise when he speaks, because of the accent.' A big grin split Joe's face. 'Why are you laughing?'

'He's the most recognisable man I've seen in Somerset. He won't need to say a word. He's an African American, about seven feet tall and bald as a coot. Used to play basketball. He's fit – very fit.'

11

CAT WOMAN

The Cedars. Despite the grand name, Mrs Marchant's Wells home turned out to be a tiny two bedroom house in the middle of a small terrace, a few streets away from the cathedral. Libby checked the address, turned off the ignition and climbed out of the car, mentally reducing the fee she'd been about to charge. Whoever lived here was unlikely to be rich.

Mrs Marchant opened her door a few inches and peered at Libby through round John Lennon spectacles. A pungent smell crept through the gap.

Libby recoiled. 'I've come about your cat.' In the distance, a cacophony of wails and squeals suggested several animals shared the house. 'One of your cats.'

'You'd better come in, then.' Mrs Marchant closed the door with a sharp click. The chain rattled for a full minute before the door opened. As Libby stepped inside, the overpowering smell of cats caught in her throat. She coughed as discreetly as possible and followed the woman down a narrow, dark passage.

'Mind your feet.' Mrs Marchant waved at an oblong litter

tray covering half the width of the passage. Libby trod with care, skidding on the light dressing of litter scattered over an expanse of ancient brown, cracked linoleum, saving herself with a hand on the wall. Her fingers stuck to the dull brown wallpaper.

'Elsie,' the woman shouted. A fat grey moggy appeared at the top of a short flight of stairs, green eyes twinkling through the gloom, and picked her way downstairs, sedate as a Victorian miss. She wound in and out of Libby's legs, purring.

Two medium sized tabbies, a tiny black kitten, and a big marmalade giant followed. 'How many cats do you have?' Libby untangled herself and stepped into a small kitchen to find two large cages full of cats. Every remaining inch of floor held bowls of water and cat food.

Mrs Marchant pulled the sides of a grey cardigan across her thin chest, retied the knot in a belt of the same material, and picked a tiny white kitten out of one of the cages. 'Lost count, m'dear. All strays, you know.' She spoke with the deep, cut-glass accent Libby remembered from the phone call. 'They come here when they're lost. Impossible to keep count.'

The cats looked healthy and happy, but the smell was almost unbearable and Mrs Marchant's clothes struck Libby as shabby and threadbare. Beneath the cat stink, Libby detected the scent of unwashed garments. The woman was painfully thin. 'Cup of tea?'

Libby glanced at the sink where dirty dishes teetered in a pile and cracked mugs lay tumbled on the draining board. 'No, thanks. I can't stop long. You rang about a missing cat?'

'Oh yes, Mildred. She went out a few nights ago. Hasn't been back.'

'Was she a stray, too?'

'That's right, she's lived with me for a year or so. All my

darlings are strays, except Emily, here.' She dropped the white kitten back in its cage and picked up the plump grey Emily, addressing the next remarks to the cat. 'You were my first cat, weren't you, my love. You came with me when I moved. We used to live in a lovely house called The Cedars. Just brought two things with me, don't you know – the name and the cat.'

Mrs Marchant put Emily down on a kitchen counter, where the animal picked a delicate route among teetering piles of tins, purring. 'Anyway, mustn't keep you. There's a picture of Mildred – the one that's lost – in one of these drawers.'

She moved to a shabby brown cabinet and pulled open one drawer after another. Scraps of paper, pens, spoons and elastic bands cascaded to the floor. Libby bent to retrieve them, trying not to touch the grubby floor. 'Here it is.'

The photo Mrs Marchant pushed under Libby's nose showed a plumper self, looking down an aristocratic nose at the camera. Libby, surprised, barely noticed the cat. 'Who took the photo?'

'My son. Terence.' She tossed the photo back in the drawer.

'Has he been here, lately?' Did he know his mother was living in squalor?

Mrs Marchant's eyes narrowed. 'Huh. What does he care? Children,' she glared, and Libby caught a brief glimpse of the handsome, haughty woman of the photo, 'are ungrateful little beasts.'

Surprised by such sudden vehemence, Libby's curiosity took over. 'Ungrateful?' she prompted.

'His father left everything to Terence on the understanding he'd look after me. Instead, what did my dear son do? Sold the house out from under my feet and left me in this place.'

'Does he realise you need help?' Mrs Marchant was a difficult and demanding woman, but surely no son would leave their mother in this state. She must have gone downhill fast and Terence deserved to be told. 'Where does he live?'

'Can't remember. Not far. Thirty miles or so.' Mrs Marchant gave an elaborate shrug. 'Lost the address, didn't I? Last time he came to see me was just after Mildred arrived. The day he took the photograph.' Libby groaned, inwardly. She couldn't let this state of affairs continue. She'd have to challenge Terence.

The temptation to walk away almost overwhelmed Libby. She could refuse the commission, leave Mrs Marchant to find her own cat, and forget about the ungrateful son. She already felt like a size eight foot in a size six shoe.

Instead, she added the task to her long mental to-do list and asked, 'May I keep Mildred's photo?' The cat woman shrugged, pulled it from the drawer among another shower of odds and ends, and handed it over.

'Has she been lost before?'

'Of course not. Well, just one night, shut in a neighbour's garage. She's not there now. I looked.'

The smell in the house sickened Libby. She had to get away. 'I'll arrange for some prints of the photo and distribute them around Wells. Would you like me to put an ad in the local paper? It might be expensive.'

'You may do as you wish. The cost,' Mrs Marchant raised both eyebrows, looking down the aristocratic nose at such vulgar talk of money, 'is of no consequence.'

12

SAMANTHA

The news of Angela Miles' interview under caution had travelled fast. On Thursday morning, half the inhabitants of Exham on Sea discovered they needed a loaf of bread or a cake, and Libby tuned in to every conversation, listening hard.

Gladys had been at school with Angela. 'She wouldn't harm a fly, and that's a fact.'

'Who knows.' The estate agent slouched by the counter. 'Middle-aged women—'

The florist cut him off, standing full square, hands on hips, eyes blazing. 'Middle-aged women what?'

'Nothing.' He backed away, stammering. 'I just meant she might be lonely. You know. Living alone. Maybe this Giles Temple took advantage of her.' He edged towards the door.

Mandy held out a paper bag. 'Don't forget your sandwich.' Red faced, he grabbed it and shot out of the shop, narrowly avoiding a collision with Samantha Watson.

'Well, really. Some people have no manners.' Patting her hair into place, the solicitor stalked to the counter to order smoked trout with mustard.

'It seems your friend Angela Miles is our killer, Libby. I'm surprised you missed that. You're supposed to be the local sleuth. But you're an amateur, of course. Perhaps you'll leave inquiries to the professionals, in future. Chief Inspector Arnold tells me the evidence against Mrs Miles is most compelling.'

Mandy slapped the solicitor's food on the counter. 'You mean that scarf?' she scoffed. 'Planted. Any fool can see that.'

Samantha sneered. 'You mind your manners, Mandy. If I had your background, I'd be more careful what I said.'

The spiteful words dropped into horrified silence. Someone drew a sharp breath. Mandy's father had been in trouble with the police many times. He'd even attacked her mother and threatened Mandy. Her face twisted in fury, mouth working, she escaped into the back kitchen.

Before Libby could gather her wits, Frank made a rare public appearance. Hiding in the back, he'd heard every word. He strode to the front door, held it open, glared at Samantha, and pointed to the street. 'You've gone too far, this time. Get out. You won't be served here in future.'

Samantha gasped. 'I haven't paid, yet.'

Frank folded his arms and waited as she picked up her food, tossed a handful of coins on the counter and swept out. At the door, she stopped. 'I won't forget this. Since you came here, Libby Forest, there's been nothing but trouble. Just watch out, you and your lodger. You'll be sorry.'

As the door slammed, the hubbub in the shop swelled. 'Well,' Gladys whispered to Libby, with a wary glance at Frank, 'if your apprentice dresses like a Goth, it's hardly surprising people think the worst.'

As the last customer left, Libby confided in Mandy and

Frank. 'Sometimes I think a small town's the most vicious place in the world.'

Mandy scowled. 'Samantha Watson's got it coming. She's the one who'll be sorry.'

* * *

After the morning's drama, Libby took time alone to work in the peace of her kitchen while Mandy stayed at the bakery. Developing overdue new product lines, she forgot everything except her recipes.

Max would be home soon. It would be a relief to talk over the problems with him. 'I like my independence,' she explained to Bear and Fuzzy as she scraped food into separate bowls – fish for Fuzzy, beef for Bear, 'but I do miss him.'

Perhaps their partnership really could work. She stopped work for a moment, imagining it. If they set up as private investigators, she'd have to do a course, take exams. Butterflies swooped in her stomach, but it would be interesting. She liked a challenge. As for marriage? She shook her head. She'd think about that later. Max hadn't offered a proper proposal. A vague suggestion in a phone call didn't count.

Soon she was humming above the noise of mixer and grinder. Chocolate hearts needed filling. Libby mixed and measured, tested and tasted, until strawberry, coconut, lime, coffee and praline cream scented the air with heady sweetness and every chocolate brimmed with flavour.

She polished the kitchen until the surfaces shone, made a cheese sandwich and put her feet up. The living room reminded her of the last time Max sprawled on the sofa, Bear at his feet, stroking Fuzzy with one hand and twirling a whisky glass with the other, watching as an inch of golden liquid coated the sides.

Libby rarely sat here on her own. 'For heaven's sake,' she muttered. 'I'm getting sentimental.'

She pulled out a pair of knitting needles and a ball of wool she'd brought home from the Guild, curled up on the sofa and concentrated on producing squares. The Knitters' Guild would meet again, tomorrow, and Libby would be there.

If only Chief Inspector Arnold hadn't burst into the meeting, full of pomposity and self-importance, Libby might have discovered an important clue amongst the gossip. What had the knitters said? A vague thought, shapeless but insistent, nagged at Libby's brain. She couldn't bring it into focus. Maybe it would become clearer tomorrow.

13

DINNER

That evening, Libby felt like a mother hen with a brood of unruly chicks. Max had returned, but instead of the quiet evening together in the cottage she'd have preferred, they were eating supper at his almost-mansion, and were not alone.

Apart from Bear, snoring loudly in the corner of the room, there was Reg, Max's American colleague. Max wanted to introduce him to Libby. She suspected Max felt awkward after their phone call, and he'd brought his friend along as a buffer. Still, Libby wanted to know more about Reg's work in the cathedral library.

Max had sweetened the deal further by inviting Libby's son, Robert, his fiancée, Sarah, and Mandy. They'd arrived yesterday to stay with her parents for a few days. Sarah, a statuesque blonde, bubbly and excited, was full of wedding arrangements, but Robert had a different agenda. He told Libby he wanted to meet her 'friend'.

Libby hadn't yet confessed that Max was more than a friend.

Joe, though invited, had not come. He was on duty. Had that been an excuse? Libby hoped not. The relationship between father and policeman son had been strained since Max divorced Joe's mother, many years ago. Things had improved recently, and Libby prided herself on helping smooth the path with input to some of Joe's cases.

Since that angry scene in the bakery, Mandy had been subdued, answering questions with monosyllables. When Libby suggested she might like to attend Max's homecoming dinner, she'd pretended indifference. Libby turned away. 'Max asked me to invite you, but it's your choice.'

That did the trick. Mandy tossed her head and mumbled but she wore a sheepish grin and sounded far perkier as she said, 'You need me there to stop you talking about weddings and boring business all evening.'

To Libby's surprise, Mandy had toned down her appearance for the occasion and looked stunning in one of Libby's silk blouses over a pair of velvet trousers.

Max welcomed the guests with champagne. He discarded his apron with a flourish, as though he'd spent hours in the kitchen. In fact, the meal had come straight from Libby's freezer along with simple instructions.

'Reg's just taking a call,' he explained. 'He'll be down in a minute – Ah, here he is. Reg, let me introduce you to some of my neighbours and friends.'

Libby heard Mandy's sharp intake of breath and glanced sideways. The girl's mouth hung half open. Libby swallowed a chuckle. She didn't blame Mandy; Reg was gorgeous. He was tall enough even to dwarf Max, his body was lean and fit looking, and his skin glowed the warm colour of a summer tan. It was hard to assess his age; mid-thirties, perhaps. His head was clean-shaven. Libby disliked that fashion, but she could make an exception in Reg's case.

They shared small talk. 'I love your British weather,' Reg said. 'In my part of Texas, it's pretty much the same every day. Hot. Here, you never know what's coming. One day it's freezing, and the next you have this gentle rain.'

Max ushered them into the dining room. 'We call it drizzle.'

'The sun does shine occasionally.' Libby defended her home country.

Bear followed close behind. 'You know, I think he misses Fuzzy,' Max said, 'or Shipley.'

Robert said, 'I haven't met the notorious Shipley. Didn't he help you find the body under the lighthouse?'

'He did. I used to walk him when I first arrived in Exham. Since his owners left, he lives with the vet, hoping for a new family.'

She smiled at Sarah. 'Any takers?'

'Don't look at us. Once we're married, we might think about a dog, or maybe a cat. Robert's more of a cat person. But we need to settle down, first. With all the wedding preparations, everything seems a whirl just now.'

Libby kept an eye on Mandy. Seated opposite Reg, she'd focused her dark, kohl rimmed eyes on the American newcomer, from time to time tucking a stray lock of hair behind an ear. Maybe her gloom at Steve's defection would be short lived. Bear lay under the table, alert in case someone dropped a titbit.

Reg's biceps rippled inside a beautifully cut jacket as he stretched to offer Libby a dish of carrots roasted with cardamom and honey. 'Ma'am,' he drawled, his voice as warm and liquid as Nat King Cole's, 'I can tell Max didn't cook this up. I gather you're a professional, and I can tell why. I haven't had a meal like this in years. Why, those chefs in the city, dribbling little pools of sauce on inch long pieces of half cooked fish, ought to come out here for a few lessons.' Libby blushed, tried not to simper, and offered him a second, larger helping. 'You bet. A man my size needs a good meal.'

Robert said, 'Mum's meals were famous when I was at school. I had to rotate my friends, there were so many wanting to try her apple and ginger crumble.'

Sarah said. 'So that's how you got girls, in those days.' She leaned back in her chair, with a sigh. 'Maybe I shouldn't have eaten quite so much roast lamb. I should have saved myself for pudding.'

As the engaged couple shared smiles, their eyes on each other, Libby glanced at Reg, wondering at his interest in Giles Temple's death.

Max had insisted Libby could trust his colleague. 'I've known him for years and he's spent a long time in England. He read for a research degree at Cambridge University, something about the crossover between history and science. He likes to play up his deep south accent when he's around women, though. They swoon.'

Now she'd met him, Libby understood why. 'We still meet up from time to time when I'm in the States or he's in England.' Max had said. 'We're pretty much in the same business.'

Reg tucked into his second helping of Libby's special roast lamb and launched into an explanation of his presence in Somerset. His story was plausible and Libby relaxed a little. She'd been anxious about Robert meeting Max and Reg. She wanted to avoid involving her son and his fiancée in any undercover work, but Reg's task sounded straightforward.

'The cathedral library has some unique and ancient books, donated over the centuries by what you British call 'canons' at the cathedral. Don't you love the idea of religious men named after weapons?' Mandy's eyes were fixed in transparent adoration on the speaker. Max winked at Libby.

Reg continued, 'Why, there was a book there, from the sixteenth century, that used to belong to your Thomas Cranmer—you know, Archbishop of Canterbury when Henry VIII was king? There are notes he wrote himself. How about that?'

Max said, 'The question everyone will ask, Reg, is whether you were in the library on the night of the murder?' There was a pause, and the air grew tense, as though everyone around the table realised the implication of the question. Was Reg a suspect? Even Robert's gaze shifted to the American.

Reg sighed. 'You always were a straight talker, my friend. No, I was travelling down from my temporary office in Bristol and staying at the Swan, sampling your local brew; Butcombe Gold, I seem to recall. I think the bar staff at the hotel will back me up.'

Everyone relaxed a fraction. Reg looked from one face to another. 'Here's something you may be interested in.' He addressed Libby. 'I can tell you about the book it seems Giles Temple was reading. The police mentioned it to me, wanting to know if I'd looked at it.'

'What was it?' Mandy asked.

'A travel guide, full of maps of the world. At least, the world they knew in the seventeenth century. Not the most precious book in the collection, but still worth a pretty penny.'

Libby's mind raced. 'How do you know that's the book he was reading?'

Max said, 'It's a best guess, according to Joe Ramshore, but the police can't be sure. Giles Temple wore white gloves in the library to avoid acid from his fingers damaging some of the books, so there are no recent fingerprints, but the spine of this one stuck out a bit from the others, as though someone in a hurry had shoved it back on the shelf. That attracted the police officer's attention.'

'The murderer left the book behind? Isn't that odd?' Libby was thinking aloud. 'Why did he shove it back so carelessly? Didn't that just draw attention to it?'

Her voice trailed away as Robert queried, 'Why do you keep saying "him" for the murderer? Are you sure it was a man?'

Max nodded. 'Good question. Joe thinks it's likely. The victim was strangled with a chain, so the murderer was strong. It would take plenty of force to keep the pressure on the chain with the victim fighting for his life.' Libby winced. 'But I guess a fit woman could manage, if she took him by surprise.'

He added, 'There's something else. Chains, like the one used to strangle Mr Temple, are attached to the shelves in the library with forged steel bolts. The murderer must have brought along some hefty bolt cutters.'

'Which means,' Robert interrupted, excited, 'he had a plan. He came prepared to kill Giles Temple that night.'

14

GHOSTS

Robert and Sarah left, arms entwined, taking a taxi to Sarah's parents' home. They were still chattering about the murder.

A lump formed in Libby's throat as she stood with Max in the doorway, watching. It seemed that only yesterday Robert had been a little boy, holding Libby's hand as they walked to the park.

She leaned on Max's shoulder. 'They're almost as excited about the mystery as their wedding. Still, it's very strange to see your son with another woman. Sarah will come first in his life, from now on.'

He slipped an arm round her shoulders. 'That's how it should be. You must be proud of Robert. He does you credit.'

'I am. I used to think he was dull until Sarah brought him out of his shell. Funny, how wrong you can be about your own children. I suppose it was the contrast with Ali – she was the enthusiast, always dreaming up new projects. I never knew what she was going to do next. I shouldn't have been surprised when she left university so abruptly and dashed off to South America. At least, judging by her emails, she's forgiven me for disapproving.'

Max sounded rueful. 'It's so hard to get it right when you have children. I made every mistake possible with mine. If I'd known my daughter would have that riding accident and die so young, I'd have spent every moment with her, instead of working away from home so often.'

Libby said, 'We can't change our natures. Look at you, still working when you could be happily retired on your banking pension.'

'But what would I do all day? At least Joe and I are talking again. I wish he'd been here tonight, to meet Robert. Still, there'll be time for that. He's pleased about you and me, you know. It's almost enough to make him forgive me for the past.'

Libby leaned against Max. 'I'm pleased, too.'

'But not enough for marriage?'

'Not quite yet. Give me time. Let's go back and see how the other pair are doing.'

Mandy and Reg were tidying Max's kitchen, Reg explaining the rules of basketball while Mandy listened, open mouthed. Max whispered, 'More love-birds.'

Mandy's face glowed. She had a wine glass in each hand. 'Reg wants to know if this house is haunted.'

Max snorted. 'Don't listen to him, Mandy. Reg sees ghosts everywhere. It's his hobby.'

Mandy and Libby spoke in unison, breathless. 'Really?'

Max sighed. 'It's one of his ploys to attract women. Successful, of course.'

'That's very sexist,' Mandy objected.

'Maybe, but true. Anyway, Reg, it looks like you've already hooked these two.' Max rescued a wine glass from Mandy's grasp as she drained the other. 'You'd better explain. What makes you think I have a ghost? I can't say I've seen anyone cross the hall with his head beneath his arm.'

Reg pointed to Bear. 'You can scoff, but that dog senses something. There are parts of this house that bother him. He followed me down the hall just now, stopped at the third door and wouldn't go in.'

Libby admitted, 'I've noticed it, too. It's the drawing room that bothers him. Sometimes he won't pass the door at all. He just pokes his nose in and backs right away to the kitchen.'

Max led them into his comfortable, scruffy study. Reg stretched out in an armchair, his legs reaching halfway across the room. 'I had no idea you had a drawing room, Max. I thought it was something only your British royalty would own.'

'It comes with the house. I'll admit I hardly go in. It's far too formal. I just use it when I want to impress someone like the Lord Lieutenant on official business.'

Reg scratched his head. 'You Brits and your aristocracy; I'm not even going to ask what a Lord Lieutenant is. But I'd love to have a peek in the drawing room. Come on now, back me up, Mandy.'

'I've never been somewhere as posh as a drawing room,' Mandy giggled. 'We just had a front room, where I grew up. Should I call you Lord Ramshore?'

Libby joined in. 'Come on, Max. Haven't you ever wondered about ghosts? This is such an old house.'

Max grinned. 'Are you sure you want to start ghost hunting? You'll give yourself nightmares. You were scared enough that time you were lost on Glastonbury Tor.'

'Don't try and get out of it that way. Come on, spill the beans.'

'Okay, then, here's the story. I'll start it properly. Once upon a time...'

Mandy chortled. Max winked at her and continued. 'Once upon a time I sat in there, reading. It was soon after I moved into the house, half a dozen years ago. I was reading Dickens. Great Expectations, I think. Seemed appropriate in an old pile like this. Anyway, it was midsummer, on one of the three hot days we had that year. We call that a heat wave, Reg, by the way.'

Reg laughed, but Mandy complained, 'Get back to the story.'

'Sorry. I realised my feet were freezing cold. It felt as though they had ice packed round them. The rest of me was fine, even a bit too warm. I got up to walk around, warm the toes up a bit, and,' his voice dropped to a whisper, 'I felt something cold land on my shoulder.'

Mandy gasped. 'Like a hand?'

He nodded; his face solemn. 'It was heavy, like a dead weight. I looked round, but there was nothing to be seen. I told myself I was imagining things and tried to go on reading, but my feet just got colder. I told myself, "Don't be ridiculous. It's just a draught." These old buildings have plenty of spots where the wind gets through, even with half decent central heating. I moved across and sat in another chair, but...'

Mandy put in, 'The cold spot followed you?' She licked her lips, eyes shining.

Libby leaned forward, caught up in the story. 'What happened next?'

'Nothing. In the end, I went back into my study to get warm.'

Mandy groaned. 'That can't be the end. Was Bear with you then?'

'No, it was before I inherited him. You're right, though, Libby. He's never gone into that room. This old house has plenty of other places he prefers.'

Mandy's eyes glowed. 'Did it happen again?'

'Every time I sit in there, to tell the truth.'

Libby grinned at Mandy. 'Come on. We have to investigate this, even though I don't believe a word of it. There's nothing to beat a good ghost story. Let's go into the drawing room, right now, and see what happens.'

Max led the way down the corridor. Bear padded beside Libby, as far as the door. Max pushed on the wood. Slowly, it creaked open and Mandy gasped. Bear stopped; his legs rigid. Mandy whispered, 'He doesn't like it here, does he?'

The dog barked, once. His tail drooped and the ruff of fur round his neck stood on end. He managed to look miserable and offended at the same time. Max strode into the middle of the room and held out a dog treat. 'Come on, Bear.' The dog took a step forward, hesitated, looked from Libby to Max, barked again, turned and padded back along the corridor.

'Does that count as proof?' Libby asked, an odd feeling in the pit of her stomach.

Max took her hand. 'Come on, Reg, you're the expert. Is there a ghost in here?'

Reg paced round the room, stopping at intervals, his face serious. 'There's a strange atmosphere,' he concluded. 'There are cold spots, just as you described. Are there any records of odd happenings? Witches in the area?'

'Nothing I've been able to track down. I've looked at various histories of the house and the surrounding area, but I haven't managed to turn up anything interesting apart from the Battle of Sedgemoor.'

Reg beamed from ear to ear. 'While I'm here, maybe I can

do a little research into your local history. Tell me about this battle.'

Max wrinkled his brow. 'The Duke of Monmouth was a pretender to the throne of England, back in the eighteenth century. He landed in the West Country, fought the king's army and was defeated. Most of his followers died, and the rest ran away.'

'Maybe some got this far...'

'Before they died...' Reg and Mandy were talking over each other, Mandy's face pink with happiness.

* * *

Libby, Mandy and Reg stayed at Max's house that night. They sat up, drinking coffee, until late into the night. Max looked out of the window. 'It's freezing cold out there and I doubt you could see your hand in front of your face. Just the weather to give Bear his final walk. Coming, Libby?'

Bear appeared, miraculously, at the door. He'd been out of sight, most likely curled up in the room Max grandly called the gun room. Libby had never seen a gun in the house. Did Max own one? He'd never told her. Just one more thing she'd find out one day. She stood up, slightly tipsy. 'Wellington boots and hats needed, I think.'

No one else would leave the warmth of the blazing fire for the cutting blast of winter's east winds. Libby and Max trudged, arm in arm, down the lane, the wind in their faces, using a flashlight to avoid the worst of the puddles. 'I know you trust Reg, but do you think we should have talked about the murder so much?'

'Why, because Joe thinks he's a suspect?' Max scoffed. 'Joe's not a fool, even if his chief is. He interviewed Reg this afternoon and the alibi checks out. He was travelling all that day, with train tickets to back him up, and the woman behind the bar remembers him being there all evening. He's very distinctive, as you've seen. She almost melted while talking about him. He's been eliminated from the enquiry.'

'That's just as well. Did you see Mandy's face? I think she's in love.' She told Max about Mandy's quarrel with Steve. 'She's got this enormous inferiority complex, and it's making her miserable and jealous. I'm worried about her, to be honest.'

'You're doing all you can. Let her be. She has to make her own mistakes.'

15

GUILT

After a morning baking and an afternoon struggling with a pair of unruly knitting needles, Libby was ready for the next meeting of the Knitters' Guild. Ignoring the uneven edges of her squares, Libby stuffed them into a bag, pulled on her thickest woollen sweater, a pair of jeans and sheepskin lined boots, persuaded the engine of the Citroen to kick into action on the third attempt, and drove through the murk of a dark winter's evening.

The car sped along deserted lanes, round twists and turns. Libby loved to drive in the dark, able to see the lights of an approaching car well before it arrived. Tonight, though, the darkness seemed less dense. It would be hours before dawn broke, but the sky grew brighter every moment. Libby slowed, puzzled.

She turned another corner. Between the naked arms of a leafless hedgerow a gleam of bright orange flickered. Libby drove closer and sniffed the air. An acrid, bitter smell filled the car. The smell of fire.

Smoke billowed, a patch of denser black against the sky.

One more turn in the lane and Libby saw the fire straight ahead, bright against the night sky. With a shock of horror, she recognised the isolated eighteenth century thatched cottage where Samantha Watson lived.

She screeched to a halt, leapt from the car and ran through a gate in the white painted fence, towards the house. A light shone from one of the upstairs rooms. 'No. oh no. Samantha must be in there.' No face appeared at the window.

Searing heat beat her back. She gasped for breath; lungs full of smoke.

The fire brigade. Coughing, she grabbed the phone from her pocket and fumbled, fingers trembling, for the emergency button, bellowing the news, the roar of fire threatening to drown her voice.

Help was on its way, but the fire had taken hold and black smoke billowed from the front door. Where was Samantha? Was she inside? Why hadn't she run out? Sick with fear, Libby ran round the cottage, searching for a way in, but the fire burned even more fiercely at the back.

She shrieked Samantha's name, but all she heard in reply was the shatter of glass as a window exploded high above, driving Libby back. Glass showered like snow into the garden.

Water. She needed water to drown the flames. Desperately, she scanned the garden, the unnatural light of the fire delineating every detail. A tiny stream trickled along beside a wall, but she had no way of carrying the water. She needed a bucket. Where could she find one?

A shed stood halfway down the garden, out of range of the fire. Libby rattled the door, but it was locked. She kicked the lock once. It trembled but held. She took a run at the door and crashed painfully against the wood.

The wail of a fire engine sounded, ever closer. Libby took

another hopeless run at the shed. Hands grabbed at her arms, pulling her back. 'Leave it to us, now.'

'Thank heaven, you're here.' Howling with frustration, she screamed, 'I think Samantha's in there. It's her house and the light was on. I couldn't get in…'

She broke off, paralysed, as with a roar like a steam train, the thatched roof threw a volcano of fire into the air and collapsed, tumbling into the house.

Someone led Libby away. 'There's nothing you can do. We can't get in until the fire's under control. Keep back while the lads work.'

Sobbing, she sank to the ground as fire officers unrolled a heavy hose. A torrent of water flooded the house, until every inch was drenched. Slowly, the flames flickered and died.

For Libby, time seemed to stand still. The house was a shell, no more than four blackened walls, when at last two burly figures pushed their way through the space where the door used to stand.

Libby held her head in her hands, tears rolling down her cheeks, waiting and hoping, knowing it was impossible for Samantha to have survived the inferno, praying she'd been away from home.

The fire officers returned, shoulders drooping. An officer trudged across to Libby and removed a heavy helmet. Libby recognised a young woman who often came into the bakery. Libby didn't know her name. *Cheese and pickle baguette. That's what she buys.* Libby's thoughts shied away from the truth she read in the woman's face.

'I'm sorry, Mrs Forest.' The officer wiped a sweaty forehead with the back of her hand. 'You're right. There's someone in there.'

Libby shuddered, horror clutching her stomach. Voice

trembling, she asked the question, knowing the answer already. 'Is she dead?'

'I'm so sorry.'

'Anyone else?' had Chief Inspector Arnold been there with her?

Libby closed her eyes and sank to the ground, hardly aware of the freezing water that puddled on the lawn, soaking her jeans. 'If I'd been here sooner. If I hadn't had that last cup of coffee...'

The officer crouched at her side. 'You did all you could. Are you hurt?'

Libby shook her head, turned away and emptied the contents of her stomach on the muddy ground.

* * *

She threw her clothes into a black bin bag and dumped it in her spare room. She'd never wear them again. She showered, scrubbing every inch of her body under hot water, and shampooed her hair three times. The smell of burning lingered everywhere, in her chest and throat, in the pores of her skin. It filled the cottage.

She gargled with mouthwash and sprayed the house with Glade. All the while, a voice in her head whispered, 'You never liked Samantha Watson.' No matter how hard Libby tried, she couldn't subdue that small, persistent voice of guilt.

Max helped her onto the sofa and handed over a glass of brandy. He'd found the bottle under the sink. It had belonged to her husband. Libby hated brandy, but tipped a big slug down her throat, anyway. Maybe it would banish the smell of smoke. 'Are you feeling better?' Max asked.

She tried to smile. 'A little. My conscience is working overtime. Samantha said there's been nothing but trouble since I came to Exham. I wonder if she was right?'

'Nonsense. That's delayed shock talking. Why should the fire be your fault? You had nothing to do with it. In fact, you nearly rescued Samantha.'

'I'm afraid 'nearly' wasn't enough.' Libby shuddered. 'That chocolate-box thatched roof looked cute, but wasn't the house a disaster just waiting to happen?'

Max tucked a rug around her knees. 'In fact, thatched roofs are no more combustible than other materials, but so many things can start a fire. Candles left burning, or gas, or a cigarette.'

'Samantha didn't smoke. I don't understand why she didn't get out when the fire started'

'Who knows. Maybe she wanted an early night, perhaps had a couple of drinks that made her woozy. Once a fire takes hold, it's amazing how fast it travels. It's usually the smoke that chokes people, prevents them from escaping.'

Libby shuddered. 'What a terrible way to die. I suppose the police and fire service will be on the case, and we'll find out the full story.'

Max tried to refill her brandy glass, but she made a face and pushed it away.

He said. 'For one thing, they'll have the insurance company on their backs, trying to avoid a huge pay out. Samantha would have all the proper documentation. She was a solicitor, after all.' He frowned. 'Though any documents may have been destroyed in the fire.'

Libby struggled to sit up straight. 'There are sure to be electronic copies online.'

Max poured another slug of brandy into her glass. 'I'll bet super-efficient Samantha had a fireproof filing cabinet. Or if not, she might have left paperwork at the solicitors' office. Anyway, Chief Inspector Arnold will sort it out. Poor fellow.'

Libby shuddered. Those things she'd said about Samantha and the chief inspector in the past; if only she could take them back. 'He'll be devastated. They've been engaged for months.'

She yawned and her eyelids drooped. The brandy was doing its job. 'I'm going to bed. I can't think any more tonight. It's been such a week, what with Giles Temple, and Angela, and that scene in the shop, and...' She stopped, half way to the door, with a sharp intake of breath.

'What is it?' Max, gathering glasses, paused.

'Nothing. I just remembered...' Libby forced herself to breathe evenly. She tried a weary smile. 'It's nothing. I'm tired. Good night.'

She couldn't tell anyone, not even Max, about the picture in her head: the fury on Mandy's face and the venom in the words she'd hissed in Libby's ear as the solicitor left the bakery. 'She'll be sorry.'

16

GOSSIP

Libby woke late to find a rare beam of light flooding the room between the curtains. She rolled over and a mild pain behind her eyes intensified until her entire head throbbed. She scrubbed at her face, eyes squeezed shut, desperate to erase the memory of last night's fire.

She sat up, pulse racing, as she remembered Mandy's fury. Could her apprentice possibly have anything to do with the fire? Libby shuddered. Mandy would never, ever do such a thing. Of course, she wouldn't.

Libby paused to think. Yesterday was Mandy's day off. She'd muttered something about visiting friends before going to The Dark Side, the club frequented by Somerset's small Goth community, for the evening. Libby could easily check on her movements. All she had to do was talk to Mandy's friends.

She chewed her lip. Go behind her apprentice's back? What was she thinking? She must ask Mandy herself. She swung her legs out of bed, threw on a dressing gown, grabbed her phone and looked at the time. Too late. Mandy must have left the house by now.

Libby fought down a stab of panic. *Think logically.* She took a deep breath and sank on to the bed. There were plenty of other possible causes of the fire. A kitchen fire? The organised Samantha would have a fire blanket in the house. Candles, or a spark from an open hearth? Possibly. What about cigarettes? Samantha did not smoke, but maybe someone else had been with her earlier, dropping a lighted cigarette end behind a chair, or near a curtain, where it could smoulder, unnoticed, before bursting into flame. A single half extinguished cigarette could burn down a house.

Libby sighed. This was all hopeful nonsense. Controlling, superior Samantha would never let anyone smoke in her home, and the fire officers had only found one body.

Two suspicious deaths within a week was too much of a coincidence. They could be connected, and Libby wouldn't find the link by sitting upstairs all morning.

She sniffed as a tantalising smell crept into the room. Bacon. Max was making breakfast. How could she have forgotten Max that had stayed overnight in the third bedroom? Her heart suddenly light, she ran downstairs.

He waved her to a stool, set down a plate of bacon and eggs and clattered cutlery. 'How are you, this morning?'

Libby, ravenously hungry, smiled. 'Much better. You're turning into quite a chef. Has Mandy gone to work?'

'Haven't seen her. I don't think she was here last night.'

Without another word, Libby turned, ran upstairs, and threw open Mandy's door. The room was empty. Either Mandy had left so quietly no one heard her go, or she hadn't slept here last night.

Libby's appetite vanished. She played with breakfast, struggling to force down the food, making light of Mandy's absence. 'She sometimes stays with her friends overnight.'

She sent Max home, pleading a long list of cake commissions. She needed to be alone to phone Mandy. She couldn't share her suspicions with Max at this stage. Not yet.

Max argued, but Libby was adamant. She had work to do. He swallowed the last of the bacon. 'If you're sure you feel OK.'

'Of course. I'm fine.' As he left, Libby's fears returned. She must speak to Mandy before she could relax. She fumbled in the diary with nervous fingers.

She ran a finger down the appointments. Mandy planned to visit Jumbles in Bath, today, discussing orders for Mrs Forest's Chocolates. Libby tried her apprentice's mobile, but it went to voice mail. She swore and tried again. Nothing. Mandy must be in the meeting already. Libby left a text message.

Ring me when you can. Need to talk. Urgent!

Near to tears, she threw the phone down, leaned on a table and buried her face in her hands.

A few long, slow breaths slowed her heart rate. Calm once more, she retrieved the phone and rang Angela's number. She could explain why she'd missed the meeting last night and talk over the horrible business of Samantha and the fire.

Angela let the call go to voice mail. Surely, the police couldn't have arrested her? But, that news would already have been around the town. Libby left a message. 'Sorry I missed the Knitters' Guild. Can we meet, later today?'

Libby's grabbed her phone as it pinged. Was it Mandy?

No, Angela. Libby read the message.

Can't talk just now. Meet later?

Libby would have to be patient. She drummed her hands on the table, frustrated, desperate for action – any action.

* * *

She showered once more, dressed in her oldest clothes, and drove out to Wells. She'd check on Mrs Marchant, to see if the cat had come home, letting Libby off the hook. She'd done almost nothing to find it, so far.

She rang the bell three times, but no one came to the door. Defeated, Libby shrugged and walked back to the car. Today was going from bad to worse.

'Libby Forest?' The hearty voice made her jump. Ruby, one of the knitters, appeared at her shoulder. 'Fancy meeting you here,' she beamed. 'I'm all alone this morning. How about a cup of coffee? Mrs Marchant's out. Taken one of her moggies to the vet, I expect. She loves those animals, bless her. Didn't know you knew her?'

Libby's spirits revived at the prospect of a dose of Ruby's cheerful gossip. 'You live near here?'

'Just over there. Vivian Marchant and I are old friends.'

She led Libby across the narrow road, flung open a red painted door and bustled inside, waving for Libby to follow.

The house, though similar in style to Mrs Marchant's, looked completely different. Floor to ceiling windows flooded the rooms with light, highlighting cushions, curtains and rugs in vibrant shades of purple and green. Libby admired a display of exotic indoor plants. 'Is that a bird of paradise plant?' Her knowledge of plants was worse than patchy, but the display was beautiful.

'My babies,' Ruby laughed. 'In winter, I can't work in the garden, so I keep plants in the house. My husband has his shed outside, to do his little bits of woodwork, but this room is mine.' She sighed. 'I can't wait to get back to my vegetable patch.'

'Your garden's very striking.' Libby joined Ruby at the window, to gaze across a space filled with a riot of bananas, palms and olive trees.

'I never want to go on holiday,' Ruby laughed. 'It's like a tropical island here. You couldn't grow these plants anywhere else in England, you know.' She laughed a good deal, and with every burst of merriment, her chins wobbled and bounced.

A pond near the house looked new. 'We dug that last summer, and we're letting it settle. In spring, we'll be adding the fish. Carp. You know, the fat ones?'

Libby nodded. 'I'd love a pond, but the ground's so heavy in my garden. I tried to dig but I got stuck a few inches down.'

'Oh, the clay! Yes, it took a few weeks to dig my pond. Practise, that's what you need. Take it slowly and build up a few muscles. It's worth it. My garden means everything to me, now my son's grown up.' Ruby's smile was sad. 'I miss him terribly. He left a gap in my life when he moved away, but he's always in my heart. I'd do anything for him. Do you have children?'

Libby told her about Ali, her daughter, saving the south American rain forest. 'My son's getting married soon,' she added, trying not to sound smug. 'In the cathedral.'

Ruby clasped her hands. 'Lucky, lucky you. I hardly see my son, these days. Just two or three times a year. I wish he'd bring a nice young lady home. Women have such a settling effect, don't you think?'

She sighed, her chest heaving. 'Still, mustn't grumble. I have all I want here, and he comes at Christmas. Now, let me get you some cake. Oh.' She collapsed in a chuckling heap on a chair. 'I suppose offering you cake is taking coals to Newcastle, as my mother used to say. Your cakes are famous. Look, I have your book.'

She sorted through a pile on a coffee table, repositioning illustrated gardening books and solid tomes on interior decorating, finally digging out *Baking at the Beach*. 'Would you sign it for me?'

Libby signed, in her usual untidy scribble, as Ruby wiped her eyes and heaved herself up. She disappeared into the kitchen, chuckling, and returned with a tray, still talking. 'Those cats, you know, over the way. Child substitutes. Did I mention that? Old Vivian Marchant drove her family away with her bad temper. The son never visits, not even at Christmas. She's on her own. Of course, Walter and I invited her here. There's always space for another neighbour beside a warm fire at Christmas, don't you agree? Our son was here, on one of his visits, but we could have squeezed a little one like Viv Marchant in. But she wouldn't have it.' Ruby fussed with plates, knives and paper napkins. 'Can't help some people, you know.'

She turned up the gas fire and the temperature rose. Sweating, Libby shrugged off her gilet. 'And another thing...' Libby longed to make notes of Ruby's unending chat, but fearing it might stem the flow of good-natured gossip, she tried to memorise every word instead. Her hostess, uninhibited, had a hint, an insinuation or a piece of downright scandal about everyone.

Ruby filled in the life and habits of every one of her neighbours and the regulars at the cathedral. 'I take flowers there, in the spring and summer. I always say, you can't have too many flowers in God's house. The Dean's wife tells me not to bother, I do too much already for the community, but I believe in giving, don't you? I can always spare time to help folk out.'

'The Dean's wife?' Libby prompted.

'Oh, yes, she's a special friend of mine, you know. "Ruby," she says. "We can always rely on you." Amelia's rather young for a Dean's wife, you know. Sometimes, she just needs a little hint.'

Libby nodded, schooling her face into seriousness, wondering whether the Dean's wife found Ruby overwhelming.

'I suspect there's been trouble in that house.' Ruby took a bite of cake, smudging a little cream on her upper lip. Libby tried not to stare. 'I'm afraid dear Amelia is just a little too welcoming to newcomers, if you get my drift. Especially gentlemen.'

She favoured Libby with a warm, conspiratorial grin. 'A very nice lady, of course. Very nice indeed. I've got a lovely anthurium I promised to give her. She adores the plants in this room, you see, and she wants to have something similar. They say imitation is the sincerest form of flattery, don't they?'

She laughed gaily. Libby, glad of the perfect excuse to talk to Amelia Weir, offered to help. 'Would you like me to deliver the plant for you? I'm going over that way.'

Ruby beamed, swooped on a plant nearby and pushed it into Libby's arms.

Libby, arms full of plant, took that as a signal to leave, but before she could move, the door opened. A bald head slid into view, whispering, 'Anything you want from the shops, dear?' A wiry body followed the head into the room.

'Walter,' Ruby cried. 'Where have you been all morning? In that poky old shed, I suppose, up to your usual nonsense.'

Walter shuffled closer and halted, one foot poised for escape. He shot a longing glance at the door. 'Just finishing that cloche you wanted, dear.' The gentle voice had a soft, Welsh lilt.

'This is Mrs Forest, the *Baking at the Beach* author. She's signed my book.'

He squinted at Libby. 'The famous Mrs Forest, is it? I've heard about your exploits. On the track of a mystery, are you? The killer at the cathedral?'

'I'm looking for a missing cat. It belongs to Mrs Marchant.'

'Not here, I'm afraid. Not allowed in the garden. Lion droppings, that's the answer. Get 'em from the internet, sprinkle on the flower beds. Works a treat.' He rubbed strong hands together. 'Not looking into this affair at the cathedral, then?'

'Sad business, isn't it?'

'So it is. Ah well, no peace for the wicked. Back to the grindstone.' Walter headed for the door and Libby grasped the opportunity to follow.

Ruby lurched to her feet, still chattering. 'We'll be on the lookout for stray cats, Walter and I. Always keen to help our neighbours. Isn't that right, Walter?'

He disappeared, the musical voice floating behind. 'Yes, dear.'

17

CATHEDRAL

Amelia Weir seemed far from pleased to see her visitor. 'If you're looking for the Dean, he's in his office at the cathedral.' Her voice was distant and chilly.

Libby pasted the warmest smile she could manage on her face. 'I was just taking to Ruby. She wanted to send you this plant. It's an anthurium, apparently.'

Stony faced, the Dean's wife took the plant, and deposited it on a semi-circular table in the hall. 'Thank you for delivering it.' She smiled without showing her teeth. 'Ruby is far too generous.'

Amelia Weir was an attractive woman with dark brown hair. Chestnut lights reflected the glow from an impressive chandelier in the cavernous entrance hall. The Dean's second wife, according to Ruby, was many years younger than her widowed husband.

'I know who you are, Mrs Forest. I suppose you've decided to undertake an amateur investigation.' The Dean's wife folded her arms across her chest, the gesture uncertain, defensive. 'I expect you want to know about my relationship with Giles Temple.'

'If you're prepared to tell me, it would certainly save a lot of time.'

'I expect it's all over Wells by now. I was friendly with Giles Temple, but I'm sorry to have to disappoint you. My husband knows about it and there's no mystery.'

She watched Libby's face. Libby, keeping her expression blank, waited in silence. The Dean's wife clicked her tongue as if irritated and continued. 'Giles and I were at university together. Giles studied for a PhD while I was an undergraduate. We had a brief romance, just a few dates, but it didn't go anywhere. We stayed friends and kept in touch. He was happily married and so am I. Our relationship was no secret, and I didn't kill my old friend.'

Amelia's wide blue eyes looked Libby full in the face. Either she was telling the truth, or she was a very accomplished liar.

Libby began, 'I didn't say—'

Amelia interrupted. 'I expect your informants told you I met Giles for a drink a few days ago.' Libby smiled, hoping she looked enigmatic. 'We discussed my husband's birthday. He'll be sixty next month. Giles found a book my husband might enjoy.'

She looked beyond Libby, fingering a gold hoop earring. 'The Dean enjoys medieval history. Giles discovered a fifteenth century Book of Hours for auction next week in Bridgwater. He offered to accompany me, although it will probably fetch a huge amount of money. From internet bidders, you know. Far too much for my pocket. Anyway, I won't be going now. Not on my own. I'll have to think of another gift.'

A slight tremor of Amelia Weir's lips betrayed hidden feeling. Was Giles Temple just a friend, as she claimed? 'If that's all?' The door was already closing and Libby had to step away. She could hardly jam her foot against the elegant grey paintwork.

Thoughtful, she returned to the car. Amelia Weir had gone to considerable trouble to set out the story. Libby could easily check the facts. The Knitters' Guild would know whether the Dean's birthday was imminent, and the local auction house used a catalogue. Amelia had anticipated the need to explain her relationship with the murder victim. However, she'd not supplied an alibi for the time of his death. Libby could not remove either the Dean or his wife from the list of suspects. Not yet.

As Libby started the engine, Angela Miles returned her call. 'Sorry I couldn't talk when you rang. I had an appointment with Joe Ramshore at the station, and he tells me the inquiry's moved on. I'm no longer the only police suspect.' She laughed. 'I'm so relieved. I wish I hadn't bothered you with it all...'

'Don't worry,' Libby said. 'I'm sure hounding you was just spite on the chief inspector's part. He's probably not at work now, after—after the fire. Poor man. It must be devastating for him.'

Angela's tone changed. 'That fire. What a terrible thing to happen. Samantha was difficult, of course, but fire is such a terrible way to go. She must have left candles burning, I suppose. And a thatched roof. Ooh, it makes me shiver to think of it. And you were there, I hear? Poor you.'

'I'd like to talk to you. Where are you? Could we meet?'

'I'm at the cathedral. This is one of the days I volunteer. The library's still closed, but I came to see if I could help out, as everyone's still upset, but to be honest, there's hardly anything for me to do.'

* * *

They found a corner of the cathedral in the South Transept, near the steps of the library entrance. Yellow tape still blocked entry to the library, but the police presence had gone. The organist played something quiet and gentle, and the friends could talk without being overheard.

'I love it in here,' said Angela. 'Even after – you know – what happened, there's a wonderful feeling of peace in a cathedral. I think it's the light. Today's weather is miserable, yet the building looks bright.'

Libby took a deep breath. 'I need you to tell the truth about Giles. I'm not prying or judging you, but if you were more than friends, it suggests a motive for his death. The killer may have been jealous.'

Angela's eyes opened wide. 'I hadn't thought of that.' She sat in silence for a moment. 'Very well, I'll be honest. The truth is, I was attracted to Giles. More than just attracted. For a while, I thought he felt the same.' She swallowed. 'Finally, I had to admit he wasn't in love with me. We were just friends. Giles had plenty of friends. Mostly women. He liked women.'

Libby touched her friend's hand. 'You were in love with him.'

Angela nodded. 'I've been very foolish.' She sighed. 'Giles asked me to meet him the night he died. That's why he was working late. He pretended he was behind with his research and needed to work after hours, and the verger gave him a key. He wanted to be alone with me. He said people were always watching...'

She bit her thumbnail. 'The trouble is...' She looked round, as if expecting to be overheard. 'The trouble is, I didn't go. I was getting ready, putting on makeup. I saw myself in the mirror and I realised what I was doing.' Her voice broke. 'I'd been behaving like a silly middle-aged woman, infatuated with a younger man.' Tears sparkled in her eyes. 'I'm ashamed of myself.'

'Did you tell him you weren't coming?'

Angela looked away. 'I rang him, but when he answered, I lost my nerve. I couldn't explain and I felt so stupid. I just switched off my phone.'

Libby was silent. The police must have checked Angela's phone records. 'Joe says they don't think I killed Giles,' Angela said, 'no matter how bad it looks.'

'I imagine,' Libby was thinking aloud, 'the police are spending more energy on Samantha Watson's death at the moment.'

Angela dabbed at her eyes. 'So dreadful. Poor Samantha...'

She blew her nose. At that moment, a sharp crack echoed round the cathedral. Startled, Libby glanced up. The noise had come from high above her head. A tremor shook the building, like an earthquake, just as Angela shoved Libby hard.

She fell, cracking her arm painfully on the stone floor. Something heavy crashed to the ground inches away, shattering into hundreds of pieces. A cloud of dust rose round Libby's head. 'What the—'

She scrambled to her feet, rubbing an arm. Angela clutched at her. 'I think someone just tried to kill us.'

Horrified onlookers appeared from all over the cathedral.

'Did – did anyone see what happened?' Libby managed to keep her voice steady.

The verger took her arm. 'I've never known one of those fall before. It's unbelievable.'

Libby looked up at the empty space from which a gargoyle used to leer at the congregation. 'Could anyone get up there?'

'Not any more. At one time, you could walk there, but we closed off the passageway a while ago. We decided it was too dangerous for visitors.'

'There's no one up here.' One of the cathedral guides called down.

The verger frowned. 'You could have been badly hurt. I can't understand how such an accident happened.'

'Accident?' Libby fell silent, thinking. *That was no accident. It was deliberate.*

She brushed plaster dust from her hair and Angela's. A circle of worried faces surrounded them. Two guides, a couple of flower arrangers, one clutching a pair of secateurs, and the verger. They looked shocked, not shifty. Whoever deliberately dislodged the gargoyle had escaped in the confusion.

'Neither of us is hurt,' said Libby, suddenly wanting to get out of there. 'Let's go home, shall we?'

* * *

Libby refused offers of tea and trips to hospital. She insisted on driving home, though her hands shook, and her arm ached from the fall. A couple of aspirin would fix that. She was on the right track. If someone tried to kill her, she must have been asking the right questions.

She opened the door and froze, hitting a solid wall of sound, wincing as Joy Division, Mandy's current favourite band, battered her ears. After a moment of total shock, she laughed. Mandy was home now, so they could talk and clear the air. Mandy could put Libby's anxieties to rest. She was bound to have an alibi for the fire. 'Hey,' Libby called. 'I'm back.'

Mandy slouched downstairs, pale face inscrutable, avoiding Libby's eyes. Libby hung up her coat. 'You didn't reply to my messages. I was worried. Did your phone battery run out?'

Mandy shrugged. 'I was with Mum in Bristol. She's getting a divorce. Dad's gone off with another woman and Mum rang yesterday, in a state. She says she never wants another man in her house as long as she lives.'

Mandy's father had a history of violent behaviour. Libby thought he'd left the area long ago. Was Mandy lying? 'I'm sorry to hear that, but you should have called me. I was worried. Did you go to Jumbles today?'

'I rang them. Changed the appointment. No need to fuss.'

Libby's patience ran out. 'Mandy,' she snapped. 'I'm your boss and I'm running a business. You have to tell me when you take a day off, even if it's a family emergency.' She threw her keys on a table, losing her temper. 'The least you can do is text. In future, when I call during working hours, you answer the phone. Got it?'

Mandy shrugged, sullen. 'Sorry.' She turned away, one foot on the lowest stair.

Libby's voice shook with anger. 'Wait just a moment. I suppose you heard about Samantha Watson?'

'I'm sorry she died. Nothing we can do about it though.' Mandy threw the words over her shoulder.

The hairs on the back of Libby's neck rose. She didn't

recognise this Mandy, and the suspicions she'd tried so hard to overcome returned. 'Are you sure you were with your mother all day, and overnight as well?'

'Of course.'

Libby couldn't see her lodger's face. 'The police are checking alibis.' She grabbed Mandy's shoulder to swing her round. 'This is serious, Mandy. I can't help if you don't tell the truth.'

Mandy shrugged the hand away. Her eyes flashed. 'I know you're my boss and I should have let you know what I was doing. I'll make the time up.'

Libby stopped her. 'That's not my point—'

Mandy's furious face shocked Libby. 'I know what you're suggesting. You think I set fire to the cottage. How could you, Mrs F? Don't you know me at all?'

'I don't think that. At least, I don't want to, but you quarrelled with Samantha, you disappeared for the day, and you're – you're different. Mandy, what's happened?'

Mandy sank onto the stair. 'I think maybe I ought to look for somewhere else to live.' Her voice grated. 'You don't trust me.'

'Don't be daft. I like you living here. Anyway, my opinion doesn't matter. Sooner or later the police will interview you. Half of Exham was in the bakery when you quarrelled with Samantha. She was rude and you were furious.'

Libby tried to speak calmly. 'No one blames you for being angry, but the police will need to know everything; where you were yesterday, what you were doing. Everything. It's their job.'

Mandy glared; eyes narrowed. 'I'll talk to the police when I have to. You're my boss, not my mother. I've apologised to Jumbles, and they don't mind. It won't make any difference to your precious business, so leave me alone. And I'll start looking for a flat tomorrow.'

She thundered up the stairs and the bedroom door slammed. Libby wandered into the sitting room and flopped on the sofa, exhausted. A little later, she heard Mandy's rapid footsteps leaving the house. Fear welled in Libby's chest, like sickness. Where had Mandy been yesterday? And where was she going now? Surely, *surely,* Mandy could have nothing to do with Samantha's death.

18

BEACH

Despite a sky full of dark clouds, heavy with rain, Max and Libby refused to cancel their plans for a walk on the beach the next morning. Libby, still shaken by Mandy's sudden hostility, wanted to talk things over with Max. She hoped fresh air might clear her head. She'd hardly slept, disturbed by dreams of Mandy's angry face juxtaposed with images of Samantha's burning house.

Bear, free of restrictions, bounded along the sand to choose one stick after another from the driftwood left by the tide. Max gripped Libby's arm. 'Why didn't you call me? You could have been killed. Imagine how I felt when I heard about the gargoyle attack from Joe.'

'I'm sorry. I was tired. I thought I'd go home and rest before ringing you. Then, Mandy and I quarrelled.' Tears sprang to Libby's eyes. 'Oh, Max. I'm so scared. Mandy's behaviour – it's not like her.' She gulped, afraid of voicing her fears even to Max. 'I'm terrified she might know something about the fire.'

She pulled her scarf tighter against the wind. 'I've been

praying Samantha's death was an accident, but…' Her voice faded. Max had stopped walking. One glance at his face told the truth. Libby stammered, 'What did Joe say about the fire? It was deliberate, wasn't it?'

'I'm afraid so. The police found petrol residue round the front door where the fire started.'

'So, the killer poured petrol through the letter box and set fire to it.' She shivered. 'He'd only need a match, or a lighter.'

'Or one of those kitchen blow torches. Like the one you use for crème brûlée.'

Libby's breath caught in her throat. Mandy had access to the torch. She closed her eyes, thinking. Had she seen the blow torch recently? She kept it safe on a high shelf in the kitchen. If only she could remember… 'Mandy's leaving the cottage,' she blurted out, 'after the row. She says I don't trust her – that I think she killed Samantha, because they quarrelled the other day.'

A sob rose in her throat. 'It's not always easy being a sleuth, is it?'

Max gathered her close, his arms strong and comforting. Libby clung tight, breathing Max's familiar scent. 'I have to solve both murders, now. I need to discover who killed Giles Temple and Samantha, but even if I prove Mandy's innocence, she may never want to speak to me again.'

Max swung Libby round to look into her face as she dragged a hand across damp eyes. 'You're not responsible for Mandy. She's your apprentice and your lodger, but she's an independent woman, not a child. If she set the fire, she must take the consequences. You can't protect her, and you shouldn't try.'

Libby swallowed. 'You're right, I suppose. In any case, it's not my call. The police came about my – er – accident. Actually, Detective Sergeant Filbert-Smythe arrived, just as I was falling asleep. He cross questioned me for ages, and he wants to talk to Mandy when she comes home.'

'Leave it to the police, then. Tell me what happened yesterday, in the cathedral. You don't suspect Mandy of that, do you?'

Libby managed a shaky smile. 'No, of course not. At least, I don't know what to think any more. My head's like cotton wool. Still, this cold wind is helping clear it.'

Her arm ached, and the quarrel with Mandy had left her devastated, but Max's embrace was comforting. Tension seeped away from the muscles in Libby's back and the hard knot in her chest eased. She yawned. 'I'm assuming the gargoyle attack was designed to scare me away. There's a corridor in the cathedral that runs high up behind the carvings. Whoever broke off the gargoyle must have been up there, but they made a quick exit. To be honest, I could almost believe it was an accident. The carvings have been up there since the twelfth century, so I suppose they couldn't last for ever.'

'An accident? When you've been investigating two murders? I don't think so.'

'No.' Libby took a moment to think. 'I must be asking the right questions, but unfortunately, they haven't taken me very far.'

'The killer thinks you know something.'

'The trouble is, I really don't. I've hardly discovered anything, except that Giles Temple was one for the ladies. He could probably take his pick, from the women who do the flowers, through the Knitters' Guild, to the members of the amateur choirs.'

'Well, you must watch your step and keep your eyes open.'

Libby giggled. 'And keep my wits about me, and tread with care...'

Max squeezed her shoulder. 'Well, you know what I mean. Good to know your sense of humour's survived. And you've got some colour in your cheeks, now.'

'The truth is, I'm finding it hard to sort out gossip and rumour from facts,' Libby confessed.

'Use that brain of yours. Think. Why would someone want to kill both Giles Temple and Samantha Watson? What connects them? If we can find a link, we'll have the answer. You've been out and about, talking to the local gossips. What are people saying?'

Libby described her visits. 'I picked up plenty of scandal from Ruby, one of the knitters. She knows everyone at the cathedral and gave me a rundown on who's doing what with whom. Most of it was just gossip. Ruby likes to chat.'

Libby threw a stick for Bear. Concentrating on the facts helped. She felt better, back in control. 'I thought I'd never escape her clutches. She mentioned the Dean's wife, Amelia Weir. Vera, another knitter, had spotted Amelia out and about with the victim, so I made an excuse to visit the Dean's wife. She wasn't pleased to see me, but she has a plausible explanation for the evening she spent with Giles Temple.'

Max asked, 'What about Angela? Was she one of Mr Temple's conquests?'

'That's why Chief Inspector Arnold suspected her at first. Mind you, half the middle-aged ladies in Wells could have been involved with Giles Temple, by all accounts.'

Max was quiet for a moment, whistling. 'Let's consider opportunity. We know where and when Giles died. Who else might stay late in the library?'

'There's the librarian. I'd suspect him, except he's so small and thin, he'd never have beaten Giles Temple in a struggle.' She thought about the cathedral. 'The place is full of vergers and volunteers, not to mention worshippers and visitors. Dozens of people have legitimate business there. It would be easy to hide until the building emptied, and if you were already inside you wouldn't set off the alarms.'

'Let's look at the detail. Giles Temple was strangled with a chain while reading a book. What do we know about the book and chain?'

'The book was old and full of maps. The police have it, but I'm planning to revisit the librarian. Dr Phillips and I got off to rather a bad start, but I think he may have more information. No one knows the library better.'

'Good idea. While you do that, I'll talk to Joe again.'

A watery sun peeped out between the clouds. Libby loosened her scarf and raised her face to the warmth. In a few weeks, spring would arrive, and then Robert's wedding. He and Sarah had returned to London, but he texted Libby almost every day, wanting to know more about her investigation. She would make sure he didn't hear about the episode in the cathedral.

Thinking of Robert reminded her of Max's relationship with his son. 'I'm pleased to see you and Joe getting along so well.'

'That's your influence. Joe admires you. You've made his work easier, and you tolerate me, so I can't be all bad. He's thinking about going for promotion, by the way.

'Good for Joe. He deserves it.'

'Your son seems happy. He and Sarah make a fine couple.'

Libby made a face. 'I wish Ali would come home.'

'Where you can keep her under your wing?'

She laughed. 'You're right. I'm a mother hen, but she' so

far away, and there's no sign she'll be home any time soon. Not even for her brother's wedding. You'd think Robert would be upset, but he just says, "typical Ali."'

'And as if your own children weren't enough, now you worry about Mandy.'

'It started before the fire.' Libby told him about Mandy's break-up with Steve.

Max stopped walking. 'Something just occurred to me. You say Mandy disappeared for the day?'

'On the day of the fire, and overnight. She said she went to see her mother. An emergency.'

Max rubbed his chin. 'I should have realised. That day, I visited Reg in Bristol. He works from an office there and he asked me to review a set of financial documents. At Temple Meads Station, someone climbed out of a taxi and into another car. I thought it was Mandy, but I assumed I was mistaken.'

'Really?' A slow smile spread over Libby's face. Mandy was telling the truth, after all. 'So, she really was visiting her mother in Bristol, though why she left the taxi at the station, I have no idea. Perhaps her mother was picking her up there.'

Max nodded. 'Why didn't she take the train to Bristol? Do you offer such generous expenses for taxis?'

'Not likely. The problem is, Mandy's got a thing about trains. A sort of claustrophobia.'

'Is she getting therapy?'

Libby shrugged. 'I don't know. I suggested it, but I think the idea fell on deaf ears. Still, if you saw her in Bristol, you can provide her alibi for the day of the fire.' Libby took a deep breath, letting it out with a sigh. 'What a relief.'

'Hold on a minute. There's no proof. I can't put my hand on my heart and swear I saw Mandy. The best I can say is that the person I saw looked similar. She wore black clothes, like Mandy's, but she had a scarf wrapped round her head so I couldn't see her face. She moved like Mandy, though, and she had big, heavy boots.'

'Well, your description sounds right. Maybe I don't have to suspect her any more, so you've put my mind at rest.'

'In that case, can we please leave this freezing beach and go home?'

19

KNITTERS' GUILD

The day of the yarnbomb extravaganza was drawing close, so the members of the Knitters' Guild planned to meet on several extra evenings. 'We want to make a splash,' Angela said. 'After all this misery, Wells needs cheering up.' Libby was determined to be there, so she set off once more through the lanes, taking a new route to avoid any sight of the burnt-out shell of Samantha's house.

The Guild had expanded. Several members, new to Libby and all experienced and competent knitters, had added their contributions. Knitted items swamped the trestle tables. Libby, embarrassed, tried to hide her uneven squares, but Angela grabbed them. 'They don't have to be perfect.'

June scooped fingers through the green stripe in her hair until it stood on end. 'Pop them on the table, my love. We're all friends, here. Colour and spectacle matter, but the odd dropped stitch won't hurt.'

Vera sniffed. 'At least they're bright.' Angela grouped colours together, shifting them around until even Libby saw a pattern emerging.

Ruby threw her arms around Angela. 'You have a wonderful eye, my dear.' Angela wrinkled her nose at Libby over Ruby's shoulder.

As the ladies sewed squares together to make blankets, Vera led the gossip. 'I heard about the gargoyles. Now, what do you think? Was it an accident or did Giles Temple's killer set a trap?'

June shook her head. 'In a cathedral. Unbelievable.'

Ruby munched a fruity scone. 'You're so brave, both of you. If it had been me, I'd stay safe at home and I wouldn't set foot in the cathedral until the police caught the killer.'

Vera interrupted. 'I forgot to tell you. The Dean said he'd drop in this evening. He's very excited about our little event.'

On cue, the door opened, and the Dean made an entrance, smiling at each lady in turn, stroking a mane of neat, groomed grey hair. Libby nudged Angela. 'I wonder how long he spends every morning blow-drying his hair,' she whispered.

'Good evening, ladies.' The voice was resonant. Libby could imagine the Dean reading a lesson, filling the cathedral with sound. The effect on some of the ladies made her smile. They fluttered around the room, searching out the prettiest cup and offering scones piled high with cream and jam.

The Dean sank gracefully into a chair, inspected manicured nails, and turned his attention to the knitted goods. 'The Bishop is most impressed with your work, good ladies. He's looking forward to the yarnbombing.'

'He doesn't think it's inappropriate after the murder?' Vera asked.

'Good heavens, no. We need a happy event to encourage community spirit. Have you decided on the date?'

'Next Wednesday,' June boomed. 'Which means we'll get

together on Tuesday evening and work through the night, decorating the city.'

The Dean extracted a diary from his pocket and made a note. 'Excellent. Please come to the cathedral after Evensong on Tuesday, for a short blessing.' He turned to Libby and Angela. 'I must apologise most sincerely to you two, on behalf of everyone at the cathedral, for your dreadful accident.'

Angela thanked him. 'No lasting harm done. The statue missed us both. I suppose it will need repair?'

He raised a hand. 'No need to worry. We have a contract with a firm of masons. The Bishop asked me to tell you how sorry he is for your fright.' He'd decided the event was an accident, and there was little point in arguing.

'Now,' he continued, 'to the other reason I came. I bring invitations to a special lunch tomorrow. It's a small thank you for such hard work.' He beamed at Libby. 'My wife asked me to give a special welcome to you, Mrs Forest and Mrs Miles, after your fright. Please bring that charming dog.'

Libby gulped. 'Do you mean Bear? He's very big.'

Angela giggled. 'I'm afraid 'big' doesn't do him justice. The creature's enormous.'

The Dean smiled. 'Amelia, my wife, is exceedingly fond of dogs.'

20

CATS

With so many events crowding into the past few days, Libby had done nothing about Mrs Marchant's missing cat. To put matters right next morning, she set off early to distribute posters. She had plenty of time before lunch with the Dean.

She walked the streets of Wells, fixing photographs of the missing cat to lamp posts. She called into almost every shop near the town centre as they opened, begging the owners to display posters. 'Have you seen this cat?' the text read, alongside a cute photo of Mrs Marchant's missing Mildred. When Libby told the sad story of the anonymous elderly lady who rescued cats, most shopkeepers agreed to help.

The proprietor of one antique shop seemed inclined to talk. Her store was stacked high with brass instruments and fishing tackle, but empty of customers. 'I think I know who you mean. Mrs Marchant, isn't it? I feel sorry for the woman. She looks lonely and I sometimes offer her a cup of tea.' She grew confidential. 'She's gone downhill, you know. I met her at the school gates when our children were young. She was beautifully dressed and, well, to be honest, too posh to talk much to the likes of me. I don't know what happened in her life. How the mighty are fallen.'

The woman leaned on the counter while Libby, keen to keep the conversation going, admired a telescope. 'Mrs Marchant has a son, I believe, but he doesn't live round here.' Libby shuddered at the price on the telescope's ticket and moved on to a blue glass fishing float.

The store keeper continued, 'They quarrelled a few years ago. Her son lives a few miles away, I think, but I don't know the address.'

Libby visited more shops, and although almost everyone was sympathetic, and several recognised her description of Mrs Marchant, none had seen the cat.

At last, feet aching, she taped the final photograph to a lamp post near the marketplace. It had all taken far longer than she'd expected, she was freezing cold, it was starting to rain, the cold drizzle sliding inside Libby's collar, and she was beginning to doubt the efficacy of this approach to finding Mildred.

'Excuse me.'

Libby turned. 'Can I help you?'

A woman in a bulky purple anorak pointed to the photograph. 'That's my cat.'

Libby frowned. 'Are you sure? Her name's Mildred. She belongs to an elderly lady and she went missing a few days ago, not far from here.'

'No. It's Jesse. She went out weeks ago and we haven't seen her since. We've been scouring the streets. My daughter was desperate, but then, Jesse arrived home the other day, all by herself.'

Libby swallowed. 'How can you tell it's Jesse?' This was all she needed – a squabble over a cat.

The woman pointed at the poster. 'You see that white mark on her nose?' Libby peered. The mark was just visible. 'That's Jesse, all right. I can show you a photo.' She pulled out a mobile phone and thrust it at Libby.

It was true. Mildred was, in fact, Jesse. Libby apologised. 'I think your cat's been rescued by mistake.'

The woman's face remained stony. 'Then your old lady should be ashamed of herself. It's a disgrace, that's what it is. You tell me where she lives. I'll go and give her a piece of my mind.'

Libby blessed the foresight that had led her to put her own contact details on the poster. A confrontation between this woman and Mrs Marchant could only end in trouble. 'I'm afraid I can't give you that information.' She spoke cheerfully, hoping to placate the angry cat owner, 'It was a genuine mistake.' She hoped she was right. 'Your cat's been well looked after. Mrs – er – the lady who rescued Jesse was convinced she was a stray.'

The anorak woman put her phone back in her pocket, mollified. 'Well, I suppose it's confusing when cats arrive on your doorstep. I expect Jesse went looking for food. She's always been greedy. She's sometimes broken into my neighbours' houses.'

She walked away, still talking and Libby wiped her wet face. The rain pelted down, harder than ever. *I suppose I'll have to collect all the posters and confront Mrs Marchant.*

Half an hour later, arms full of soggy posters, she returned to the car. She'd never imagined private investigation would be so hard on the legs.

Mrs Marchant threw the door open. 'Have you got good news?'

'Well, yes and no.' Libby explained that Mildred was in fact Jesse, owned by a different family. She coughed, broaching a difficult subject. 'Perhaps you should take your strays to the vet. She could read their microchips. You know, the cat's details, hidden under the skin.'

Mrs Marchant looked doubtful. 'Oh dear, I suppose I should.'

Libby bit her lip, telling herself to walk away. She'd finished the job, and this was none of her business. Before she could move, she heard herself say, 'How often do you go out looking for stray cats?'

'Oh, most evenings. There's nothing else to do now my television's broken.'

The poor woman was lonely. 'Do you know many of your neighbours? I was here the other day and I spoke to Ruby, who lives across the road. She's very friendly and I'm sure she'd love to meet up for tea or coffee.'

She'd made a mistake. Mrs Marchant snorted. 'Ruby Harris? She's no better than she should be, that one. Thinks herself so perfect. Well, she wasn't so high and mighty when she had that son of hers.' Mrs Marchant dropped her magnificent voice to a feline hiss as she repeated, 'No better than she should be.' Libby hid a smile. She'd heard that expression years ago, about an unmarried woman with a child.

'Oh, yes.' Mrs Marchant was getting into her stride. 'Shacked up with a man from the railway, she was. He ran off with a foreign dancer and left the country. I'll give her credit; Ruby made a good job of bringing up her son alone. Then she met her husband. Weak as water, Walter Harris, taking on another man's child.'

She sniffed. 'Of course, she wants me visiting her. She asked at Christmas, you know. Wanting to show off that enormous television, I suppose.'

Libby abandoned the subject of neighbours. 'Talking of television,' she ventured. 'Maybe your Terence could buy a new one.'

Mrs Marchant emitted a noise somewhere between a cough and a grunt. 'Not he.'

Libby wasn't giving up, yet, although it was hard to help this awkward old lady. She had an idea. 'The Cats Protection League. They collect strays. Why not get in touch with them? They'd help you check the microchips and you wouldn't have to pay.' Perhaps the League would find better homes for some of those cats.

She'd at last hit on something of which Mrs Marchant approved. 'I can't bear to think of those poor homeless animals. Someone must save them, but I sometimes wish I had help. It's cold and dark in the winter. A few nights ago, I had the fright of my life. I was on the green by the cathedral, heading for Vicar's Close. I like walking down there. Sometimes, you hear children from the school practising their music, you know.'

Libby often walked Bear along the medieval cobbles of the Close. She understood its attraction. Mrs Marchant talked on. 'A man and a woman were whispering. When I came near, they hid under the archway. I thought they might jump out and rob me so I hurried past as fast as I could.' She tutted, loudly. 'All these people begging, that's the trouble these days.'

'What night was that?'

'I remember it well, because the next day I heard about that dreadful murder. Imagine. I was near the cathedral at the same time as the killer. I said to myself, "Vivian, that could have been you." Made me shiver to think of it.'

'Have you told the police? Given descriptions?'

'They haven't bothered to ask. No one takes any notice of me, these days.' Mrs Marchant was on her high horse again. The mood changes were unpredictable and disconcerting.

'The police don't know you were there,' Libby pointed out.

The woman shrugged. 'If you like I'll tell you about them and you can pass it on.'

Libby took that as a compliment. 'Go on.'

'Well, one was big and fat and the other tall and thin. I couldn't see what they were wearing because it was dark.'

The descriptions were disappointing. Libby tried another question. 'You said they were whispering. Did you catch what they said?'

'Not really. The tall, thin one wore a hoodie. I remember that. It muffled the words, you see.'

Libby suspected Mrs Marchant's hearing might be failing, but pride would prevent the woman admitting it. 'You're sure it was a man?'

'Oh, yes, definitely.' The old lady paused. 'I'm not sure about the fat one. Could have been male or female. They all dress the same, these days.' She held a finger in the air. 'Now, wait. I remember they had a bag. The thin one handed it over to the other before they split up. The thin one went along Vicar's Close and the fat one crossed over the road towards the cathedral.'

'Really?' Two people behaving suspiciously in the dark, on the night Giles Temple was murdered. Libby could hardly speak for excitement. What a good thing she'd taken on the job of finding the missing cat.

Unfortunately, despite Libby's efforts to help her remember, Mrs Marchant was unable to add more detail. Taking a different approach, Libby tried to persuade her to tell Joe about the two mysterious figures. In the end, she turned to bribery. 'While you speak to the police officer, I'll see if I can find a new television for you.'

'One with a bit of sound. Everyone mutters, these days.'

21

LUNCH

'I'm not invited to the Dean's lunch?' Max lay in an armchair, feet on Libby's coffee table.

'Members of the Knitters' Guild only, I'm afraid. Unless you bring proof of your knitting ability, I'm afraid you're excluded.'

'Just as well, I suppose. But I'm offended that Bear's invited while I'm not.'

'Bear is much fluffier and cuddlier.'

Max stretched out a foot to trip Libby and she fell into his lap. 'Don't mess my hair. I must look respectable for the Dean.' She preened. She'd chosen her favourite bright jade silk blouse and skin-tight embroidered trousers. 'Not too dressy for lunch, is it?'

'You look beautiful. I'm jealous.'

Libby snorted. 'Don't forget, his wife will be there. I'm not convinced the so-called special invitation came from her, though. She seemed hostile when I called at the house. Still, I can't refuse. She's near the top of my list of suspects, though I'm hoping Mrs Marchant's suspicious lurkers are a better bet. I wonder what they were up to in the dark, that night.'

'Probably drug dealers.'

'You could be right. Anyway, I rang Joe, and he promised to pay a visit to Mrs Marchant, and not send one of the team.' She laughed. 'Meanwhile, I have to find a TV for the old lady. Somehow, I found myself promising I would.'

'Typical. Making work for yourself.'

'Maybe, but I mean to persuade her son to contribute. I think it's time he gave her a helping hand, don't you? I'll see if I can track him down. But, in the meantime, I'm off to the Dean's lunch party. It's a wonderful opportunity to snoop.'

She glanced at her watch and struggled away. 'Look at the time. I need to go. It won't do to be late and I agreed to take Angela.'

It felt strange, leaving Max alone in the little cottage. He'd stayed there before, and one day he even cleaned the bathroom. Libby almost died of shock. Her husband had never lifted a duster. Since the gargoyle affair, Max had spent every spare moment in the cottage and Libby, to her surprise, enjoyed his constant presence.

At the Dean's imposing property, Amelia played the gracious hostess, more glamorous than ever in a multicoloured silk blouse and blue harem pants. She stretched out a hand. 'Thank you so much for coming,' she said. 'I was in a rush, that day you brought Ruby's plant. I didn't have time to chat. I hope I wasn't rude.'

Libby stitched a smile on her face and lied. 'Of course not. And thank you for inviting Bear today. He's very honoured and on his best behaviour. So far.' Amelia pat ted Bear. Maybe she really had insisted he attend. She certainly looked pleased to see him.

The ladies sat, subdued, nursing a variety of drinks. Vera restricted herself to water, but June gulped gin and tonic, drained the glass and looked round for more. Other ladies held glasses of white wine while Ruby sipped from a tumbler of orange juice.

Libby, soft drink in hand, mindful she must soon drive home, settled next to Ruby. 'I'm so glad you're here. I wanted to tell you we found Mrs Marchant's missing cat. Except, as it turned out, the cat wasn't a stray. It was all a mistake. Anyway, all's well that ends well.'

Ruby beamed. 'I went to see Mrs Marchant yesterday and took her one of my sausage casseroles. I pride myself on being a good neighbour and letting bygones be bygones. She wasn't very grateful, but we must persevere with those less fortunate than ourselves. I never want thanks. The deed is enough reward.'

Vera overheard. 'Playing Lady Bountiful again, Ruby?'

Libby excused herself and moved next to June. Amelia perched on her other side, clutching a wine glass so tightly Libby feared the stem would snap.

Bear, who until then had lounged behind a chair, chose that moment to glance through the French doors. He caught sight of a black and white cat digging under an apple tree at the bottom of the garden, leapt to his feet, galloped to the doors and barked at the top of his voice.

Amelia followed and threw open the doors. A blast of cold air rushed into the overheated drawing room. 'He can run in the garden. Maybe he'll stop the local cats using it as a litter tray. I wish your Mrs Marchant would collect more of those animals. They're forever digging up our plants.'

Angela said, in her gentle voice, 'I think Mrs Marchant is lonely and looking for something to love.'

'Perhaps,' Vera suggested, an edge to her voice, 'she should have stayed on better terms with her son.'

They gathered to admire the garden. 'The pond will soon be full of frogs,' Amelia said. 'I can't thank you enough for helping me dig, Ruby. I'd never have managed it alone.'

Vera sniggered. 'Do you keep fish in it? No wonder cats come.'

'We did, but they were eaten. It was very sad.'

Libby thought the lunch party would never end. By the time they'd finished the last chocolate mousse and risen from the table, she felt uncomfortably full. She was tired of listening to Vera and Ruby sniping and nothing she'd heard today seemed at all useful.

The sky hung grey and heavy as the early winter evening closed in. Libby longed to make excuses and leave, just as Amelia whispered in her ear. 'Bear's still having a wonderful time in the garden. Shall we throw balls for him?'

Libby glanced round. The other guests were in small huddles, discussing the yarnbombing. Amelia had seized the opportunity for a private talk, so perhaps the day could still be productive.

She wasted no time. 'I want to apologise again for the way I behaved.' She tossed a brand-new tennis ball from hand to hand, finally throwing it for Bear to chase. Thrilled, he galloped in its wake. 'You see, I wasn't entirely honest with you about Giles Temple.'

Libby nodded, trying to hide her excitement. Did the Dean's wife mean to confess?

'It's perfectly true we've been friends since university,' Amelia continued, 'but we became much closer a few years ago.' She looked across the garden, eyes unfocused, as though gazing into the past.

Bear returned with a well-chewed tennis ball. Amelia, startled, took a step back, hands raised to protect her clothes. Drool dripped from Bear's jaws as he offered the sodden object, and Amelia winced as she held it at arm's length. 'I'm afraid my husband doesn't know that Giles and I had – well...' She hesitated. 'I suppose you could say we had an affair.'

Libby held her breath as she continued, 'I told you I knew Giles at university. We bumped into each other again several years ago. He was married, but I wasn't. I worked in Manchester at the time – in the library.' Amelia seemed to be struggling for words.

'Giles came in, quite by chance, looking for some book or other. He was a very attractive man, as I'm sure you've heard.' She looked Libby in the eye. 'I believe your friend Angela had some feelings for him.'

The sudden hint of malice was over in a flash. 'Our affair lasted for over a year.'

Amelia concentrated on folding the hem of her blouse into tiny pleats. 'He didn't tell me he was married, but I became suspicious. There was a pattern. For example, he never saw me during half term or school holidays. When it came to Christmas, he made one excuse after another, and wouldn't spend the day with me. I still didn't understand. At least, I didn't let myself see the truth. I suppose that's what happens when a woman imagines herself in love.' Giles Temple was turning out to be a real piece of work.

'After that, I followed Giles a few times, without his knowledge, until one Saturday morning I saw him in the park with some children. Two girls. They called him Daddy.' Amelia's cheeks turned crimson. 'I'm not proud of spying on him but at least I found out the truth.' She shot a glance at Libby. 'Of course, you know about following people and spying on their lives. You do it in your line of work, as an investigator.' She almost spat the word.

'Later, I confronted him, and he confessed. He told me I wasn't the only other woman.' She sniffed. 'He wasn't the man I thought. Not at all. I felt used and dirty and I planned to tell his wife the truth.'

'But you didn't.'

'No, I wasn't that cruel. Instead, a wonderful thing happened, like a fairy tale. I went into the local church. It was quiet and I wanted to think. I was very unhappy. Quite by chance I dropped my handbag and a stranger picked it up. That man became my husband. We fell in love and he saved me.'

She blew her nose on a lace handkerchief and gave a watery smile. 'The trouble is, he's such a moral person. I never told him about Giles and I don't want him to know. He might not forgive me.'

Libby frowned. Wouldn't a man of the church forgive her sins? 'You must have been horrified when Giles appeared in Wells.'

'The word horrified hardly covers my feelings.' Amelia hid her eyes behind one hand. 'I spoke to him after a service and asked him to meet me. We met in the pub and I begged him not to tell my husband. I knew meeting in public was risky, but I couldn't have him in my husband's house, and I certainly wasn't going to visit him in rented rooms.'

She gave a sad little laugh. 'I couldn't understand what I'd seen in him. He was still handsome and full of compliments, but he made me shiver.' Her shoulders twitched at the memory. 'Soon after, Vera told me Angela had been seeing him. I meant to warn her – tell her what Giles was like – but before I could say anything, someone killed him.'

She looked at Libby through wide eyes. 'I had no need to kill him. He'd agreed not to tell my husband. Why would he? He didn't want trouble any more than I did.'

She clutched Libby's arm. 'Please, promise you won't tell a soul.'

Libby shook her away, gently. 'I can't promise. I shall Max, because we work together, and Joe needs to know. I won't mention it to the Dean, though, and Joe will only tell him if it becomes necessary for the case.' She took a long breath. 'But, maybe you should think about telling the truth to your husband. After all, you weren't married when you knew Giles.'

Amelia shook her head. 'I can't tell him. I just can't...'

Libby shrugged. 'I'll leave that to you. The real question is, do you have an alibi for the evening Giles Temple died?'

'That's the trouble.' Amelia's face was creased with anxiety. 'I was alone at home and my husband was at a prayer meeting, so I have no alibi at all.'

22

CLIFTON

Mrs Marchant's situation weighed on Libby's conscience. The woman was suffering. She wasn't the kind to fit in with her neighbours, go to classes or join groups and societies. She'd be unlikely to turn up at the Knitters' Guild armed with a pair of sharp needles and several balls of brightly coloured wool. Living alone in a house unhealthily full of cats, though, was no life. Libby had played a part in bringing Max and Joe together. Why couldn't she do the same with Mrs Marchant and Terence?

First, she had to find the woman's son. That shouldn't be too difficult. She thought back to the conversation in Mrs Marchant's house. Had she told Libby where her son might be living? Libby flipped through the notes she'd made and grinned, pleased with her attention to detail. Terence Marchant lived about thirty miles away. She pulled out a road map and drew a circle round Exham. There weren't many places within range.

'South Somerset,' she murmured. 'Wiltshire and Dorset, plus a bit of Devon, and in the other direction, Weston-Super-

Mare and Bristol. Well, that shouldn't take too long.' After an hour's research she had two Marchants on her list living in the right area. The on-line census made it clear one resident was far too old to be Mrs Marchant's son. That left just one candidate. Triumphant, Libby set off in the purple Citroen to visit Terence.

She found a comfortable, detached house in Clifton with two expensive cars parked on the drive: a Jaguar XJ series and a BMW 7 series. A handsome, blond god with very white, even teeth came to the front door. Libby mentioned cats and he raised his eyes to the sky. 'You'd better come in. My mother adores those ghastly creatures. I tried to convince her to give them away and clean the house but she took no notice. Now why don't you sit down and tell me all about it. How did you become involved?'

He seemed friendly but Libby wasn't sure she trusted the man. His eyes were very sharp and his lips rather red and full. Not her type. Still, she wasn't there for pleasure. She'd say her piece and leave as soon as possible.

She sat on a pale couch in a minimalist room. No photos or ornaments cluttered the surfaces and she saw no sign of any books. Libby wondered if the room had a sliding wall to hide shelving. She'd seen one in a magazine. She looked in vain for traces of another person in the house. Terence Marchant appeared to live alone.

'I don't want to interfere, but I'm worried about your mother,' Libby confessed. 'She asked me to look for her lost cat, but it turned out it didn't belong to her at all.'

'I suppose she'd rescued it,' her son groaned. 'No cat's safe from my mother.'

'Well, I'm not sure she's looking after herself properly, never mind the cats. There are so many of them.'

'I'm afraid it's her own choice.' His voice sounded harsh. 'I offered to pay for a cleaning woman and have regular meals delivered but she won't let me. Was she forgetful when you were there?'

Libby thought back. 'No, not really. I think she's deaf, though.' No harm in taking the bull by the horns. 'Have you seen her recently?'

He leaned back in his chair, quite at ease. 'I can't visit as often as I'd like. I have to earn a living you know.' Something about his bright blue eyes made Libby uncomfortable. They held her gaze a little too long and his smile couldn't disguise their cold stare. 'Let me get you a cup of coffee.'

'No, thank you.' She didn't want to spend a moment longer than necessary in this cold, featureless room. She forced herself not to stammer. 'I thought I'd get in touch with the Cats Protection League and maybe ask Age UK to visit.' Was she overstepping the line?

On the contrary, Terence Marchant nodded, happy for her to take responsibility. 'That would be wonderful. I'm afraid I don't know what's available for old people once they go doolally.' He clamped his mouth shut, as though he'd let his true feelings show.

Libby decided to probe a little more. 'What a beautiful room.' She resisted the temptation to cross her fingers behind her back. She'd hate to live in such soulless surroundings.

He smiled, unnaturally white teeth gleaming. His skin was light orange, either from trips abroad or visits to the tanning parlour. Pretending to search for a handkerchief in her bag, Libby leaned forward to inspect his shoes. The soft brown leather had been polished to a gloss. 'You're lucky to catch me at home today. I'm not often here. My business is based in London and I'm away most of the week. The train ride from

Paddington leaves much to be desired, so I come back to Bristol as rarely as possible. I'm here this week for the opening of one of my shops.'

Libby's bag slipped from her fingers and fell to the floor. She'd thought the name was familiar. 'You own Marchant's coffee shops?' The chain sold overpriced espressos and a range of exotic teas. There was one in Taunton.

'That's me. We're about to open more branches in the West Country, starting with Axminster and Exham.' Libby stifled a gasp as he went on, oblivious to her shock. 'A decent up-market café and patisserie should wake those sleepy little places up.'

Libby bridled. 'Do you think there's room for another patisserie? I live in Exham and it seems quite happy as it is.'

He laughed. 'Of course, that's what residents think. They're always scared of change in an old-fashioned town like Exham. I've done my research, I can assure you. As soon as my place is open, customers will flood in. I quite understand your concerns, Mrs Forest.'

He gave a thin smile, and Libby realised he'd been goading her into a reaction. His research had identified Libby as the competition. 'We'll be offering high concept pastries. There's no need to be worried.'

Libby's head buzzed with fury as she left the house and made her way to her Citroen. The aging car looked small and battered alongside Terence Marchant's highly polished, expensive vehicles.

She rang Max. 'Condescending, calculating brute,' she fumed. 'He'll be trying to put us out of business. High concept pastries, indeed. What's more, he has no intention of looking after his own mother.'

'Mrs Marchant's not your problem, Libby. Let it go.'

'I can't. He could at least pay for her new television. He's loaded.'

'Did you ask him to?'

Libby fidgeted, uncomfortable. 'Well, no. He distracted me with all that talk of pastries.' She kicked a stone down the road. 'I suppose that's what he intended. He took me for a ride.'

'Libby, if it will calm you down, I'll pay for a new television for the woman. It'll be worth it. But you have to promise to stop trying to solve every problem in Somerset.'

'I could kiss you.'

'Then that's my mission accomplished. Come and have lunch. Reg is here and he's dying to talk to you. I'll get Joe to come if he can.'

'I'll be there, but I've a job to do first. I'm visiting the librarian. It's time we got to the bottom of all this.'

23

LIBRARIAN

On the way into the cathedral, Libby almost bumped into the Dean. He aimed a cool nod in her direction. Perhaps Bear's antics in the garden had annoyed him.

She searched for the librarian. Deprived of access to his beloved library, he'd moped around until someone found space for him in a tiny office, where he sat at a desk, tapping his bald head with the fingers of one hand. His cheeks had faded and shrunk since she last saw him.

Remembering their unfortunate meeting on the stairs, Libby exhibited her most perfect manners. 'Thank you so much for agreeing to see me. As you know, my friend Angela has been caught up in this sad business of Giles Temple's death. She was friendly with Giles.'

The librarian acknowledged that with an inclination of the head, and Libby continued, 'Angela told me a little about the books he was interested in, but she doesn't know much. I don't think they discussed literature. Can you tell me any more? What was his research area?'

'Ah.' She'd hit on the right topic. The little librarian's

cheeks glowed and his eyes lit up. 'Giles was a scholar, you know. A real enthusiast for ancient texts. He planned to work here for another three or four weeks, fact checking.'

'I gather his interest was history. Something about Thomas Cranmer?'

'That's right, he was working through Thomas Cranmer's student books.'

Libby smiled. 'They must be incredibly valuable.'

'Priceless, I'd say, although not illuminated like some of the other books we have. Still, they're full of Cranmer's notes, in his own handwriting.'

Dr Phillips warmed to his topic, excited by Libby's interest. 'I'd be glad to show you some of our most beautiful books. You could return under happier circumstances, when all this is over.' He waved a hand vaguely.

'What were the books about?'

'Where's your history, my dear?' He sighed, his tone hinting at years of disappointment with ignorant students. 'They dealt with the old beliefs in relics and other superstitions of the Catholic Church before the Reformation.'

He rubbed his hands. 'You see, in those days, people thought they needed sacred objects to ward off evil. They believed in the devil then.'

Libby thought about the murders. 'They might have been right. Perhaps we should pay more attention to wickedness.'

'Ah, well, we do,' he exclaimed. 'Every archbishopric has someone delegated and trained whose job it is to deal with the devil.'

'You mean, providing – what is it – exorcism? Does that still go on?'

'Yes, indeed.'

Libby moved on. 'I wondered if you could say any more

about the chain used to kill Mr Temple. It's such an unusual way to store books.'

'Oh, yes, the chain. This is one of the few chained libraries in England, you know. Let me show you.' He pulled a photo out of his jacket pocket. 'I can't show you the books themselves as the library's still off-limits, but this picture illustrates the mechanism.' Libby scrutinised the picture. 'You see, one end of the chain is attached to the book and the other end to the shelf. The position of the chain makes it easy to pull the book from the shelf and read it, but it prevents people from borrowing a book, wandering away with it, and forgetting to bring it back.'

'Like forgetting to return library books?'

'Exactly. You'd be amazed at the number of upright citizens with old library books in their houses; books they should have returned years ago. Well, the canons of the seventeenth century were just as bad. Hence the chain.'

Libby pointed to the photograph. 'That chain looks incredibly strong. It would take a lot of force to break it away from the book, wouldn't it? And how would the murderer remove it from the shelf?' She frowned. 'It seems a crazy way to kill anyone.'

The librarian jumped up and snapped his fingers. 'Why didn't I think of this before? The killer didn't have to remove a chain from a book. I keep spares in a box.'

'Spare chains?' Libby's heart thumped. 'Where's the box?'

'At the back of the library.'

'So, anyone could grab one of the spare chains?'

'Of course. The box isn't hidden. The chains have no value in themselves.'

Libby laughed aloud. She'd supposed the killer had planned the murder with care and taken along heavy-duty cutters for the chain. Dr Phillips' revelation changed all that. Perhaps the murder had not been planned, after all. Giles Temple was simply in the wrong place at the wrong time.

* * *

Over cheese, salad and crusty bread, Libby recounted her meeting with the librarian to Max, Reg and Joe. She put her worries over the sad cat woman and the unpleasant Terence to one side. 'You see, we've been concentrating on the victim, trying to work out why someone would want to kill Giles Temple. That's why we were so interested in Amelia Weir, and why the police suspected Angela, but perhaps we've all been on the wrong track. What if this isn't about Giles, but the library itself?'

Reg, eating with appreciative gusto from a heaped plate, grinned. 'That's exactly what I wanted to talk to you about. Did you know there's a huge international market in stolen books?'

'Like the art market? You often hear about the theft of paintings, but I've never heard much about books.'

'That's true, ma'am. It happens pretty much under the radar. I shouldn't tell you this, but that's why I'm in the area. On behalf of the International League of Antiquarian Booksellers.'

Libby tried not to laugh. 'Seriously? That's a thing?'

'Sure is. They maintain a database of stolen books and manuscripts.'

'Are you about to tell me the book Giles Temple was reading is on the stolen list? Wouldn't the librarian know?'

'The book didn't come from Wells. It's on the list, but it was reported missing from another library.'

'Let me get this straight. On the day Giles Temple died, a book appeared in the library, from nowhere. No one in Wells noticed it, but the killer knew it was there.'

She spoke slowly, trying to figure it out. 'Giles happened to be there, for an assignation with Angela, when the killer arrived. He was murdered to stop him talking.'

She shivered. 'If Angela had gone to meet him as planned, she could have been killed as well. But why would anyone kill over an old book? It doesn't make sense. We must be missing something.'

Max said, 'All this leaves us no further on. We still don't know the identity of the two people seen by the cat woman, and we don't know who stole the book, or why it matters so much. I don't even think we can discount Amelia Weir. No one can support her explanation of the meeting with Giles Temple. What other suspects do we have?'

'The cat woman saw two figures that night. One took something from the other and disappeared in the direction of the cathedral. It's only circumstantial but I bet that was the murderer.'

Joe mused aloud. 'Amelia Weir could be the small, thin person seen in Wells that night. Could the Dean be the other?'

Libby leapt to her feet. 'I've had an idea. I've been wondering about the connection between Giles and Samantha. What if I couldn't find one because it doesn't exist? Maybe the connection is between Samantha and the book thief. She was a solicitor, after all. She worked with criminals. I think a visit to her chambers is the next step.'

Joe was thoughtful. 'Good idea. We've already interviewed the head of chambers and looked through the files, but no one's found any cases handled by Samantha, other than divorces and a few minor criminals. My men are cross-checking, but it's a slow job and there's nothing to stop you poking around as well.'

He looked at his watch. 'I've got to get back to the station. It's awkward as the moment. Some of my colleagues are like headless chickens. Chief Inspector Arnold's gone on sick leave. He came back in for a few hours, but he couldn't cope. There's no way he could work on Samantha's case. He handed over to another chief, drafted in from an inner-city police service.'

'That'll be a shock to his system,' Libby said, remembering how strange Exham on Sea had felt when she first arrived.

'He's come down from Birmingham with a great record but precious little feel for country ways. Let me know how you get on.'

Joe paused on the way out. 'By the way, officially, we haven't talked.'

24

SOLICITORS

The solicitors' offices filled the ground floor of a Victorian building in the oldest part of Exham. Painted bright blue, the building overlooked the beach. As Libby and Max sat in a stuffy waiting room, they could see along the beach as far as the nine legged lighthouse. 'It seems such a long time since the murder at the lighthouse. I was walking Shipley, Marina's dog. I miss that crazy springer spaniel, you know, and I think Bear does, too, since Marina went. I walked past her house the other day. There's a sale sign on the drive, and Shipley is still homeless.'

'I think Exham on Sea can live without Marina and her overbearing ways,' said Max. 'What will happen to Shipley?'

'The vet's looking after him. I'd like to adopt him but he's so wild. He needs more training.' Shipley was quite a handful. 'I'm thinking about it.'

'Because you have so much time to spare?' Max raised his eyebrows. 'Maybe I could help.'

'Help? You mean?'

'I love having Bear around, and I have space. Why not find a companion for him?'

'Would you really? Bear would be thrilled.'

Libby forgot about dogs as the receptionist returned to the waiting room. 'I'll ask Mr Scruggs to come in. He's the senior partner and he might be able to help you.'

Libby tried her best smile on Mr Scruggs, a formidable man with a hooked nose and rapidly receding hair. He nodded a greeting, his attention on Max. 'Mr Ramshore. We haven't seen you at the Rotary Club for a while.'

Max introduced Libby, a half-smile on his face. 'This is my associate, Mrs Forest.'

Mr Scruggs looked Libby over from top to toe. 'The chocolate lady, I believe.' The corner of his lip lifted in a smile that was almost a sneer. Libby found the atmosphere oppressive. How had Samantha worked in this place, where women were second best?

Reluctantly, Libby allowed Max to ask the questions. Mr Scruggs would give more information to a fellow member of the Rotary Club. 'As you know, Mr Scruggs, I've worked with the police on several matters of interest to the government,' Max began.

'Oh yes, indeed. I remember.'

'You've been very helpful in the past.' Mr Scruggs laughed in a 'man-to-man' kind of way. 'Now, we're keen to find out more about this sad business of Samantha Watson's death.'

The warm smile disappeared from the solicitor's face, replaced by an expression of well-practised, profound sorrow. 'Mrs Watson worked here for many years and was a most valued member of our team.' The condescension in his voice grated on Libby's ears but she pressed her lips together, kept quiet and let Max do the talking.

'I'm afraid,' the solicitor continued in a hushed voice, full of self-importance. 'I'm unable to tell you much about Mrs Watson's work. Client confidentiality, you see.'

'Of course. You understand, though, I'm privy to the highest level of secrets in my government work?'

Mr Scruggs beamed. 'In that case I'm sure I can help you a little, although I would need an official warrant to show you any case files. The police have already searched them.'

'That won't be necessary. I just want a feel for the cases Mrs Watson might have worked on when she died, to consider why someone might bear her a grudge.'

The solicitor frowned. At least he was thinking about Samantha now, rather than himself. 'Mrs Watson dealt with the more domestic areas of our work. She had a successful caseload including many divorces, people wishing to change their name by deed poll, wills, all that sort of thing, and a little minor crime. She never handled anything of a serious nature, such as murder.'

'Perhaps I could have a list of her most recent clients?'

Mr Scruggs shook his head. 'I'm so sorry, Mr Ramshore. Not even for you.'

'Were there any cases she was particularly concerned about, to your knowledge?' Max tried a different tack.

'Not really. I tried not to overburden her with difficult work. We left that for the senior partners.'

Libby coughed gently and forced herself to sound deferential. 'Perhaps there were personal issues that Samantha discussed with colleagues in the office. Is there anyone in whom she might have confided?'

The solicitor drew himself up. 'I can assure you, if Mrs Watson had any worries or concerns, she was quite at liberty to speak to me. My door is always open to my team.'

As he spoke, a young woman appeared. 'I'm sorry to interrupt, Mr Scruggs. Lord Haversham is on the telephone for you.'

Her boss rose to his feet, face pink with pride. 'Then I must come and talk to his lordship at once. Mustn't keep the aristocracy waiting, must we? Was there anything else, Mr Ramshore? Or Mrs – er... If so, perhaps Mary here can help. She was Samantha's personal assistant.' He gave a perfunctory wave in the direction of an attractive young woman of around thirty, who sat just out of earshot on the other side of a glass partition.

Libby knew her face was a picture of outrage. She'd known many condescending males – her husband had been one of the worst – but Mr Scruggs took the prize. On the other hand, she'd probably learn more about Samantha from the personal assistant than from an out-of-touch boss.

'Max, I wonder if I could have a minute or two alone with Mary. I'd like to know more about Samantha's time here, and it may be easier on my own. Sort of a water-cooler chat.'

'You mean, no men allowed. Feminists only.' Max chuckled. 'Fair enough. You get on with your girl talk and I'll meet you back at the car.'

Libby introduced herself to Mary. 'I'm sorry for your loss.'

'Thank you. It's very strange here without Mrs Watson.'

'I thought you might be able to tell me about her. Did you know her well?'

'I'm just a personal assistant and she shared me with one of the other solicitors, but I've worked for her for a while. She gave me some lovely presents at Christmas.' Mary broke eye contact, examining her own hands. The nails were beautifully French polished and neatly squared off. Libby liked the woman already. Long nails on computer keyboards made her shudder.

'To be honest,' Mary said, 'Mrs Watson wasn't always easy to deal with, but her heart was in the right place.'

Libby wasn't so sure. She'd had plenty of spats with Samantha.

Mary fiddled with a ring, winding it round her finger. Libby asked, 'Is there something you think I should know? Anything that struck you as odd in the last few weeks?'

The PA squared her shoulders as if she'd made a decision. 'It's not much really, but it hadn't happened before, and it was the day before she – she...' Mary's lip trembled.

Libby waited a second to let her regain control, pleased to find someone genuinely upset for Samantha. Mr Scruggs had hardly acknowledged her death. After a moment, she said, 'What did you want to tell me?'

Mary concentrated on her hands once more. 'I think she was worried about something. It started with that business in the cathedral. The – the murder.' She drew her breath in with a shudder. Libby nodded, taking care not to interrupt Mary's train of thought as the young woman said, 'Every Monday I give – gave – her a list of appointments for the week. Of course, they'd often change as the week went on and I'd update her on-line calendar, but she liked to have a printed copy to pin up by her desk.'

She raised an eyebrow at Libby, as though checking she understood, and continued, 'The Monday before Mr Temple died, I gave Mrs Watson the list as usual and she pinned it up. Then the day we heard about the murder, she took it down and put it through the shredder. She'd never done that before. Not ever. She always gave things to me if she wanted them shredded. I'm surprised she even knew where the machine was.' Mary smiled, as though this was an office joke.

'Do you have a copy of the list?'

'It's still on my computer. I keep the originals as well as the updates.' Mary shot a glance over her shoulder. 'I shouldn't really give it to you, though. It belongs to the partnership. Mr Scruggs...'

'Of course.' Libby waited. Mary glanced over one shoulder. No one stood nearby. She typed a few rapid strokes, her fingers flying over the keys.

She looked up again, a hint of conspiracy in her smile. 'Perhaps I can get you a glass of water?'

'That would be lovely.' Mary stood up, touched her computer screen, glanced at Libby and left the room. Libby leant towards the screen, scanning the list of names, dates and times. She pulled out her phone to take a picture, but a message told her the memory was full. She swore under her breath. So much for technology.

She grabbed her notebook from her bag and scribbled as fast as she could. As she copied the last name, she heard a discreet cough, heralding Mary's return. 'Thanks,' Libby murmured, already on her way out.

25

GHOSTS

Reg, Libby and Max settled in Max's study, nursing mugs of coffee and plates of lemon shortbread. 'Did you or Joe find anything useful in the list of Samantha's clients?' Libby asked.

'Afraid not. There were a couple of minor criminals, Wayne Evans and Ricky de Havilland, but neither appeared to have any interest in the cathedral.'

'No links to anyone we know?' Libby was disappointed.

'No. Samantha's clients were small fry. A spot of criminal damage, cannabis, minor vehicle thefts. She wasn't allowed to represent any of the big boys. Her boss saw to that. Both her clients were given suspended sentences, by the way.'

'Would either have a motive to kill her?'

'Quite the opposite, I would have thought. They got off lightly. Joe thinks the judge had a soft spot for Samantha, so he was disposed to give her clients another chance.'

'She was certainly lovely to look at,' Libby admitted. 'Funny, I couldn't stand the woman when she was around, but now she's died in such a dreadful way, I just remember the good things about her. She had sharp wits. She often made me laugh, even when she used them against me.'

She swallowed the last crumbs of shortbread, brushing sugar from her fingers. 'It's disappointing. I had high hopes of a link between Samantha's clients and the cathedral.'

'Joe's team have been running the names through the police computer. They may come up with something useful, but it all takes time.'

'It's so frustrating.' Libby laughed. 'There are plenty of threads, all tangled, like my knitting. Everyone we follow seems to break off. I feel if only I could pull on the right one...'

'Stop thinking so hard,' Max suggested. 'Let your subconscious do the work.'

Bear was stretched out across Reg's feet, snoring. Reg had sat in silence as Libby and Max talked. Now, he shifted in his seat. Bear wriggled and went back to sleep. Reg asked, 'On another subject, has this guy ventured into the drawing room yet? I'd back him against any ghost.'

Max dribbled cream on his coffee. 'Won't put a paw across the threshold. Our ghost still seems to worry him. I sat in the room for an hour the other day and I must admit it's uncomfortable. Cold, as much as anything.'

Libby drained her cup. 'It's broad daylight. Why don't we go in there now and see if we can't get a sighting? Reg, you know about ghosts. You could tell it to go, or something.'

'Not me. I've researched plenty of old houses, and spent the night in some, and I've learned enough not to take them lightly.'

'But things don't happen in daylight, do they? I mean, people see the odd white shape flit across a hall, but I never heard of anyone coming to harm.'

Reg shook his head. 'You need to be properly equipped if you're going ghost hunting. Microphones, infrared cameras. Or, if you want to chase the ghost out, you need an expert.'

'Dr Phillips told me there are exorcists working in churches. I suppose we could get in touch with one of those.'

Max put in, 'Why would we want to? It hasn't hurt us.'

'But you can't use the drawing room in your own house. Aren't you curious? Wouldn't you like to know why the house is haunted?'

Max and Reg exchanged glances. They were hiding something.

'What is it? You know something, don't you? Reg, you were going to do some research. What did you find out?'

Max moved across to sit beside Libby on the sofa. 'Go on, Reg. She won't give up. You'd better tell her what you know.' He took Libby's hand. 'You won't like it.'

A chill ran down Libby's spine. 'But I love ghost stories. Anyway, you must tell me about the ghost, now you've mentioned it. I'm imagining all sorts of things.'

Reg said, 'It's sad, rather than frightening. You see, one of the men fighting for the Duke of Monmouth, the pretender to the throne in the seventeenth century Battle of Sedgemoor, escaped the battle and ran away, getting as far as Exham. He was a local man, and he made the mistake of returning to his own house, where his mother hid him as best she could.'

'The village was divided, with half backing Monmouth, the others loyal to the King, and our soldier was careless. A neighbour saw him and told the King's men. Informing on enemies could be lucrative in those days. When the King's men arrived, the soldier hid in a trunk under his mother's bed. She pretended illness and said she couldn't walk.'

Libby groaned as Reg continued, 'Needless to say, the

soldiers took no notice, dragged the old woman from the bed, levered the top off the trunk and found her son curled up, cowering in his mother's linen. The woman pleaded for her son's life. She fell on her knees and begged the captain to kill her instead.'

Max took up the tale. 'The captain paused, thinking about his own mother. He said to the prisoner. "You hold your mother's fate in your hands. Choose your path."'

Libby bit her lip. 'Did he do the right thing?'

Max leant forward, bright eyes exploring Libby's face. 'You'd expect him to man up, submit to his fate and save his mother, wouldn't you?'

'But he didn't?'

Reg scoffed. 'The coward fell to the ground, snivelling, begging to be saved.' A thought began to stir in the back of Libby's mind as Reg finished the story. 'The captain shrugged and gestured to his men. "Do as you will with her. Why should we take more care of an old woman than her son does?" They tied her up and hanged her from the gallows. This place was built a century or so later for the local Lord of the Manor, on the spot where the gallows stood.'

Libby groaned. 'Did they let the soldier go?'

Reg laughed. 'Not a chance. They let him watch his mother die, then strung him up as well.'

Libby gripped Max's hand. 'That's cruel.'

'The old woman thought she'd saved her son. She died happy, I suppose, though his cowardice must have broken her heart.'

'Is that why she haunts the house?'

'She doesn't. It's her son. He can't leave, because he can't forgive himself for letting his mother die.' Max was thoughtful. 'He's ashamed.'

The story reminded Libby of something she'd heard. What could it be? She screwed her eyes tight, trying to recall the words.

A moment later, she leapt to her feet. 'That's it. I understand what happened.'

He frowned. 'You mean, with the soldier?'

'No, not that. Giles Temple's death. You were right. Once I stopped thinking so hard, everything fell into place in my head. Where's that copy of Samantha's client list? And I'll need your computer.'

She clicked through to the on-line census she'd used to find Terence Marchant. 'There it is. I can't prove it, though. Not yet.' She ran into the hall, ignoring Max's shout, and pulled on her outdoor clothes. 'I'll tell you later. Meanwhile, I have to bomb Wells with my appalling knitting.'

26

YARNBOMBING

Libby and Angela arrived at the cathedral in time for the Bishop's blessing. 'I'm glad you're here,' Angela admitted. 'I haven't been back since that – that thing fell on us.' They stared into the roof. 'Do you think someone was really trying to kill us?'

'It's an inefficient way to do it,' Libby said. 'I see they've sealed the area where the gargoyle fell. They don't want a whole row of statues landing on people's heads.'

'If anything else happens in the building, they'll have to rope off the whole cathedral.' Angela giggled.

The moment of tension broken, they joined Vera, Ruby, June and the other members of the Knitters' Guild. Each carried an enormous bag stuffed with knitted items. They fidgeted, checking watches, keen to get to work.

The Bishop beamed, kept his blessing brief, and let them go. 'I can see you're all keen to begin your task.'

Outside, a cold wind sliced into Libby's face. 'Let's split up,' she said to Angela. 'It'll be quicker.'

'Don't you think we should stay together?'

'We'll be fine. It's a clear night. You go down the High Street and I'll cover Vicar's Close.'

Lights shone from houses on either side, like beacons reflected on the cobbles. Libby tied a knitted scarf to a gate and moved on. Music spilled all around. She paused to listen to a quiet guitar. A piano joined in, then a saxophone. Libby walked on, her feet moving to the rhythm of a tango.

She stiffened. Was that a footstep? She waited, breath held, heart thudding in time with the dance. She took one more step, every sense alert.

Another footfall. Should she turn and look? Libby tensed, waiting, listening. Another footstep sounded, and another, close by. *Not yet. Wait.*

Now! She spun round, arms outstretched, fingers clutching. A heavy object swung towards her head. Libby caught the bag, tugged, and a figure lost its balance, slipped on the cobbles and fell among the pile of knitting tumbling from Ruby's red holdall. Metal clattered on the path.

Ruby, scrabbling to rise, lunged sideways, but Libby was first. She stamped on the knife. 'I don't think so,' she gasped. 'Leave it. It's all over.'

Defeated, Ruby curled into a sobbing ball. Libby's eyes searched the empty street. She shivered, searching for help, but Vicars Close was deserted. Only the invisible music played on, the oblivious musicians safe and warm.

Libby scrabbled in her bag, but before she could pull out her phone, Joe Ramshore and a uniformed constable appeared from the shadows. The constable pulled the distraught, weeping Ruby to her feet while Joe retrieved the knife from the cobbles. 'Mrs Forest, when will you learn to let the police handle things?'

Ruby hiccuped. 'I didn't want to hurt anyone. I was just trying to help.'

Joe spun round. 'Help? Help who?'

'My boy. My son.' She howled. 'I only wanted to stop him going to prison.'

* * *

The yarnbombing had to wait. The Knitters' Guild crowded into the verger's office to drink tea and demand explanations from Libby. 'How did you know Ruby had a knife?'

'I didn't, but I guessed she'd try something tonight. Giles' killer failed to get rid of me in the cathedral, so once I'd worked out it was her, I gave her the opportunity to try again.'

June was aghast. 'Ruby's been a friend for years. She's the kindest soul I know, always looking after others. I can't believe she'd kill.'

Libby, trembling, accepted a cup of hot, sweet tea from Angela. Her friend glared. 'I'm so angry with you, Libby. You knew Ruby wanted to kill you and never said a word. You should have let me come with you.'

'I didn't know for sure, but yarnbombing in the dark was the perfect time to attack me. She'd already tried once, with the gargoyle, and nearly killed you as well. I chose Vicars Close, because I thought I'd hear her footsteps on the cobbles. I'd told Joe my suspicions, earlier. I knew he'd come.'

'I bet he told you to wait for him in the cathedral.'

Libby stirred sugar into her mug to avoid answering. Angela was right. Joe had made Libby promise to stay away from Ruby. She'd have to face his anger later, and Max would be furious, as well.

Angela laughed. 'Anyway, you'd better tell us all about it. We won't move until you do.'

Libby began the story. 'At first, I thought Giles Temple's murder was about the man himself. He had something of a past.' Libby caught a glimpse of Angela's flushed face and moved on. 'His murder seemed carefully planned. I supposed the killer slipped into the library armed with wire cutters, planning to cut the chain from a book and use it to kill Giles.'

Angela shuddered. 'What kind of twisted mind would want to use a book as a murder weapon?'

'Exactly. It was very puzzling. Then, the librarian told me he kept a box of spare chains in the library. That changed everything. It meant the murder could be a spur of the moment crime, not planned at all. Ruby wasn't there to kill anyone. She was just returning a book.'

Everyone gasped. June said, 'Why didn't she just take the book back during the day? And why did she have one of the books from the cathedral library, anyway?'

'She didn't have it. It was her son, Wayne Evans, and it didn't come from the cathedral library.'

'Evans? Ruby's name is Harris.'

'Wayne was born before Ruby married her husband, so the name meant nothing. Her son had stolen the book, and not even from Wells. From Hereford, perhaps. There's another chained library there. Rare books are worth a great deal of money, and there are gangs of thieves, like art thieves. Wayne was a persistent criminal. He'd been in trouble with the law for cannabis crimes and he already had a suspended sentence. If he were caught with the book, he'd end up in prison.'

Libby looked from one puzzled face to another. 'Let me explain...'

A loud clatter from the other end of the building interrupted her. Reg and Max arrived, and Libby's heart lifted. Max said, 'Joe told me what's been going on, and to get over here if I didn't want to miss all the fun.'

Reg drawled. 'I guess you're going to need help with the yarnbombing if you're going to get it all done. We're here to help.'

Libby let Max settle next to her. 'I was just explaining about the book theft, but Reg can tell the story better.'

Reg inclined his head. 'There's a lucrative market in old books. I've been working secretly on behalf of the International League of Antiquarian Booksellers, searching for items on the Stolen Books database. I hoped I'd kept it quiet, but somehow I was outed.'

'You're pretty distinctive to look at,' Max pointed out. 'Half the criminals in the West Country must know who you are. News travels fast down here in the sticks.'

June interrupted. 'So, Ruby's son heard you were on the trail of books. He was scared. He thought you'd catch him with one of the stolen books in his possession, so he hatched a plan to take the book to the library. He thought Reg would find it and stop investigating. But what did that have to do with Ruby?'

Libby took up the tale once more. 'Ruby has one goal in life. She needs to be loved. You said it just now, June. Ruby was "always looking after others." She told me her son is the apple of her eye. She'd do anything for him. He confessed he had a stolen book and begged his mother to return it, so he couldn't be caught. If the police discovered he'd stolen it, he'd be back in court, and as his last sentence was suspended, he'd end up in jail. Ruby couldn't allow that to happen.'

Angela frowned. 'But why did Ruby kill Giles? He had nothing to do with the stolen book.'

'I'm afraid he was just unlucky. When Ruby slipped into the cathedral at the end of Evensong, she must have been astonished to find the library unlocked. She was even more surprised when she saw Giles Temple there, probably with his head in a book, waiting for – er – an assignation with someone.'

Angela's sigh was so quiet only Libby heard it. 'Ruby panicked, thinking everything would come out if Giles saw the book. She looked around, wondering what to do, saw the chains, crept up behind Giles, threw one round his neck and twisted.'

Someone gasped.

'Yes,' Libby agreed. 'Horrible. We thought it was a man, because you'd need such strength, but Ruby's a strong woman. She works in her garden most days.'

Amelia murmured. 'She helped dig my pond. It was amazing. She's got enormous muscles under her twin sets.'

Angela said, 'Giles was wearing my scarf.' Head high, she looked straight at Amelia. 'Yes, he was waiting for me to come, that night, but I'd had second thoughts. Ruby wrapped the scarf around his neck on the spur of the moment, I suppose, to incriminate me.'

There was a pause. 'Wait a moment.' Vera, beaming at the evening's excitement and no doubt pondering when to tell the story to her acquaintances, was still puzzled. 'That explains why Ruby killed Giles Temple, but what about Samantha Watson? Surely, Ruby didn't kill her as well?'

Max said, 'I think she did, and I can explain why, although it's only conjecture. Samantha was Wayne's solicitor. She suspected his guilt and she was very foolish. She contacted him and shredded her calendar for the week to hide the fact she'd made a secret appointment to meet him. She's always been jealous of Libby, and I bet she was trying to solve the case first.

'Wayne told his mother he was going to see Samantha. Ruby, thinking Samantha suspected Wayne of the murder, set the fire. She'd already killed one person and I suppose murder is easier the second time.'

Libby added, 'Ruby became totally ruthless. I visited her quite by chance about a missing cat, but she thought I was suspicious. She must have grabbed a weapon, probably a hammer, and followed my car. I met Angela in the cathedral and Ruby saw us under the gargoyle, climbed up to the passage above and gave the gargoyle a good whack, hoping it would fall on me. It was a desperate thing to do.'

She took a long breath. Two of Ruby's wild plans had succeeded. It was only a matter of luck that the third failed.

June said, 'How did you know it was Ruby? Even the police hadn't realised she was the killer.'

'This afternoon I heard the story of a mother who gave her life to save her son.' Libby smiled at Max. 'The ghost in your house. Ruby once told me she'd do anything for Wayne and I realised she might even kill. After that, everything fell into place.'

Max took her arm. 'Come on, Libby. Let's leave the others to finish the yarnbombing. I'm taking you home.' As they walked out of the building, he laughed. 'By the way, as I drove here, I saw a flashy BMW outside Mrs Marchant's house. Looks like her son's been to visit. Which means, I hope, I won't have to buy that television for her, after all.'

27

MANDY

Max removed the wine glass from Libby's hand. 'After today's success, can I assume you won't stop investigating?'

Libby laughed. 'How can I? I'm just too nosy. I've decided to stop dithering. I'm ready to turn professional. There's training, apparently, for private investigators and I put my name down, earlier today. I'm ready to take the plunge.'

'That's great. By the way, I have news for you.'

Libby's pulse raced. 'Good, or bad?'

'Depends.'

She pulled a cushion from under Fuzzy and hugged it close, suddenly nervous. 'Is it about us? You and me? The other thing?'

'Don't look so worried. You know I want to marry you, but I'm not going to bully you today. Maybe tomorrow.'

'Oh. Good.' Libby frowned. What was causing that tightness in her chest? Surely it wasn't disappointment. 'Can I have my wine back, please?'

'Only if you promise you won't throw the contents over my head.'

'I promise. Now, tell me your news. No, wait. I can guess from your smug expression. It's Mandy, isn't it?'

She watched as Max topped up red wine in both glasses and pushed the cork back in the bottle. 'We haven't been in touch since the quarrel. Not even a text. She's been in the bakery, but I don't often go there, these days. Frank's doing well. He's taken on more staff so all he needs from me are new ideas and recipes.'

'And chocolates.'

'Exactly. Mandy hasn't been home at night, so I haven't seen her. I thought we needed a cooling off period. I'm dying to know where she's staying, so tell me. What do you know?'

'Why don't you just text her?'

'Max, you're wriggling. You know something.'

'I have a suspicion. I was saving it for tomorrow when you're no longer tired.'

'Tired? Me? I'm wide awake. I insist you tell me, or I'll throw you out of the cottage.'

'OK. Reg is planning to stay in the area much longer than originally planned. Wayne's stolen book's not the only one. He has a list of books he wants to track down. He's renting a house in Bristol.'

'Oh.' Libby exhaled. 'That's where Mandy's staying? Where she went on the day of the fire?'

'I'm guessing, but it makes good sense.'

Libby pulled threads from the cushion. 'That's why she wouldn't tell me, because I'd disapprove. I knew she had a thing for Reg, but he's much too old for her. She's had her heart broken once—' Max's hand on her mouth cut off the words.

'There you go again. Will you never learn? Repeat after me, Mandy is a grown-up.'

She moved Max's hand so she could talk but held it tight against her cheek. 'Do you think, if I talk to Mandy tomorrow, things will work out? I miss her. She's also very good at her job and I don't want to lose her from the business. You have lovely, warm hands, by the way.'

Max kissed her forehead. 'Quite the entrepreneur, aren't you? Ring her tomorrow.'

Libby pushed him away and grabbed her phone. 'Sorry. Can't wait. I have to talk to her now.'

'It's past eleven.'

'She's young. She stays up late. Don't worry, I won't call. I'll text.'

Heart pounding, Libby typed;

Hope all's well. Talk tomorrow. Have new idea for chocs.

'There.' She showed it to Max, crossed her fingers and hit the button. 'It's done.'

Seconds later her phone beeped. Max hooted. 'How does she text so fast?'

Libby read Mandy's reply aloud.

Count me in. Luv u Mrs F. See u tomoz.

ACKNOWLEDGMENTS

So many readers and reviewers have given their time generously to help with reading, revising and editing the books in this compilation. I've received a host of useful comments from Pippa Dunbar, Nick Evesham, Barbara Jensen, Kate McCormick, Doreen Pechey, Mary Robinson, Susan Schuman, and Frank Wright, and I'd like to thank them all for their time, trouble, eagle eyes, and kind support.

A special thank you also to Wendy Janes, and to the terrific team at Boldwood Books.

MORE FROM FRANCES EVESHAM

We hope you enjoyed reading *Murder on the Tor* and *Murder at the Cathedral.* If you did, please leave a review.

Sign up to become a Frances Evesham VIP and receive a free copy of the Lazy Gardener's Cheat Sheet. You will also receive news, competitions and updates on future books:

https://bit.ly/FrancesEveshamSignUp

ALSO BY FRANCES EVESHAM

The Exham-On-Sea Murder Mysteries

Murder at the Lighthouse

Murder on the Levels

Murder on the Tor

Murder at the Cathedral

Murder at the Bridge

Murder at the Castle

Murder at the Gorge

The Ham Hill Murder Mysteries

A Village Murder

ABOUT THE AUTHOR

Frances Evesham is the author of the hugely successful Exham-on-Sea Murder Mysteries set in her home county of Somerset. In her spare time, she collects poison recipes and other ways of dispatching her unfortunate victims. She likes to cook with a glass of wine in one hand and a bunch of chillies in the other, her head full of murder—fictional only.

Visit Frances' website: https://francesevesham.com/

Follow Frances on social media:

twitter.com/francesevesham

facebook.com/frances.evesham.writer

bookbub.com/authors/frances-evesham

instagram.com/francesevesham

ABOUT BOLDWOOD BOOKS

Boldwood Books is a fiction publishing company seeking out the best stories from around the world.

Find out more at www.boldwoodbooks.com

Sign up to the Book and Tonic newsletter for news, offers and competitions from Boldwood Books!

http://www.bit.ly/bookandtonic

We'd love to hear from you, follow us on social media:

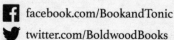

facebook.com/BookandTonic

twitter.com/BoldwoodBooks

instagram.com/BookandTonic